# THE TREE HOUSE

By Timothy Kyle

# Dedication

This story is dedicated to being different and not just noticing the good in the world, but looking for it.

This book is also devoted to my grandparents: Jean and Palmer. You've taught me that impressions last for much more than just a lifetime. Thank you for smiling down upon us every single day.

And lastly to my wife. Yes, the same woman I met in a hot tub while on my college Spring Break. You are my ride or die! You are my everything! Thank you for always being in my corner. I will forever be in yours. I love you, Emmy!

"Don't change."

# Trigger Warnings

As the author of this book, I value the sensitivity of the reader. This is a contemporary adult romance novel with some dark and disturbing themes. If you are easily triggered by the below content then please take that under serious consideration before reading. Thank you.

**Extreme Acts of Racism**

**Racial Slurs**

**Child Abandonment/Neglect**

**Violence/Physical Assault**

**Graphic Sex**

# Other Work by Timothy Kyle

*The Girl in the Red Wig*

# PROLOGUE

## Benny

## *1956*

*Don't say kiss her!*

*Don't say kiss her!*

"And one other thing..." Marcus pauses, already cringing. "You'll need to kiss her…on the lips."

I shake my head emphatically. I'd do anything for my best friend. But kissing his seven-year-old sister is crazy. She's two years younger than me, annoying as fuck, and the worst of it is she's already in love with me.

The plan was simple at first. I put on the tux. Then I put the plastic ring on her finger, say "I do," and give her a hug. That was the plan I begrudgingly agreed to.

"No, Marcus!" I shout, seeing Penny's expression wilt out of the corner of my eye.

"Come on, Benny. She needs this. Please do it," he begs.

The first tear runs down the cheek of Penny Jones. Then comes the droopy, puppy dog eyes. Her dark skin can't blush like mine, but this poor girl sure knows how to cry when she needs attention.

"Fine," I sigh, feeling suddenly nervous because I've never kissed anyone.

It's one thing to play pretend games in my red treehouse. But this is no ordinary treehouse. It's a safe haven for my neighbors.

Marcus and Penny Jones come up here most nights to escape the rage of their mother. My grandparents gave them a key to our back gate a couple years ago. They also gave them a key to our house, but they prefer the treehouse most days. Perhaps part of the reason is black kids don't just walk into a white person's house. Maybe it happens in other places, but not in Birmingham, Alabama.

I turn to face Penny. The first thing I notice is one of her eyes is still slightly swollen from her mother's latest attack. But I know the pain she feels on the inside is the worst part. It's the reason I'm up here doing a pretend wedding.

"Here's your vows, Benny," Penny says, handing me a sheet of paper.

I read it in my head, but even doing that makes me want to vomit.

"I can't say this—"

"Just do it," Marcus interrupts, gritting his teeth with a glare.

I let out a loud exhale. "Fine."

Marcus hands me the ring. I glance at Penny, whose wilted face has quickly blossomed into a giddy woman on her wedding day.

I still don't get it. She's just a kid. She may be cute, like how I'd describe most puppies. But she's looking at me like this feels real to her.

Marcus starts giving his sermon. I zone out by staring at my dress shoes. Eventually my gaze comes up to meet Penny's brown eyes. I quickly notice the brimming moisture in them. But she's not gearing up for her usual cry. These are about to be happy tears.

For a brief moment I have a funny feeling in my chest and tummy. It's hard to understand what I'm feeling. All I know is it feels heavy and warm. But it also feels oddly comfortable, and good for a change. Maybe it's okay that I don't understand it. All I do know is it feels really good to make Penny happy. Happiness is typically something only Marcus can bring out of her.

Marcus gives a forced clearing of his throat. "Hello. Um, guys. Can you hear me. Now you can read your vows," he says, looking at us like we're deaf.

I guess we didn't hear him the first time. It's like our eyes were caught in some type of trance with one another.

"You can go first," Marcus says, nodding to Penny.

"Dear, Benny. Thank you for marrying me and for having children with me. I want three boys and one girl. That's all. Love, Penny."

My throat locks up. I was not expecting her to demand children. I want to laugh at her, but I also don't want her crying again. Besides, she seemed dead serious and overly confident with her demands. Does she still think babies come from a stork?

"Your turn, Benny. And remember to first put the ring on her," Marcus says.

My hands starts shaking. Then I slowly slide the ring up her finger. Her eyes widen once the ring is on. The smile on her face is an illumination of happiness like I've never seen.

I pull out my vows, taking a deep breath. "Dear, Penny. You are the only girl I will ever love. I promise to love you to the moon and back. And to the moon and back again. Love, Benny."

I want to breathe out a sigh of relief, but the next part is the most nerve-wracking.

"You may kiss the bride," Marcus says. "On the lips."

I take a step towards her. Penny closes her eyes and puckers her lips. Then I lean down for my first-ever kiss.

# CHAPTER ONE

## Benny

### *Two Years Later*

"Kindness, hmm," Grandpa sighs, taking a long swig of his coffee.

His stare goes over my head, to a place in another time. His eyes are already glossy with remembering, like he's wanting to freeze so many moments of his past all at once.

"Okay, here it is," Grandpa says, shooting his glare down to me. "True kindness…is willingness."

"Willingness?"

"Yes, Benny. It's the willingness to want to do good without recognition or praise. It's doing it because your heart is overflowing with love. And remember, it's the giver of kindness who gets the most out of it."

Grandpa smiles at Grammy as she walks in. "I've only known one person on this earth who did it better than anyone else. Isn't that right, Honey?"

Grammy doesn't blush or bat an eye. She just smiles at Grandpa. She gets compliments like these every day. Then he grabs her hand, pulling her onto his lap. They share a long smooch that makes me want to vomit.

"Yuck," I complain, looking away.

"Well, I think the best form of kindness is the one born from courage. Are you courageous, Benny McClain?" Grammy asks.

How does an 11-year-old boy know if he's courageous or not?

*I guess.*

"Sure, I think so."

Grandpa softly chuckles. "Oh Benny boy, it's already within you. It's always going to be there, no matter what. You're a McClain. Look, here's how I know. Take your hand and place it over your heart. You feel that?"

I do as Grandpa says, feeling the rhythmic thud beneath my chest. "So, what? It's beating. It's no different than anyone else," I explain, feeling confused.

"Ah!" Grandpa raises one finger in the air. "That's where you're wrong. Your heart doesn't just beat. It speaks to you!" he raises his voice as his glare intensifies. "You just have to learn how to hear it. Now close your eyes. Tell me, Benny. What is your heart telling you right now?"

I close my eyes as the thunder roars outside. I can't help but sigh in frustration at my grandpa's lesson. It's a lesson I get every year on my birthday. This year is no different than the rest.

Most grandparents shower their grandchildren with gifts or money. Not mine. I get the yearly Grandpa McClain life lesson.

The loud footsteps and panicked breathing suddenly break my concentration. I open my eyes as my younger brother wraps his arms around me, grasping for dear life. He digs his face into my chest. My arms go tighter around him because it's the only way to calm him down.

"You're okay, Jimmy. I'm here. You're okay."

"Oh, Jimmy. Your big brother loves you so much," Grandpa says, smiling with admiration. "Now Benny, let's try this again. Close your eyes and put your hand over your heart."

I slowly let Jimmy go. He stays seated on the edge of my chair while I do as Grandpa says.

"Ah, ah, Benny. Your brother is here, too. Help him out."

"Sorry, Grandpa."

Jimmy may be different. But my grandparents have always been adamant that he gets the same opportunities as anyone else: "No differences and no excuses." It's what I've been hearing for every day of my waking life.

When I can't get Jimmy to hold his shaking hand over his heart, I settle on pulling it over my chest as our hands interweave.

"Okay. Now close your eyes, boys."

I try my best to concentrate on the sound of my heart. It's a little less frenetic. Perhaps it's because I have my brother's closeness at my side.

I try hearing through the pain and noise in my head. If only it could go away for a second. If only I could will people back from the dead. If only I could console my brother and help him find his words.

*That's it!*

My eyes flash open, and hope courses through my veins. I take a deep breath, feeling like I understand the meaning of life.

"So…?" Grandpa asks.

"I know the meaning of kindness, Grandpa. I'm going to change the world," I proclaim, taking my gaze from Grandpa to my brother. "I mean, we're going to change the world, together, me and Jimmy."

I hug my brother closer into my side, smiling wide at my grandpa. His eyes squint. His hand itches the grey and white stubble on his chin.

"How?" he challenges.

*How? How? How?*

The word pinballs around in my head, adding to the noise and fog in my brain.

I think I have an idea. But how does someone change the world? I mean, I'm only a kid. I'm not an expert on anything. My abilities in the classroom are average at best. The only thing I've known since a young age is running like a cheetah and throwing the football like Bart Starr.

*That's it!*

"I'm going to be the best there ever was, Grandpa. I'll win National Championships. I'll win Super Bowls. Then I'll start a charity for people like Jimmy," I declare, puffing my chest with pride.

Jimmy's hand grasps tighter around mine. His smile slowly forms across his face with the usual bit of underlying tension.

"That's great you want to be a champion and start a charity, but dig deeper, Benny. What do you really want to do?"

I glance at Jimmy as he looks away from me. I pull his hand back into my chest. Then his eyes come back to mine. His smile is gone. His thoughts on the inside feel like a broken puzzle. It makes me want to piece him together from the inside. Or maybe just understand what's going on inside his head. But I don't have superpowers like Penny.

Then Jimmy pulls my hand into his chest. The emotions on his face are still hidden. The only thing I notice is his eyes looking the slightest bit glossy. He stares into my eyes with new intentions.

It's at that moment I know. The answer to my grandpa's question is right in front of me, broken puzzle pieces and all.

"I get it, Grandpa. I'm going to be the most devoted big brother for Jimmy. I'm going to make other people see the true him. I'm going to help him be heard. And I'm always going to protect him, no matter what."

Grandpa just nods his head smiling. Then the doorbell rings. I groan right away, knowing who it is.

"Come on, Benny. A promise is a promise," Grandpa scolds. "Be nice to her."

It's almost 8 a.m. on a school day. It could only be one person—my next-door neighbor, Penny Jones.

My grandparents have been providing free daycare to Penny for the last few years. But it's become much more regular ever since her brother Marcus, my best friend, died about a year ago.

Another big reason is Penny's mom. She's been an off-and-on alcoholic for as long as I can remember. However, now that her son is gone, her alcoholism has been the definition of who she is. She loves her whiskey more than her only living child.

The story of Penny's dad is more of a mystery. All I know is he left her when she was about four years old. The only somewhat dependable parental figure she has is her Aunt Mary. She does her best to look after her, but she's always working, and she has her own family to tend to.

The doorbell rings again. I huff out another long sigh as I make my way to the front door.

*A promise is a promise.*

"Hi, Benny!"

She marches past me like she owns the place. I roll my eyes at her flirting grin.

"Jimmy!" she screams, running into the kitchen. She tackles Jimmy with a hug that almost knocks the air out of him.

"Penny! Penny! Penny!" Jimmy keeps shouting with an ear-to-ear grin.

My brother typically doesn't talk much at all. But around Penny, he's able to find his words more easily.

We all settle in at the kitchen table for a light breakfast.

"No, no, no, Jimmy. You have to use the fork," Penny instructs, guiding his hand to the handle of his fork.

Jimmy usually knows how to use his fork. He just loves having Penny's doting attention.

Grammy walks into the kitchen, giving me a glare I can't ignore.

"What?"

She leans down into my ear.

"Did you not hear your grandpa. It's willingness, Benny. Take a lesson here from Penny," she says, smiling her direction. "Penny has willingness."

"But Grammy, Jimmy does just fine eating with his hands."

"Manners, Benny!" Grammy's eyebrows raise up. "Last I checked, you're the big brother. And everything you're capable of, so is Jimmy. Besides, we're not savages."

I exhale, thinking of the million things I already do for Jimmy on a daily basis. It's gotten easier now that he's nine years old and doing most of his daily tasks on his own. The only challenge for him is processing the emotions around him and learning how to communicate.

"It's okay, Mrs. McClain. Me and Jimmy are best friends for life. I don't mind helping him out. Besides, one day he'll be my brother-in-law," Penny says, flashing a bright smile my way.

I can't help myself as I start making gagging noises. "You're nine, for god's sake! And I'm not going to marry you, Penny Jones. I'm sorry."

"Manners, Benny," Grammy demands, pinching my shoulder. "And Penny, please call me Grammy. You're family, Sweetheart."

"I was just kidding, Benny," Penny mutters, looking embarrassed.

Penny Jones was not kidding. She declared her love for me the first time Marcus and I invited her up into my treehouse. At the time she was five and I was only seven years old. Then a couple years later I mistakenly agreed to a fake wedding that I should have never shown up for.

Maybe it was the peer pressure from her brother that day. Marcus wanted to do something to cheer her up. She'd been crying all day because her mama abandoned her for the thousandth time. Either way she loves reminding me every single day of our treehouse wedding.

I still wish I had just said no that day. It's not that I don't care for her or know how much the McClain family means to her. But I don't like her like that. I only see her as an annoying younger sister.

Besides, Penny's been through enough in life. She lives in a town where people hurl insults at her just because her skin is black. She also watched her brother Marcus die suddenly from a rare form of bone cancer. But the worst part is never having a real mother or father figure in her life. The closest thing she has to a parent are my grandparents. And the closest thing she has to a brother is Jimmy and me. And I promised Marcus I'd look after Penny like a brother. It's a promise I'll no doubt take to the grave with me.

I watch Penny as she walks back to the table with a glass of water for herself and Jimmy. She helps him dish up seconds on his scrambled eggs. Then she whispers something in his ear that makes him giggle.

Grammy and Grandpa think that Penny will one day become a teacher to the differently abled. I could see it. She's more patient with Jimmy than my grandparents and me combined.

Jimmy is just a different person around Penny. His smile typically has a bit of confusion in it. But around Penny, his smile is wider and more natural looking. I'm a bit jealous that I can't always bring that side out of him, but I know he loves me regardless.

"Ah Penny, you're an angel darling. Thank you," Grandpa compliments her.

"Thanks, Penny," I barely mumble the words.

I do my best to pay her as little compliments as possible. Whenever I say something nice to her, she takes it as an opportunity to unapologetically swoon and give me googly eyes. Today feels no different. She keeps flashing crooked smiles at me from across the table.

"So, Benny. What did you get for your birthday?" Penny asks.

"Nothing," I mutter, rolling my eyes.

Penny's face wilts with empathy.

"We don't give presents, Honey. We made an exception for you the last couple years—you know, with all you've been through. But Benny doesn't need anything. He's got the love of his family, the roof over his head, oxygen to breathe and food in his belly," Grammy boasts with pride.

"And he's got my eleventh life lesson on kindness. A lesson Penny just performed perfectly. Here it is for the record, Benny. Now go file it with the rest of them," Grandpa says, handing over a single sheet of paper.

I read it again, rolling my eyes.

**Happy 11<sup>th</sup> Birthday, Benny. And remember, true kindness is willingness.**

"Thanks, Grandpa."

I head upstairs to grab my backpack, cleats, and helmet for football practice. I file my grandpa's note in my birthday folder. Then I quickly flip through all 11 of his notes, smiling and laughing at my grandpa's one-liners. Each sheet is identical in form, a single sheet of paper with only one or two sentences. But each message is unique to my grandpa's lesson on that specific birthday.

Maybe one day I'll understand his point. Besides, I already know that I'm a good person. I take on more responsibility than any one 11-year-old kid in this town. And if I complain or act ungrateful on occasion—oh well.

"You're going to be late for school!" Grammy shouts.

I put my birthday folder away and rush downstairs. "You ready, Penny?"

The question is rhetorical because she's never ready to walk to school with me. Penny loves doing long goodbyes. But I don't blame her. She knows how sad Jimmy gets each day we go to school.

It's the loneliness that gets to me. He stays home to learn things with Grammy and Grandpa, but it's not the same social experience. It hurts seeing him so isolated from others. It's too bad our hillbilly town doesn't offer educational opportunities for people like Jimmy. Instead, the people of this town look down on him like he's some pariah that should be institutionalized. Little do they know that Jimmy is academically smarter than most of them.

In some ways it's no different than the treatment of black people here in Birmingham. We're probably the most segregated city in America. There's only a handful of schools like the one me and Penny go to that are desegregated.

"Hey, wait up!" Penny yells as I rush out the door.

"Hurry up, slow poke."

It only takes a few steps out the door until I hear the thud. It's heavy and unlike anything I've ever heard in my life. I quickly turn around as I hear Penny's blood curdling scream. Then Jimmy shrills out a terrifying scream of his own.

I rush into the house as Grandpa is huddled over Grammy, holding her head in his lap. He keeps screaming her name, begging for her to wake up. Meanwhile, my body is frozen. My eyes can't look away from the pool of red beneath her head.

# CHAPTER TWO

## Penny

### *Three Years Later*

"Oh, shit! I'm too old for this stuff, Penny," Mr. McClain groans.

"You got it, Mr. McClain. You're almost there."

He finally makes it to the top. Then he collapses on his side, catching his breath.

"I did it," he says, breathing rapidly. "Not bad for a 70-something old chap. Wouldn't you say?"

Once Mr. McClain catches his breath, he stands up in the treehouse. The ceiling barely misses the top of his head. It's odd seeing him up here. This is the first time I've ever seen him in the treehouse that he built when Benny was just a little kid.

"I'm impressed. Now, what was it you wanted to tell me?" I ask.

"Well, we're up here because I know how much this treehouse makes you feel safe. And I want you feeling safe when you see what I have for you. Can you do that for me?"

I nod pensively while he reaches into his back pocket, then hands over an envelope. I grab it, noticing his hand trembling the slightest bit.

"Go ahead. Read it."

It's two sheets of paper with all sorts of fancy words, names, and signatures. It's all one big jumble, but the familiar name at the top makes no sense.

"What is this?" I ask, looking at my name—well, part of my name. "Penny...McClain?"

Those two words feel disconnected, leaving my mouth. There's butterflies in my tummy. Chills covering my body. My lips begin to quiver as I see the first tear run down Mr. McClain's face.

*What's happening?*

"Are you crying?" I ask, not believing what I'm seeing.

"Of course not. It's allergies," Mr. McClain says, quickly wiping his eyes.

"I... I...uh."

"You don't need to say anything, Penny. I've already spoken with your Aunt Mary. And she got the signature from your mom. It's all done. It's been a long time coming. I'm sorry we didn't ask you. But this will keep you safe. It makes things easier for all of us. And it's not just what Grammy wanted..." His voice trails off, lost in the memory of his wife.

It's been three years since I watched Grammy collapse in the McClain family kitchen. Madeline, his wife of over 50 years, was gone quicker than I could blink my eyes. It was a massive stroke, and it took her life for no good reason at all.

None of the McClain's have been the same since she died. It's been especially tough for Benny, because his grandpa is constantly grieving. Mr. McClain has these moments where his eyes glaze over and he's no longer with us—just like he is in this very moment.

Things are just different now. Benny's responsibilities with looking after Jimmy, keeping his grades up, and training for football have made him more angsty than usual. He barely pays attention to me, or even talks to me.

"I'm sorry," Mr. McClain says, clearing his throat. "Can I tell you why we're really doing this, Sweetheart?"

I nod my head, swallowing back the lump in my throat.

"Well, you know how much we love you. Right?"

I nod again, feeling the first wet trickle glide down my face. I want to tell him yes, and that I love their family more than anything, but my voice is rendered useless by my emotions.

"And I want you to know that the seed of this plan was not from me or Grammy. I mean, I'm sure we both thought about it. But the first person to want this was Benny. He's been asking us to adopt you for the past couple years. This year we're surprising him for his birthday. He doesn't know it yet."

"Benny wanted this?"

I can't hide the shock in my voice. Meanwhile, Mr. McClain just nods his head with a crooked smile.

Benny McClain is the last person on earth I'd guess to come up with such an idea. He thinks I'm annoying. I can't help that I like him. He shouldn't have ever married me in the treehouse when I was younger. Yeah, even at that age I knew it was fake, but I'll never forget the nine-year-old version of Benny McClain dressed in his Sunday's best. I fell in love with him on that day and I can't shake off the feeling. He may only love me as a sister, but he's terrible at showing it.

I still don't know the best way to get his attention. Even when we walk to school each morning he barely looks at me. I'm lucky if I can even get him to answer a question or mutter more than two words. Any attempt I make in talking to him feels more like a monologue.

The bigger reality is Benny is married to football. It's always been his passion. He's been in love with football ever since he met my brother. That's all he ever wants to do or talk about.

"Why would Benny want this?" I finally ask.

Mr. McClain steps forward, slowly leaning down on one knee.

"Penny dear, we all wanted this—even Jimmy. And Benny's just having a hard time like me with processing emotions. But believe me, Benny loves you like a sister, and sometimes big brothers have funny ways of showing it."

I sigh, knowing I don't want Benny to love me like a sister. Then I close my eyes, feeling uneasy by so many other things.

"But Mr. McClain, aren't you worried what others will think. I mean—"

"Ah, ah, stop it right there," he interrupts, extending his hand out to me.

"Give me your hand," he demands.

I extend my hand to Mr. McClain. He quickly grabs onto my wrist with a tight grip that startles me.

"Ow!"

"Oh, you're fine. Now, you grab my wrist too." he demands. "And squeeze it tight. Come on. Do it like you mean it."

I do as I'm told. I strangle his arm with all my might. After about 20 seconds I notice the change in color. Then I notice his veins becoming more inflated, just like mine. It hurts a little, but I'm starting to get used to it.

"So. What do you see?" he asks.

"Well, you're cutting off my blood supply for one. And my veins."

"Yes! You're getting it," he says with excitement. "And what runs through our veins?"

"Blood."

"Yes, Penny. Our blood pumps through our bodies the same way. And what do you see on the surface of our skin?"

I glance up to his eyes, feeling confused. He loves teaching lessons, but I don't know where he's going with this.

"Well, I see my black skin, and your white skin."

"No, you're wrong!" he tersely replies.

"But—"

"Think about it, Penny," his voice becomes hoarser. "You're a McClain now. But even before you were a McClain we were no different. Don't let the people in this bigoted town convince you otherwise. And now that you're a McClain, we don't see skin color. Others will, that's their problem. And others may try to bring you down, but you're mentally stronger than all of them. You have to believe it."

I stare into Mr. McClain's face, noticing the fire in his eyes, and the trail of emotion in his words. Every part of me wants to believe that I'm strong enough, but this new reality scares me.

"But Mr. McClain, black kids don't have white parents—especially in this town. It's hard enough seeing how some people treat Jimmy. And aren't you worried about how others may treat you and Benny? It's not safe."

He takes a long, agitated breath. Then he takes another one. I don't mean to frustrate him or ruin this moment, but I couldn't live with the idea of bringing harm to any of the McClains.

Then he smiles, letting his large hands grab hold of my shoulders. "It's going to be okay. I won't let anyone hurt you, and neither will Benny, or Jimmy. We love you and want you to be a part of our family—all of us want it. Because you deserve the love of a father…and two brothers." His voice breaks.

The trail of tears begins flowing down his face. There's more than just pride in those tears. There's love.

*He wants me! They want me!*

"I love you, Mr. McClain. I love you so much," I cry.

We embrace. The tears pour out of me like I have a never-ending supply. It's years of abandonment, verbal abuse and physical abuse coming out in heaps.

The crying eventually subsides. A new reality sets in. It's a weight I've never known, because now I have a last name I'm proud of.

"Thank you, Mr. McClain."

"Ah, ah, no more of that either. From this day forward you can call me Dad, or Grandpa. Whatever you feel fits best. That is…if you're ready."

I think about what feels right and natural. Benny and Jimmy know him as Grandpa. But he feels like more to me—*much more!*

"I'm ready. Thank you, Dad," I say, hugging him and crying even harder.

*Dad!*

It's a word I can barely remember using in my life. It should feel weird and unnatural, but it's fitting. There's not a more perfect word for my hero.

----

"When can we eat cake?" Jimmy asks, peering into the kitchen at the homemade carrot cake I made.

"After you eat your salad," Dad replies.

"But why?"

"Here Jimmy, put more ranch dressing on it. It'll make it taste better," I say, passing the dressing to him.

Watching him pour the dressing on his salad is such a little thing. But it shows the growth in his fine motor skills. Three years ago Jimmy wouldn't have been able to do this on his own. Nor would he have been able to communicate his likes and dislikes at the dinner table.

I watch as Jimmy tells a story from yesterday about playing football with the neighbors and his big brother. His face lights up, boasting about how jealous the neighbors are of Benny's athletic prowess.

Jimmy is still learning how to play football. It's cute seeing Benny include his little brother, even though the other neighbors typically want nothing to do with Jimmy. He's also a patient teacher to Jimmy. And Jimmy eats up that attention because he sees Benny like a mythical god.

No one knows why Jimmy was born the way he is. I for one don't care. I like that he's different. And it's amazing seeing his growth as a person over the last couple years. He can carry a conversation with people as long as he knows them and trusts them. He only shuts down when he doesn't understand something or if he's around an agitating situation. And he still struggles with understanding the social cues that come natural for most people.

We all deserve credit for Jimmy's growth as a person. However, most of it is due to Clara Green, or Ms. Green as she asks to be called. She's an older black woman who moved in across the street shortly after Mrs. McClain died. She lives with her cousin—Christine.

It's a slow process getting to know Ms. Green. All I do know is she's a recent widow like Dad and she was never able to have kids of her own. But she worked the greater part of her life as a nurse in a psychiatric ward, helping people like Jimmy. And she's voluntarily become a therapist for him. She comes over on a daily basis to help him with his motor skills, communicating, and with his overall cognitive processing. It's been a regular thing now for the last couple years.

Every day she comes, Dad offers to pay her for her time. But every single time she gives him the same answer: "I don't need a dime. I do it because people like Jimmy deserve to be heard and seen."

Benny thinks Dad likes Ms. Green. Most days she stays longer at our house to have a cup of coffee with Dad on the front porch. And on special occasions like today she'll stay for dinner. But the relationship between my dad and Ms. Green is a funny thing to see. They say very little to each other. When they sit on the front porch they just sip their coffee in silence. If they do like each other's company, they have a weird way of showing it.

"Isn't this a great birthday dinner Penny put together for you, Benny?" Dad asks, flashing a grin at me.

"I asked for pork chops," Benny mutters, looking away from me with his usual scowl. "Can you pass the salad, Penny?"

I feel Dad's glare at Benny from across the table.

"But thanks, Penny. The chicken is pretty good," he mumbles.

When I hand Benny the salad, Dad's long arm shoots across the table to latch onto Benny's wrist.

"Again?" Dad asks, assessing his scuffed-up pink and blue knuckles.

19

Benny's eyes droop, staring into his lap. "Yes, Grandpa. But don't worry, I took care of it."

"You should've walked away!" he quickly reprimands. "Those Monroe boys ain't worth you getting in trouble."

"I know. But I had no choice, they hit me first. And they called Penny a…" Benny pauses. I feel Grandpa now glaring at me. "Never mind. I'm sorry, Grandpa," he quietly mutters.

"Did you know about this, Penny?"

I just nod my head, feeling deflated. I'm the one to blame for everything. I shouldn't have stood up for myself. It only incited Benny's rage. I've told Benny so many times that I can walk to school by myself, but he always refuses, and it's always because of the Monroe brothers.

"What happened?" Dad demands.

Jimmy suddenly bolts out of his chair to the front door. Dad and Ms. Green chase after him.

"We'll talk about it later, Benny!" Dad shouts.

After dinner things settle down. Jimmy goes to sleep early after getting upset over Dad raising his voice at Benny. It's just the four of us, eating carrot cake in complete silence.

"Do you like the cake?" I ask.

"It's dry, but not terrible," Benny remarks, avoiding eye contact.

His plate is just about clean of any cake crumbs, but his ambivalent reply hurts. These snide comments always get under my skin, but I do my best to ignore it. It's not the real Benny. I get glimpses of the one not simmering in anger, and then I fall in love all over again. But those times are becoming rarer. And when he finds out I'm his sister tonight, who knows how he'll react. Even though Dad said it's what he wants, I don't fully trust it. I know he wants to protect me, but I just want him to like me, too.

"Is it present time," Dad says after we finish cake.

Benny groans. "I guess. Let's get this over with."

Dad hands over an envelope. Benny opens it up looking supremely confused.

"I don't get it. What is this?" he asks, looking perturbed.

"That's your gift, Son. I've finally adopted Penny. She's your sister now, and my daughter. She's going to take your room and you can shack up with Jimmy."

"Excuse me?" he raises his voice.

"Benny, I know this is what you wanted."

"Yeah, I wanted it after Marcus died. But are you sure? I mean, is it even legal?"

"It's done, Benny. Penny's always been family. Now it's just official."

I glance at Benny. His eyebrows push up, creating wrinkles in his forehead I didn't know existed. Then I notice the deep swallow in his throat. I can tell he wants to speak against this, and I don't blame him. Maybe he never really wanted this. Perhaps he said it a long time ago and wants to take it back.

Benny finally lets out a long sigh, shaking his head, muttering expletives under his breath. Then he crumbles up the sheet of paper, throwing it across the table past Dad's head.

*Oh fuck!*

"Benjamin Joseph McClain!" Dad shouts, standing over him with his fists balled up.

"Fuck this! I'm out of here!" Benny shouts back, looking unfazed by Dad's murderous stare.

He walks straight out the door. Dad's redder than a beet. Ms. Green is catatonic on what to do. I know better than to chase after Benny. Instead, I head into the backyard, going straight up to the treehouse.

Once up there, I crawl into a ball. I feel as if my heart is shattering into pieces that can't be put back together. All at once I begin to cry. It goes on and on until I have no more tears in me. Then my tears become secondary to the pain in my chest.

It no longer matters that Dad and Jimmy want me in their family. It feels incomplete without Benny's blessing. But this is my life. People don't want me in it—whether it be my skin color, or the shitty hand I was dealt with my biological parents.

About an hour later I hear shouting. Benny has returned home. The shouting lasts a minute or two, then I hear only quiet conversation. I'm too high up to hear what they're saying. I don't know if they stopped shouting because they made up or if they're just staying quiet to not wake up Jimmy.

The events of his birthday dinner replay in my mind. I've never seen Benny look at his grandpa with such disgust. Nor have I ever seen Dad look at Benny like he wanted to hit him. I know he would never lay a hand on Benny. It's not who he is.

Even with all the rioting and segregation in the south, Richard McClain sticks to his ways of being a pacifist. He thinks it's the only way will get through the 1960's decade unscathed.

"Acts of kindness are one of the many blossoms from the roots of love." It's been his mantra no matter the injustices occurring every day to those of color. Benny's never taken to his ways. He's always been apt to protect others through the physical means he's been blessed with.

The night drags on as the sounds drift away from inside the house. Their quiet conversing becomes intermittent background noise. Eventually my pain and tears run their course. I slowly drift into a deep slumber on the cold wood.

----

First, I feel it on my legs. It's warmth that slowly envelops my whole body. It wraps tighter and tighter around me. It feels good until a hand lightly touches the top of my head.

"Oh fuck!" I scream, choking the air out of my larynx.

The figure in front of me calmly takes a seat by the open window in the treehouse. The silhouette of a person is unmoved by my scream, or the spasm of shock. I blink a couple more times before realizing I'm not in a dream.

"Benny," I whisper. "What are you doing here?"

"You were cold, so I got you a blanket and a pillow. My room's all cleaned out, too. Maybe I can help you move the rest of your stuff in tomorrow. If that's okay with you."

Benny McClain just spoke more words to me in the past ten seconds then he has in the last ten days. I'm stuck trying to process his words.

I sit there in awe, looking at his face. The full moon behind him lights up the treehouse just enough to see my favorite features. The sharp jaw line, broad shoulders, fluffy hair, tiny nose and the dimples that go concave with effortless beauty.

*Say something, Penny!*

"Um…thanks, Benny."

"Come sit with me?" Benny says, patting the chair next to him.

I sit down next to him, feeling the tension in the air. Boys in general make no sense, but Benny is a different breed of a 14-year-old boy. He buries his feelings on the inside. He doesn't show that he's in pain, but I can see it. He misses his parents and his grandmother. He worries for his brother. And he worries for his still-grieving grandfather. Now, I've only added more worry and responsibility to his life.

When Benny puts his hand on my shoulder, my body shudders at his touch. Seeing through the darkness, I can somehow still see how perfectly green his eyes are. It's beauty that's too utterly effortless.

"The truth is, it was my idea to adopt you a couple years ago. I remember so many nights being woken up by the screams when your mom was drunk. I don't know how you and Marcus handled those nights. My grandpa wouldn't let me go over there. And I know sometimes he went and helped, but that was my job, too. It was a promise I made to your brother. And for that, I'm so sorry. I've let him down, and I've let you down too many times—just like tonight."

"But Benny—"

"No, no, no. Just let me finish," he says, leaning closer. "The truth is there's many nights I thought about going over there to kill your mom or find some way to rescue you. Then your aunt came along, and things settled down a bit. But I still worry if she comes back and tries to hurt you. And now you're my sister.

It's not that I don't want that, but now I'm worried that others will find out and bring even more trouble to all of us. It's like the target on our backs just got bigger. There's the Klan and there's every other racist asshole in this town that we have to deal with, including those Monroe motherfuckers."

"I'm sorry. I don't mind not signing the papers. It's still not official. If that's what you want, I'll do it. I can take care of myself," I lie.

"No!" he raises his voice. "You'll sign it, and you won't ever think twice about regretting it. You hear me."

I want to argue with him, but I can't. I need Benny.

"Okay," I whisper, feeling my breath go shallow.

"Give me your hand, Penny," he demands, pulling it into his chest.

I can feel the warmth coming from him. His heartbeat races, but not like mine. My heart is manic with desire and so many other emotions I've never felt until this moment of real touch.

Benny may not love me like I love him. But for now, I don't care. His closeness is all I need.

My life is now full of so many uncertain tomorrows. But at least I have a real family now. It's the only thing I've ever dreamed of having. And it always felt impossible, until today.

"Penny McClain, I will never let you down again. But we have to stick together. You won't leave this house without me. We have to all look out for each other. You promise?"

"I promise."

Benny stands up. He hugs my head into his chest. Then he kisses me on the top of my head and leans down to my ear.

"I'm sorry, Sis," he whispers.

That night I learned that there's two kinds of love. There's love for things I thought I could never have, like family. And there's love that you feel for a boy. Each one hurts, but it's the best kind of hurt. It's the only kind of hurt I want to feel…forever.

# CHAPTER THREE

## Benny

### *6 months later*

"Where the fuck is she? You know if we don't get going in the next few minutes we could cross paths with them," Paul complains.

"I know. I know. She said she'd be here. Something must've happened."

Not having control bothers the shit out of me. I take a deep breath, still not knowing what to do.

The routine of picking up my sister has always been followed to a T. She meets Paul and me by the same flagpole outside Westchester High school at 4 p.m. Then we pick up Jimmy at the Day Center and weave our way around the Monroe Farm to get home safe and sound before nightfall.

This is unlike Penny. The one consistency with her is she's never late, and I never leave without her.

"Just go ahead," I tell Paul.

"Buddy, I ain't leaving you. You may be strong, but if you come up on two Monroe brothers, you'll need me."

Paul is right. I've gotten faster and stronger in the last couple years, but so have they. I'd have no chance at protecting myself if the Monroe twins ganged up on me. But it doesn't mean I'm afraid of them.

Things have been better of late. We know the proper routes and time frames to get home safely. If we stick to the schedule, it means avoiding the Monroes and some of the other lowlifes in this town. It's also been easier now that the Monroe twins go to a different school.

"Didn't you say it's her birthday today?" Paul asks.

"Yeah, which is why this makes no sense. I've been nothing but nice to her all day," I defend myself.

Paul shoots me a disbelieving look.

"Okay, maybe I could have been a little nicer this morning," I mutter. "But did you see what she was wearing?"

"Whatever you say, Benny."

Paul Bates is right. I'm just too stubborn to admit it. He's also more than just my best friend. He's my extra security detail when I walk home with Penny and Jimmy. We have each other's back, on and off the football field.

It helps that Paul is the only freshman in our high school that's six foot two and carries enough weight that he's almost two of me. He plays left tackle on our Junior Varsity team. It's a big deal for me as the starting quarterback, because on the football field he protects my blind side.

"Alright, wait right here. I'll run over to the nurse's office to see if something happened. I'll be right back."

Paul nods as I sprint my way back to school grounds. Once on the middle school part of the campus, I hear a familiar whimper by the girls bathroom. I freeze in my tracks, slowly walking towards the entrance.

"Penny!" I shout.

The crying quickly comes to a halt. I wait a little bit longer, only to hear complete silence.

"Penny!" I shout again.

"Go away!" Penny yells.

"What are you doing crying in there. Please, come out!"

"I said go away!"

I let out a long sigh, unsure of what to do. I can't leave her here. But I also can't go inside. Or can I?

"Are you alone in there?"

She starts crying again. I look at my watch, knowing we don't have time for this.

"Okay, I'm coming in."

I take my first trip ever into a girl's bathroom. I turn the corner seeing Penny sitting on the ground crying. She's hugging her backpack over her legs.

"Benny, you have to leave!" she screams, looking terrified by something.

"I'm not leaving." I squat down to sit next to her.

She hugs her backpack tighter over her lap, looking away. It's then I notice the smallest streak of blood on her hands. I reach to grab her hand, but she pulls it out of my grasp.

"You don't want to touch me. Trust me, Benny McClain! Not today!" Her shrill scream leaves her body shuddering in fear.

"Did someone hurt you? I swear, whoever laid a hand on you is going to—"

"No one hurt me, Benny," she quickly interjects. "But something happened to me. And I don't know what to do, or how to get home…like this."

She hugs her backpack tighter into her crotch. My eyes glance down for a split second. Then it clicks in my head.

*Oh fuck!*

"Don't look at me," she reprimands.

"Penny, I know what's going on. And you're going to be okay. Is this the first time?"

She looks away, nodding her head the slightest bit.

"I'll just run to the nurses office and—"

"It's locked. She left at 3:30. You need to just hurry home and get Ms. Green to come get me. But only her. Don't have Dad come all the way out here and see me like this."

I've never heard Penny sound so mortified and embarrassed. I want to tell her she's going to be okay, and this is totally normal. But for now, I feel like my words are only going to incite her even more.

I also know that Ms. Green rarely drives; her eyesight isn't great. And if I leave Penny here in the bathroom, it will take me at least an hour and a half to get back here. And by then we'll be walking home in the dark, which isn't an option.

Running out of ideas I take my jacket off. "Just take it, Penny. Wrap it around your waist and we'll walk to the drugstore."

"But Benny, this is your favorite jacket. You realize it's going to get ruined."

*It's also my only jacket.*

"Don't worry about it. Wrap it around your waist and let's get out of here. Everything is going to be okay."

I sit there looking at her, while she just stares back with a dumbfounded look.

"What?"

Her eyes suddenly widen. "Um, I need privacy. I'll do it, but give me a minute," she complains, rolling her eyes.

I head out of the bathroom feeling like an idiot that I didn't leave sooner. We eventually walk our way back to the flagpole to rejoin Paul.

"Where have you guys been?" Paul groans, raising his hands in the air.

"Don't worry about it, Paul. We have to make a quick stop off at the drugstore, and if you ask why, Penny will probably kick you in the balls."

Penny chuckles under her breath. Luckily, Paul doesn't utter a word to Penny the whole way to the drugstore. He has sisters, so he probably knows.

The closest drugstore is for whites only. Penny doesn't know the specifics of what she needs, so she asks me to get different kinds. I feel mortified as I walk up to the cashier and slide my quarters to the woman. She smiles at me, then glances outside where Paul and Penny wait.

"Are you with them?" she nods toward my friends.

I see the slight change in this lady's facial expression. It's like she's suddenly scowling or feeling confused by something. I want to say yes and tell her it's my sister and my best friend. But I can't be stupid.

"I don't uh, I don't know who they are, ma'am," I mutter. "I'm just getting this for my mom."

Her face becomes congenial again. She hands over my change, then puts the maxi pads in a brown paper bag. "That's good to hear. You don't want no nigger getting close to you. They're the poison in our world," she nonchalantly says, glaring out the window.

My throat freezes up. The tension in my chest is something greater than anger. It's hard to suppress, but I swallow it down, fighting the dire need to defend my family.

"Hey! Hey! You two! No fucking niggers on my sidewalk!"

I watch Penny and Paul calmly walk away. They're doing as their told, being treated like a couple of stray animals.

*Walk away! Walk away!*

I put my hand on the door to leave, but the fire in my belly becomes too much. I turn around, looking at the cashier with the most disingenuous smile.

"That's my sister and my best friend, you fucking redneck racist bitch. Have a great day, you fucking low-life."

The woman's jaw drops. I push the door open, yelling for Paul and Penny to run. We run all the way home, not looking back once.

Once we're home, Penny goes to Ms. Green's house. Paul, Jimmy and I head in to get ready for supper.

It's Penny's 13th birthday today. Grandpa splurged by buying steaks and Ms. Green is bringing over her famous peach cobbler.

This day has been as weird as can be. Nevertheless, I haven't felt as happy as I do today. Maybe I'm on a high for defending my family at the drugstore. But there's also a lot of good in my life to be thankful for.

Penny and I are getting along better. I just got promoted to starting quarterback. And Grandpa's been more of himself, learning to move on from the loss of Grammy.

It helps that he and Ms. Green spend a lot more time with one another. She comes over for dinner almost every single night now. They always share a glass of wine in the evening on the porch. They'll even share a coffee with one another on most mornings.

Ms. Green does more than just help Grandpa as a companion. She also still works with Jimmy every day. The therapies she's doing are helping him cognitively and with his motor skills. She even found a day program for Jimmy to attend three times a week. It's basically a school for people like him.

Feeling good on the inside is a rarity for me. Grandpa tells me I worry too much. He may be right, but when you grow up losing so much that's close to you, it's hard not to. My mind has been programmed for some time now to worry about losing what I already have. It makes life a constant balancing act, because it's hard to relish the good that's right in front of me.

However, tonight is different. I look across the table at Penny laughing it up with Jimmy and Sarah. Sarah is her best friend and Paul's younger sister. Penny's laughing so hard she starts to cry.

It sounds weird, but sometimes I get jealous of her relationship with Jimmy. She's so fond of him. Penny's connection with him comes so naturally. The first time she met Jimmy was up in my treehouse. All she did was smile, hold his hand, and talk to him. She couldn't understand a word of his gibberish, but it didn't matter. She never cared that he was different, she just wanted to help him.

Jimmy is still growing into such a beautiful person. He tells Penny and others what he wants. But more importantly, he expresses so much love to our sister, which Penny always returns.

The pure heart of Penny McClain doesn't make sense to me. How does a young girl who's dealt with abuse, abandonment and bigotry still have a heart this big? And now she's becoming a woman. She's only 13, but she's developing curves in areas that make me uneasy.

I know I usually act cold to her, but it's only because lately she's had a big mouth. Maybe it's hormones, or maybe it's payback for all the years I've been ignoring her. I'd never tell her this, but I like that she's standing up for herself. She'll need the gumption when she ventures out on her own one day.

The thought of her and Jimmy being on their own scares the shit out of me. Even though it may never be a reality for Jimmy, I know Penny will one day go her own way. It'll be the best thing because she'll probably get out of this godforsaken town. She may not know it, but I'll miss her more than she'll ever imagine. But the most troubling part is not knowing how I'll look after her when she leaves.

*"A promise is a promise,"* Marcus had said.

I told Marcus I'd always look after her. "Forever." It was his final dying word.

"How's football going, boys?" Ms. Green asks.

"I pancaked a varsity linebacker today. It was bee – you – tiful!" Paul boasts. "Then Benny hit a receiver on a 60-yard fly right in the breadbasket."

I see Penny looking confused.

"It means I threw a perfect pass and Paul knocked the living shit out of a guy," I clarify.

"Language!" Ms. Green reprimands.

"Sorry, Ms. Green. Paul knocked the bowel movement out of that guy."

I do my best to stifle a giggle. I know better than to use foul language in front of her, but I couldn't help it. Thinking about how good it felt to be on that football field today puts me in a different state of mind. It's like everything in my world becomes copacetic. All I have is my athletic gift, doing what others on the field can't stop.

"You think you boys could jump up to varsity?" Grandpa asks.

"Benny might be able to," Paul says. "I ain't got a chance in hell. Sorry, Ms. Green."

Paul's better than any offensive linemen at Westchester High School. He could probably be one of the best in the state with the quickness and size he has. The only thing he has working against him is Coach Jansen and the color of his skin.

Paul is one of only a handful of black students on the team. All of the black kids play junior varsity, when most of them should all be starters on the varsity team. It wasn't until last year that they were even allowed to play sports.

"Stay with it, son. Just keep your head down and outwork everyone else. Good things will come. Give it time," Grandpa encourages Paul. "Now, who's ready for peach cobbler?"

"Me! Me! Me!" Jimmy shouts.

"Settle down, Jimmy. The birthday girl gets served first," I say.

"Can I be excused for a minute?" Penny asks, standing suddenly at the table.

"But we haven't even sang you—"

"Of course, Penny," Ms. Green interrupts Grandpa, raising her eyebrows at him. "Take your time, Sweetheart. Do you need—"

"No, no, no. I'll be fine," Penny politely says, forcing out a smile.

I seize the opportunity to run out back to get the treehouse ready. I've never gotten her a present for her birthday, but I felt compelled to make this year different. I hope she likes it. It took four weeks' worth of work at the hardware store to pull it off.

After singing "Happy Birthday" and loading up on cobbler, Penny opens Ms. Green's gift. It's a necklace with a purple butterfly attached to it.

"You didn't have to—"

"Uh, uh," Ms. Green interrupts. "The butterfly is a symbol for change and transformation. You're becoming a beautiful young woman. You're going to help shape and change people for the better. My mama gave it to me when I was younger. I don't need it anymore. I've done enough changing and transforming in my life. It's your turn now. Now I'm just a grouchy old lady," she says, chuckling to herself.

Penny wipes her eyes, smiling at Ms. Green.

"Open mine, Penny," Grandpa insists. "It's from all of us boys."

"It is?" I ask.

Grandpa shoots me a glare.

I clear my throat. "I mean, of course. It's from all of us."

Penny rips off the wrapping paper, still smiling ear to ear after opening Ms. Green's gift. Then she pulls out a small picture frame. Her brown eyes widen as she stares at the picture. Then her mouth falls open the slightest bit, letting out a gasp of air.

"It's so beautiful!" She exclaims, rotating the picture so we can all see it.

The symbol is two hands embracing at the wrist, with the words "Penny's Place" at the top. One arm is a pale looking white, and the other is a dark shade of black.

"It'll go great in your treehouse once you see what your brother did up there," Grandpa explains.

Penny glances around the table, still looking shocked. Then she dashes out of her chair and into Grandpa's waiting arms. I can hear him whispering something in her ear. There's only one word I can hear: "remember."

"What did you do to the treehouse, Benny?" Penny asks, wiping her eyes again.

"You'll see."

"I hate surprises. Can I go look at it now?" she eagerly asks.

"Of course. But once you go up there, I guarantee you won't want to leave," I playfully taunt.

Penny giggles. "May I be excused, Dad?"

"Of course."

Penny dashes her way through the living room, giddy with excitement. I get up to follow until the explosion of glass jolts me from my feet. I instinctively dive to the ground, tackling my body over Penny's as glass rains down. I cradle my arms tightly around her body like a shield.

All I hear next is a distant scream from the front yard. "Nigger lovers!" Then a car peels out while Jimmy screams a shrill of panic.

# CHAPTER FOUR

# Penny

"You said what?"

Grandpa's tongue-lashing echoes through the backyard. He's finding out for the first time what Benny said to the lady at the drugstore.

I want to defend Benny, but I know it'll just make him and Grandpa more upset. It's possible that Benny's actions had nothing to do with the three bricks smashing through our window and whizzing by my head. But deep down I know that's wishful thinking. Regardless, those three bricks sent a much bigger message.

*We'll never be safe!*

It was only a matter of time before people in this town found out how Grandpa took me in as one of his own. We don't advertise my adoption to very many, and the few that do know in our community would never mention it to anyone else. I don't even know if the adoption was done legally.

It all doesn't matter. At the end of the day, I've been living with the McClain's for some time now. It's who I am, and I wouldn't want it any other way. Besides, the adoption is probably a minor detail when you consider there's multiple black people and one mentally challenged kid going in and out of this house every single day.

Rung by rung, I begin making my way up the Aleppo pine tree. I've been making this trip ever since the McClain's gave me and my brother the key to their back yard gate. I was only five years old at the time, but that key symbolized something much bigger. It symbolized the path to my safe place above the noise of my mom.

I haven't seen my mom in well over two years. My Aunt Mary no longer lives in Birmingham. She moved with her new husband to Mather Air Force Base in Sacramento last year. She'll call on occasion to check in, but she has her own family and her own life to worry about now.

My mind plays back the events of today. Physically I'm unharmed, but emotionally, I feel scarred. The day was an ebb and flow of so many emotions. I got my period for the first time in front of Benny and Paul. Then I spent time at Ms. Green's house. She walked me through the early stages of menstruation. Then she patiently answered my millions of questions.

During my early encounters with Ms. Green, she seemed like a bit of a grouch. But she's mellowed out over the last year. And today I saw a different side of her. She hugged me so many times I lost count. She also kept telling me how she is so proud of my becoming a woman. I don't feel proud, but something inside me feels different.

I get to the top of the treehouse with my mind still drowning in pain and guilt. I worry for my family's safety more than my own. Benny's not going to let this slide without getting revenge, no matter what Dad is telling him right now.

Once in the treehouse I rub my tired eyes before turning on the lamp. Then I freeze, looking around the treehouse. Everything feels different. It's no longer the same treehouse. Usually there's a dusty old wicker chair and some blankets and pillows scattered on the floor along with my books. But I don't recognize any of it.

The treehouse is immaculately clean, from floor to ceiling. The makeover includes a brand-new daybed and desk in opposite corners. There's also a new bookshelf with all of my favorite books neatly arranged. The wicker chair has brand new purple cushions and a glossy new finish along the arms and legs. I run my hands along different parts of the treehouse wondering how much time and money was put into this.

Then I walk closer to the new desk. There's a small picture frame of all four of us kids. Jimmy's resting his head on Benny's chest. Next to them is Marcus and me with our arms around each other. The smiles on our faces are priceless.

I hug the picture to my chest. I close my eyes remembering that pain-free day. It was a rarity for me and Marcus. The pressure in my chest becomes warm and heavy. The feeling slowly rises in my body until it rests heavy behind my eyes.

*Benny did all of this…for me!*

"Knock, knock," his voice startles me from behind.

His voice has changed a lot in the last couple years. It's more hoarse and manly than before. I like it, *a lot*.

I try to stifle my sniffles, wiping at my eyes before I turn around.

"Hey, Benny. What are you doing up here?"

"Don't mind me. Just putting up your sign. I'll be in and out."

Benny goes straight to work, putting up the beautiful sign that Dad made me.

I stand there in silence, my questions hanging on the tip of my tongue.

*Did you see who threw the bricks? Was it the Monroe brothers?*

*Is Ms. Green okay? How are Jimmy and Dad? How are you?*

All of the questions in my head would be played down by Benny. He'd give me the same kind of answers that Dad would by telling me to not worry. But how could I not worry?

"Thank you for the treehouse. I love it."

"Welcome," he quietly mutters.

"Benny, are you—"

"I'm fine," he interrupts. "Don't worry about a thing. Paul and I will handle it."

He continues to hammer away, his voice so even-keeled. I know it's the opposite of how his insides feel right now. He's human, there's no way he's not scared. Beneath those stubborn and callous layers beats a heart I wish I could understand, or at least find.

I take a long frustrating sigh. There's just no hope with Benny. He never lets me in on how he's really feeling. If I do get a glimpse, it passes faster than a bolt of lightning.

I take a seat in my new armchair and crack open my favorite Claire Forrester novel. Benny continues to straighten things up after putting up my sign. He says nothing as he lays down under my desk. He must be tightening some loose screws. But all I see is his shirt sliding up past his belly button, revealing indentations in his stomach. I pull my book down a couple inches. I'm no longer reading my book. My eyes are reading Benny's body. I feel my mouth watering at the sight of his hardened stomach muscles and the bulge in his pants. It feels wrong to be staring at my brother like that, but I can't stop. The feelings fluttering around in my belly feel too good to stop.

Time passes as I admire so many other things about his body. The only thing I wish I could see from this angle is the glimmer of his green eyes. His eyelashes are long like most girls would only dream of, and it further enhances the beauty of those emerald irises.

Benny's a naturally beautiful boy. But his eyes are my favorite part. They're the only part of him that tells me how he feels on the inside. Right now, if I could see them, they'd tell me he's hurting on the inside like the rest of us.

I've only seen him cry twice in my life: when Grammy and Marcus died. He doesn't talk much about his parent's passing, but he was only five years old at the time.

When Benny slides out from under the desk I quickly dart my eyes back to my book. I'm still reading his body, just with my imagination now.

"All done," he says, getting up to leave.

"Thanks, Benny."

I try smiling in his direction, but he walks past me like I'm a ghost.

My eyes try to read the words in my book, but it all looks like a jumble of letters. Then, out of the corner of my eye, I notice Benny stop. He slowly turns to look back.

"You know…" He pauses, letting out a long sigh. "What happened today is not your fault."

"I know," I lie.

"Are you okay?" Benny asks.

I feel the shuddering emotion ripple through my body. His words have a conscientious tone I rarely hear.

"I'll be okay," I lie again.

I feel the tears behind my eyes. I slide my book up a couple inches to shield my eyes from Benny. It makes him uncomfortable when I cry.

The creaking of wood gets louder. I can feel him getting closer, so I shut my eyes, trying to stop the tears. Then I feel his hand on my shoulder. His flesh feels so warm and comforting on mine, but it breaks me at my core.

My book falls into my lap. I bury my face in my hands, reliving the terrifying moment of glass raining down all around me. The images in my mind feel too vivid. Then I focus on my angel shielding me from harm. His willingness to protect makes the tears pour out harder. Benny says nothing, instead, he just wraps his arms tighter around me. His hands glide up and down my back to make our embrace even more unforgettable.

I can't remember the last time Benny McClain gave me a hug. But I don't want it to ever end. I want to feel more of him, so I wrap my arms tighter around his hardened waist. He lets my tears drench his shoulder and neck. He leans into me with a suffocating pressure I'm starving for.

Time passes and I imagine a clock, the hands frozen in time. The whole world stops to Benny McClain's rare showing of affection. The feelings of safety and love become a never-ending part of my dream world.

Then it's gone in a flash. He lets go suddenly, rising tall over my head. He leans down to press his lips into the top of my head. His lips meld into my hair with the bottom lip barely touching the skin of my forehead. The warmth on my skin sends a special kind of shiver through my body. Then his lips lift off as he quickly turns away.

My mouth falls open, but the words don't come out. I want to scream for him to stay. I want to go on my hands and knees, begging for him to share the words hidden beneath the layers over his heart.

*Don't leave! Please hold me, just a little longer.*

Benny's out of the treehouse before I can blink twice. He leaves as suddenly as he arrived. He came up here saying very few words. But his actions spoke with so much depth and affection. It's everything I've always dreamed of getting from him, but now I'm addicted and craving more.

----

The next day our walk to school is just the two of us. Paul's either sick or freaked out from last night. I wouldn't know because Benny refuses to tell me what's going on. He's quickly back to his old self.

Regardless, I woke up today vowing for things to be different. I'm going to get Benny McClain talking, even if I have to beg for it. But so far we're halfway to school and I don't know shit.

"How are you doing?"

"I'm fine," he tersely mutters.

"Benny, I saw paper notes wrapped around the bricks. What did they say?"

"Don't worry about it."

"No!" I raise my voice. "Please tell me what's happening," I beg.

"Mind your business. I already said I'd handle it," Benny barks back.

"No! No! Stop this!" I realize I'm screaming. But I don't care. "I'm not a little girl anymore. If you're so hell-bent on protecting me, then talk to me. Stop treating me like a defenseless child. I can fight back! I'm tough!"

Benny stops in his tracks. His head hangs down, shaking side-to-side.

"Oh, yeah. Prove it. What're you going to do?"

All it takes is Benny's mocking crooked smile. It brings out a rage in me that I didn't even know existed. I quickly charge at him like a bull going after a matador. My arms fly into his chest as my right knee flies up towards his abdomen. The collision catches Benny off guard, knocking the air out of the both of us. He falls flat on his back, suddenly gasping for air.

It takes me a second to gather my bearings as I roll onto my hands and knees. Then I realize he's still wheezing for air.

"Oh, fuck! Are you okay, Benny?"

I suddenly realize that his hands are over his crotch, writhing in pain. He slowly starts to catch his breath.

"Fuck, Penny!"

"Did I hit you in the..." I pause, realizing my question is rhetorical with his hands over his groin.

It was never my intention to knee him in the balls. I just wanted to show him that I'm strong enough to knock him to the ground.

*Mission accomplished. I guess.*

Benny slowly pulls himself up, still holding his hand over his privates. Then his scowl morphs into another crooked smile. His smile gets wider before becoming a laugh.

I'm stunned beyond belief. I don't know how this is funny, but his giggle roars into a deeper belly laugh. For some reason it annoys the shit out of me.

"Why are you laughing?" I finally ask.

"Oh, man. I don't know," he sighs, collecting his breath. "But maybe you're stronger than I thought. It still doesn't change anything, Penny. What I keep from you is only for your own safety."

*Fuck my life!*

Benny McClain is officially the most stubborn human being on earth. But so am I.

"If Marcus never died, would you still look after me?"

Benny's smirk vanishes the second I utter my brother's name. His mouth hangs open while his eyes pop out of his skull. He's paralyzed by memories, both good and bad. The question may be below the belt, but it's an answer I need from him. I know the promise made between Benny and my brother. But things have gone too far. Everyone's at risk.

Our stare-down becomes a standoff, and I refuse to blink or back down from my question. After a minute of stunned silence, Benny bends down to dust his knees off. He grabs his backpack and continues his walk to school.

I catch up to him, and we walk side-by-side in complete silence. I'm out of answers about what to do. I've stood up to him with my words and with every ounce of physicality I have. Yet, I continue to lose.

Then the tight grasp of his hand tomahawks down on my shoulder. I shudder.

"Stop walking," he demands. "It was a threat."

"What?"

"The message on the bricks. Two of them had the n-word on it. And the third one said next time we'll send bullets."

I swallow his words, trying to digest what's really happening. I'm glad I know, but I also regret it at the same time. It makes my insides feel suddenly hollow.

"Are you happy you know now?" Benny asks, letting go of my shoulder.

"Um, yes," I mutter.

"And I'd look after you no matter what. Your brother never asked me to take care of you. I know it's what he wanted, but I started that conversation on his death bed. I told him I'd look after you until the day we're both in the grave. It was my idea—

all mine!" Benny pounds his fist over his chest with gritting teeth. "And if I say I'm going to do something, you better believe I mean it. You're my family. You, Jimmy, Grandpa and Ms. Green. There's no difference. We're all the same—black, white, smart or dumb, I don't give a shit."

The gleam in his green eyes brightens. Like a Phoenix rising from the ashes, Benny McClain breathes confidence in his words. He's a man of typically few words, but there's no doubting his heart—especially in this moment.

"So, what are you going to do?" I ask.

"Nothing. I promised Grandpa I'd do nothing. He said revenge is a never-ending cycle."

Benny bites his lip, like he's wanting to take back words that aren't his own.

"But Penny, you better believe if these cowards step up to my face, I'm going to protect all of us. Even if it means cracking their skulls."

"Can you teach me?" I ask.

"Teach you what?"

"How to defend myself. Eventually you'll be off to college or living your own life. You're not going to be able to always look after me and Jimmy. Come on. Help me, Benny."

Benny runs his hand along the back of his neck as he grimaces. My eyes trace his broad shoulders, his jaw line and plump lips.

"Okay. I'll teach you what I've learned in my Judo classes. But you'll never need to use it unless there's some impossible reason I'm not around to protect you. Only if there's an emergency. Deal?"

Benny extends his hand. I reach out to grab it. Then, in a flash, my arm contorts around my body. His leg sweeps across my feet, knocking me face first towards the ground. If not for his arm flying over my chest to catch me, I would've eaten dirt.

Benny lifts me to my feet, pulling his arm and hand off my breasts. His smirk quickly morphs into embarrassment.

"Sorry about that. I didn't mean to touch you right there. I swear," he quickly apologizes with his hands in the air.

"It's okay. I did just knee you in the balls a second ago. We'll call it even."

Benny's cheeks get rosier. It's the first time I've ever seen him embarrassed. I do my best not to giggle. Besides, I'd be lying if I said it didn't feel good to be man-handled by him.

He helps me practice the self-defense move a few times until I get it right. Then we continue our long walk to school. My mind continues to race, thinking about all of the good and bad in my life. Right now, I'm thinking more about the goodness that walks next to me—always protecting me. And finally letting me in.

# CHAPTER FIVE

## Benny

"You ready?"

"I was born ready, Benny boy," Paul replies, slapping my back with an echoing thud.

Together we begin our walk from Westchester High to Monroe Farms. We're acting unfazed by the mission ahead, but we're both nervous as fuck.

The Monroe brothers are the prime suspects for smashing our window two nights ago. The tire marks by our house match the red Chevy Apache they drive. Paul also got some new intel through a couple friends this morning. Apparently, the lady I told off two days ago at the drugstore is the Monroe brother's aunt.

"So, tell me the plan?" Paul asks.

"You're not going to like it, Paul."

He frowns. "Look, I'm not afraid to teach those fuckers a lesson. Even if it comes down to three against two."

I chuckle at Paul's pompous attitude, thinking how nice it must be to be six feet tall and 250 pounds of lean muscle. It's a shame we can't use it to our advantage.

"Fighting them isn't an option. No matter what."

"What do you mean?" he asks.

"The plan is we return the bricks," I explain, repeating my grandpa's master plan.

"Like, into their skulls," Paul says with a dumbfounded look.

I shake my head. "Nope."

"What the fuck are you talking about. I don't get it."

"That's the plan. Grandpa wants us to return the bricks. He said to leave them at their doorstep along with this note he gave me," I explain, holding up the envelope.

Paul stops in his tracks, slapping his hand into my chest. "Man, your grandpa lost his damn mind!"

"I know. But we don't have a choice. He says if he has a sniff that we got into a fight, then no more football. I ain't risking their sorry asses for my love of football. He said he'd tell your parents, too. And you know your mom and dad will beat your ass. Besides, the twins will still be at football practice. Worst-case scenario is we run into their dad and their younger brother."

Paul and I have dealt with the twins on multiple occasions growing up. Early on, the Monroes served up their fair share of ass-whoopings on us. They're a year older than us and still large behemoths. But now we can match their physical stature if we need to.

We've been able to avoid them over the last couple years because we're now at different schools. We don't know much about the younger brother, Ricky. All we do know is he's a Monroe offspring, meaning he's probably a racist piece of shit.

The Monroe family name still owns some of the farmland in Birmingham. But Grandpa says they lost a good portion of their land when slaves began to gain more rights and labor costs rose. Their last name is still attached to the idea of "having money." But they're even better known for having roots in the Ku Klux Klan.

All of these things should scare my grandpa. But he grew up with the father, Clarence Monroe. Grandpa thinks he's harmless. He only believes the Monroes are misguided by the tragedy of losing their mother to a horrific car accident at such a young age.

*"Every person has a story,"* Grandpa said last night. *"Whether it's right or wrong, we always try to understand why, before placing judgment."*

"What did your grandpa put in that note?" Paul asks.

"He told me it's to schedule a meeting between the two of them."

"Seriously? Should we read it?"

"No. If Grandpa said that's what he wrote, that's what he wrote."

"Then why does he want us risking our asses coming down here to drop off their bricks? Is this another one of his life lessons?"

"Who knows? Maybe he really is losing his mind."

We turn the corner on Knob Tree Road and see the familiar house at the end of the cul-de-sac. It's a two-story Victorian style house with a wraparound porch. I breathe a sigh of relief that the twins' red Apache Truck isn't parked out front. All that's in the driveway are two tractors and their dad's blue Chevelle.

"Wait right here," I tell Paul as we approach the steps leading up to the front door.

"No way. I'm coming with you."

I want to tell him it's not a good idea. But Paul's too stubborn.

I put down my backpack, pulling all three bricks out of my bag. The notes are still attached to them. I place them on the door mat, then knock loudly on the screen door. My stomach quickly ties into knots hearing the commotion inside.

The screen door squeaks open. A tall, wrinkly old man with a filthy white shirt and faded blue jeans appears. It's Clarence Monroe. He takes a long draw on his cigarette, then blows it the direction of my face. I watch his eyes glance over to Paul. His face scowls with a look of utter disgust.

"Who the fuck are you?" he asks, looking back at me.

His voice is scratchy and strained, his eyes heavy with wrinkles and bags. He's tall but emaciated in the face and upper torso.

"My name is Benny McClain, sir."

"My name is—"

"I didn't ask you!" he shouts at Paul, staring daggers over my shoulder. "Benny who?"

"McClain, sir."

"Are you Chip's boy?"

Hearing the name of my late father hurts. I have so few memories of him, but his absence still hurts the same.

I nod, swallowing the tension in my throat. "Yes."

"A shame what happened to Chip and your mama. But I got shit to do. So tell me your business."

"Well, those three bricks came through my window two nights ago. The rumor is a red Apache your kids drive peeled out in front of my house about when this happened. The bricks almost hit my sister."

*Oh shit!*

"Sister? I thought you just had that dumb fucking retard for a brother."

*Retard!*

The word causes my fists to ball up. I close my eyes for a quick deep breath to reign in the rage.

"I have a sister too, sir. And don't call my brother a—"

"I'll call him what I want," he quickly interrupts, grimacing as he bends down to grab a brick.

He unwraps the note, reading it over. His mouth smirks the slightest bit. "This don't look like my boys' handwriting. You got no proof. Now go on. You and your gorilla need to get off my property," he says, glaring over my shoulder.

"What did you call me?" Paul asks.

I feel Paul take a step closer from behind me.

"I ain't talking to you, nigger!" he shouts, reaching to the side of his doorway.

The barrel tip of Clarence's 10 gauge brandishes a couple inches into view. I turn around to Paul, placing my hand on his chest. His eyes are wide with a fear and anger I've never seen in him. He looks like he's ready to pancake this guy and rip his head off.

"Go wait at the bottom of the steps. I got this," I quickly tell him.

My heart races as Paul stands there, looking like an immovable object.

"Come on, Paul! Just go!" I raise my voice.

He finally walks down as a younger boy appears in the doorway. He says nothing, looking unfazed by the sight of his father holding a weapon.

"You know anything about this, Ricky?" Clarence asks, handing the note over.

"Nope," he replies, staring down at his feet.

"Well, there you have it, Benny. We got nothing to do with this. Now go on before your pet monkey does something he'll regret."

"Your boys did this!" I raise my voice, taking a step closer. I hand him the envelope. "I didn't come here to start trouble. My Grandpa won't let me see the football field ever again if I do. But your boys did this for no good reason. I'm only here because my grandpa wanted me to return your bricks and give you this note. That's all. We'll be leaving now."

Clarence opens the envelope as I walk away. Paul gives one last glare over his shoulder as we head out.

The two of us say nothing. We begin our 40-minute trek home. The longer our silence lasts, the more I regret not standing up for the people I love. I don't know what I could've done, but I'm pissed. That piece of shit trashed the name of my family. It's all grandpa's fault for making me choose football.

"You okay, man?" Paul asks.

"I'm sorry," I admit.

"What are you sorry for?"

"I don't know," I reply, taking a long, frustrated breath.

There's a roaring engine sound from behind us, and dust and dirt quickly flood the air.

*It's them!*

The tall figure standing in the bed of the truck begins hurling rocks at us. I cover my head a second too late as my vision goes black. Then I hear the Apache peel out as I feel a cloud of rocks and dirt flying into my face.

----

"Aaahhh! That stings, Penny."

"Stop whining, Benny. It's just a black eye."

Penny stays intensely focused on cleaning my wounds. Then she wraps the bandage very delicately over my left eye.

I'm lucky the rock didn't go into my eyeball. It hit my left eyebrow, leaving a bump the size of a golf ball. The rocks thrown at Paul only left a couple small bruises on his back.

The conversation between Paul and Grandpa is wrapping up in the other room. He's giving the exact same story I gave my grandpa.

Eventually I hear the front door close. Grandpa must be giving Paul a ride home.

"What else happened?" Penny asks.

"I've told you everything."

She glares at me.

I raise my right hand high in the air. "I swear to god."

I really have told every bit of our story.

"Was it all three brothers throwing the rocks?" she asks.

"No, just the twins. The blond curly haired one was driving. And the one with short brown hair was in the bed of the truck."

"So what're we going to do, Benny? Should we maybe have you return the rocks back to their house?"

I look up at Penny, grinning from ear to ear.

"What? Too soon?" she chuckles.

I start giggling. "Yep, way too soon."

We begin to laugh harder. It feels good to laugh after having such a shitty day.

Jimmy barges into the bathroom.

"Are you okay, Benny?"

"I'm fine. Just a few bruises and scrapes. Are you okay?"

Jimmy's eyes go down to his feet. His hands begin fidgeting in his pockets. It's a look of embarrassment to most, but to me, I know he's just confused. He saw Penny crying earlier. He also heard the commotion with Grandpa when we recounted what happened.

I grab his wrist to slow his fidgeting. "Hey. Hey. Look at me. I'm fine. Everyone's okay. I'm not letting anything happen to any of us. You're safe. You hear me, Jimmy?"

Jimmy continues to avoid my eyes. I can tell there's something else troubling him. It's something he can't articulate with his words. Then he hands me a note and quickly walks away.

**Went to take Paul home. Then to go take care of something. I won't be home for dinner tonight. Don't wait up for me and don't worry. Be home in a couple hours. – Grandpa.**

I hand the note to Penny. Grandpa never misses dinner with his family. It's as important as church.

"What does he mean, 'take care of something'?" Penny asks, reading the note again.

"It's probably just errands."

"You don't think he'd go back to Monroe farms? Do you?"

I rub my temples, taking a deep breath. "I don't know with him anymore. But try not to worry. Whatever he's doing, I'm sure there's a good reason."

*I hope.*

The three of us begin working on dinner together. Penny walks Jimmy through the process of homemade mashed potatoes while I make the pork chops.

Jimmy's not talking much. He's completely thrown for a loop, not having Grandpa here when he's always home for dinner. Any changes in routine still affect him emotionally.

Once dinner is ready, Sarah joins us. Luckily, she doesn't bring up what happened to me and her brother.

I used to think Sarah was annoying. But now I like seeing her around Penny. She brings out the silly, fun side of Penny. It's a welcome distraction given the events over the last couple days.

The only thing I don't like about Sarah is she's boy crazy right now. And when she brings that out in Penny, it makes me uncomfortable. I think they're both too young to be even talking about dating and boys, but maybe it's just the protective, big brother part of me, overreacting.

After dinner, we all enjoy dessert before Sarah heads home. Once Jimmy goes to bed, we both get started on homework.

When nine o'clock rolls around, Penny suggests I call Ms. Green. The second I grab the phone, Grandpa strolls through the front door. He walks into the house like it's just another ho-hum day.

"Where've you been?" I ask, unable to hide my sour tone.

"Let me grab some food first," he replies, avoiding my eyes.

Penny rolls her eyes, giving me a "What the fuck is going on?" look.

We sit down with Grandpa, watching him eat his food in a laborious fashion. He says nothing until his plate is empty.

"What?" he finally asks.

"Where have you been? Me and Benny have been worried sick," Penny complains.

"I was handling something. It's something Benny and me will need to talk about in private," Grandpa explains.

He picks up his dish and walks to the sink. I glance at Penny, who looks frustrated. She pounds her hand on the table, hitting it so hard my glass falls off, shattering beneath my chair. Grandpa freezes in his tracks, with his back to Penny.

"No! No more of this, Dad! I'm done! I can't lose anyone else," she pleads, walking around to stand in front of him. "Now give me your arm. Give it to me!" she yells, leaning her face within inches of his.

Penny finally grabs his wrist. She squeezes it so tight I start to see her arm shake. "You remember this. If we really were the same, you wouldn't treat me like a child. But we're different. I'm just a lowly nigger who's your charity. Aren't I!" she screams.

The hairs on my neck stand up. I've never seen Penny stand up to Grandpa.

"You're not that, Penny," he finally says. "You're my daughter. I'm just like any other dad who protects and loves his daughter. You have to believe that."

"Bullshit," Penny says, letting go of his arm. She marches straight into the backyard. Grandpa places his dish in the sink, then turns around to face me.

"You went to Monroe Farms, didn't you?" I ask.

"I did."

"And?"

"I spoke to Clarence Monroe. Then I talked briefly to his boys. They denied throwing those bricks through our living room window. And they claimed self-defense with throwing those rocks at you and Paul. Then Clarence sent them back up to their rooms. After that I wished Clarence a good evening and walked away."

I feel my mouth fall to the floor. My insides rage with inextinguishable anger.

"You walked away. That's it. That's your story?" I ask through gritted teeth.

"Well, there's a little more that happened after that. But let's just say we came to a truce. As long as we avoid one another, Clarence assured me his boys won't cause any more trouble."

"What do you mean?"

"That's all you need to know. I'm off to bed. I'll deal with your sister in the morning," he calmly explains.

I stare at Grandpa, feeling dumbfounded. How did he create a truce with those pieces of shit? And why would he take that asshole for his word?

Grandpa walks past me, stopping at the doorway of his room. "One more thing," he says turning around. "You do remember what I taught you about revenge, don't you?"

How could I forget. He's only repeated it a thousand times in my life.

"It's a never-ending cycle. But Grandpa, I don't—"

"Ah, ah, ah," he interrupts. "Just remember that lesson. And know that Clarence Monroe is not well. That man is living with a lot of grief and anguish. I've been there many times. It clouds your judgment from right and wrong. It's not an excuse. But it's his reality he has to work through. He's not too different from us in some ways. But the only difference is, I still know how to show love and compassion to you three. Those Monroe boys don't get that from their father. And there's a lot of pain in that family—a lot of pain. That's why we'll never be ones to judge, but we'll always be ones to forgive. Don't you ever forget that, Benny McClain."

I bite my tongue to keep myself from blowing up in his face. Grandpa slowly starts to shut his bedroom door. Then he stops halfway.

"And one other thing, Benny. I'm sorry I put you boys in that situation. Your Grammy always said I have too much faith in people. I guess she was right. Goodnight, now."

I head into the backyard. My climb up the tree is slower than usual. I'm wondering if I should just let her be for the night.

"I can hear you, Benny."

"Sorry, I just wanted to make sure you're okay. You mind if I come in?" I ask.

She turns from her desk to wave me in. I take a seat on her new armchair. Then her eyes go suddenly wide with fear.

"What is it?" I ask.

"You're bleeding."

I touch the bandage and notice there's a smear of blood on my fingers.

"You okay?" Penny asks.

"Yeah, I bumped it on a branch coming up here. It's no big deal, probably just a broken scab. I'll be fine."

"Let me take care of it," Penny raises her voice, looking concerned. "I have a first aid kit up here."

"Penny, I'll be fine."

She mutters something under her breath and goes to grab the first aid kit, then sits down on the arm of my chair, slowly leaning in to remove my bandage. I close my eyes, relaxing to her careful touch. She cleans the wound again and replaces the bandage.

"There you go. You're good as new. Just make sure you ice it a little before bed."

"Thanks," I say, smiling at her.

"Of course."

I grab Penny's wrist, stopping her from getting off the arm of my chair. Her head tilts to the side, her brown eyes look suddenly confused.

"Wait. I meant what I said. Thank you for helping me."

"It's just a bruise, Benny. It's no big deal."

I look into her eyes, feeling suddenly overcome with emotions that are hard to articulate. I've never been good at it, but maybe I can find the right words.

"It's not just the eye," I say, looking down at my grip over her wrist. "There's really a lot of things I've been meaning to thank you for. You do so much for Jimmy and so much for Grandpa—for me, too. And I know I don't ever say it to you, but…" I pause, taking a long sigh.

*Just say the words, you wimp!*

Penny flashes a crooked smile. It's too dark to tell if she's blushing, but I feel like she might be.

She lightly pats my wrist. "I know, Benny. I football you too," she chuckles softly.

That night we stay up way too late. I tell her about my conversation with Grandpa. Then I answer every one of her questions, without holding back like I usually do. I can tell she appreciates my candor.

The night stretches on to us talking about so many other random topics. Some are serious and others are silly. We talk mostly about our dreams and aspirations after high school. Penny tells me about her dream of becoming a teacher for people like Jimmy. The vision she has for helping others understand people like Jimmy is awe-inspiring. It shows me a kindness I've always seen in her, but tonight, I truly appreciate it.

Her candor about her future helps me open up to her. I tell her about my worries for Jimmy after high school, and how I worry about Grandpa getting older. Penny doesn't just listen, she hears me. She shares in the responsibility and worries like I do. It helps me feel less alone.

I'm also able to tell Penny about my dreams of making it into professional football. I tell her how I want to take care of the family financially and then retire and go into coaching.

Penny doesn't doubt my lofty goals. Instead, she just smiles and says supportive things. She tells me how she believes in me.

It's after 2 a.m. when we head out of the treehouse to get to bed. We're both tired beyond belief, but I get the feeling that Penny didn't want the night to end. And the truth is, neither did I.

I may not be able to tell my sister how much I love her and how much she means to me and our family. But I feel like tonight is the first time I've truly talked to her. I let her be heard. It's what I've been denying her for far too long and for no good reason at all. I want to tell her how sorry I am, and tell her how much she means to me, but I'm not always the best with my words. Instead, I just give her a big hug before bed and a kiss on top of her head.

Tonight is the first night I go to bed realizing that Penny McClain is more than just my sister. She's my best friend, too.

# CHAPTER SIX

# Penny

## *3 years later*

The clock strikes zero. The energy of the Westchester crowd erupts. My eardrums are rattling, but I don't care. I scream at the top of my lungs. The exhilaration deep in my bones is something I've never felt before.

Benny McClain just threw the winning touchdown for his first state championship. It's my birthday of all days today.

I told him before the game all I wanted was a win and three touchdown passes. He ended up throwing four touchdowns and running one in as well. He's undoubtedly the game's most valuable player.

Jimmy holds his hands over his ears. He's elated, but also unhappy about the deafening crowd noise. I squeeze his shoulder for comfort. Years ago, he would have run from crowds and screaming noises. But now he can manage the sensory overload.

Meanwhile, Dad and Ms. Green are still on their feet screaming. Dad is so happy he's actually crying a little with Ms. Green. He still tells Benny and me that he and Ms. Green are just friends, but we know better. The way they look at each other is not the way friends do.

Life has been good for the McClains over the last three years. I'm now a sophomore in high school. My grades have been really good, and I just got my first job at the local diner that Sarah's parents own.

Our family gets our usual stares as we file out of the stadium. Jimmy's arm is hooked around mine while Ms. Green and Dad walk side by side. The stares are still bothersome, but most days I'm used to it. It helps that everyone knows we're related to the great Benny McClain.

Benny eventually meets up with us for dinner at Patty's Steakhouse. It's the only place we go out to eat because it's one of the few places that serves blacks and whites.

Benny walks in with his hair combed back and his Varsity Jacket on. He hugs each of us, one at a time. I'm last, standing next to Jimmy. I begin to tear up when I see how hard he hugs his brother. Then he whispers in his ear, "I did this for you."

He comes to me, and my arms wrap tightly around his torso as he leans down over me. His hug feels like a warm blanket on the coldest of days. The security and love I feel radiating from him feels so good. Maybe too good.

"Happy Birthday," he whispers in my ear. "I have a gift I need to give to you tonight. Will you Scrabble with me later?"

I eagerly nod my head, feeling my smile stretch wider with giddy excitement. Benny and I stay up late most nights in the treehouse. We typically play board games and chat about anything that's going on in either of our worlds.

We rarely hang out in public except when we walk to school together. This makes the time at night with Benny feel extra special. Everyone's asleep and our relationship no longer feels like brother and sister. Instead, we're just friends that enjoy each other's company.

I've slowly accepted that's all I'll ever be to Benny. It's more than me just being his sister. He's had girlfriends on and off for the last couple years and he doesn't look at me like that—even if my body is developing curves. Sarah loves telling me otherwise, but I just don't think he's attracted to me in the way that I'm attracted to him.

I wonder how any girl could not be attracted to him. His eyes are so green I could get lost in them for hours, dreaming about how they'd feel up close. His hair is a fluffy golden brown with hints of curls that I just want to bury my hands and face in. His shoulders and chest are so broad it's like he's wearing armor. All I want to do is window wash his bare skin with my hands to feel those perfect ripples. And his smile is unlike anything else, making my heart overflow every time I see it.

Throughout dinner, other diners call out "Cheetah!" It's the nickname Benny's gotten as he's become a bigger star on the football field.

Every person in this town wants to shake hands with Benny and congratulate him on his full-ride scholarship to Eastern Alabama University. But Benny is humble like Grandpa. He deflects all the praise to his teammates, especially Paul and his offensive line. It's the fair thing to do, because Paul protected his blindside all season long, allowing him to be a standout on the field.

The only bothersome part of being interrupted every minute is how most people ignore Ms. Green and myself. It's like we don't exist because of our black skin. And if we say something they pretend not to hear us, like we're ghosts. Ms. Green may not care, but today it's eating at me.

Towards the end of dinner Benny heads outside to chat with his girlfriend, Samantha. She's the head cheerleader and they've been a couple for the past few months. Her boobs are massive, and her blond hair is curly and long. It's the opposite of how I look, except I have a much nicer ass.

When I glance outside I notice that Samantha and Benny both seem tense. I'm not sure what's going on, but something's troubling them. It seems odd for them to look so upset on the night we become state champs.

Later that night I lie down on the new loveseat in the treehouse. The minute hand of my clock seems to be moving extra slow as I eagerly wait for Benny. Then I see the flash of light shine up from the kitchen.

Benny makes his way up the treehouse. The smile on his face couldn't be brighter.

"Hey, all-star," I say.

He takes a seat across from me with the Scrabble board between us.

"I've got good news, Penny."

"Oh, yeah?"

"Yeah, Paul officially has a partial athletic scholarship to Eastern Alabama. He'll be part of the team with me."

"That's great news! But why only a partial scholarship? Why not a full ride like you? You told me he was the best left tackle in the state."

Benny's smile morphs into something else. He just shakes his head staring at the ground. My question suddenly feels rhetorical.

"He is the best in the state. But the athletic director is a bigot, plain and simple. He said they don't give scholarships to the colored boys. I threatened to rescind my offer."

"You did what?"

"I told him I'd go to Northern Alabama. It was Grandpa's idea to give us leverage by threatening to go to a rival school. It didn't work because Paul deserves a full ride to play football, but a partial scholarship is better than nothing."

I begin thinking about college decisions as our Scrabble game gets going.

"Can I ask you something, Benny?"

"Sure."

"Why did you only consider going to in-state schools? You could have probably gone anywhere. And I told you I'd stay home as long as I needed to take care of Dad and Jimmy."

"I know, but that shouldn't be only your burden," he calmly explains, shuffling the tiles on his board.

Benny's offers from colleges were basically a full-ride ticket to any school in the country. There was Notre Dame, University of Southern California, and the University of Texas to name a few. And yet he chose Eastern Alabama. It's a good school only 50 miles northeast of our house. But they're not a football powerhouse and it's not one of the more prestigious educations he could be getting.

I want him close like he'll be, but I also want him to consider what's best for his future.

"You know, I mean what I said. I really don't mind taking care of Dad and Jimmy and just doing the junior college thing. It's the least I can do for all you guys have done for me. I mean, I'll be here regardless. Maybe you should reconsider a bigger school."

His eyes go from the game to mine. His brow furrows and he tilts his head.

"You know, Penny, Grandpa and Jimmy aren't the only reason I want to be close to home."

"They're not?"

My question hangs in the air. I don't want him saying he'll miss his sister. He needs to miss his best friend. The one he opens up to for late-night talks in the treehouse. The one he vows to protect. And the one who allows him to share his lofty dreams, while also believing in and supporting mine.

"You're the biggest reason. I just…I just feel the need to stay close to you. I mean you're my sister. And I just feel like we need each other. Does that make sense?"

I nod my head, not knowing if I really understand what he means. I want more of him, but I can't take his caring heart for granted. After all, he may see me as his sister, but we both know that things have felt different lately.

"Are you ready for your birthday present?" he asks, looking suddenly nervous.

Benny slides over a paper bag.

"A brown paper bag?" I ask, feeling confused.

"Sorry about that. We're out of wrapping paper. It took me a long time to finish. I had to track down some people. I wanted to make it a little more perfect, but Ms. Green told me it already is. She helped a lot with it, too. But go ahead, open it."

I slowly reach into the bag, feeling a nervous tension from Benny.

*A photo album!*

"Oh, Benny! This is so thoughtful. You didn't have to do this."

"I did, Penny. You deserve this. Go ahead, look through it."

Benny has never sounded more confident. I truly don't feel like I deserve anything. I'm happy with what I have. But tonight, his words keep touching different parts of me.

I open up the album, which is full of pictures. Some go all the way back to our preschool and kindergarten days. Others are as recent as a couple of months ago. But it's more than just pictures of family and friends. Every single photograph has a short, handwritten note by Benny.

Many of the pictures make me want to cry. Other pictures make me want to laugh. But every page I flip is a flash flood of vivid memories.

Some memories are harder to see again. The further I get into the album the more I see of Marcus. My big brother was so happy and full of life. Whether he was with the neighbors, the McClains, or with just me, he brightened our worlds.

I finally come to the last page, pasted with a picture I've never seen before. In it is a young man dressed in camouflage. He has a large afro and a baby in his arms. The caption below the picture has no names or description. It only has an address in Boston, Massachusetts.

"What's this?" I ask. "I don't, um…who is this?"

Benny scoots closer to me on the loveseat. Then his arm comes around my shoulder. "That's your dad, Penny. I found him."

I shudder at Benny's words.

The thought of finding my father has rarely been a thought since I got adopted. Richard McClain is my father. But I look at the man in the photograph, standing proudly, his baby in his arms. His smile looks just like mine. He doesn't look anything like a man who would abandon a child like my mama swore he had. He only looks like a proud father, loving his baby girl.

"But…how?" I ask.

"Your Aunt Mary helped me track down the picture. Then I did tons of research. His name is Calvin Jones and he used to live at that address in the Boston area. The phone number no longer works, but your aunt believes he's at that address or somewhere close by to that neighborhood."

Benny shrugs. I'm confused about why he did this. I've only mentioned my father once or twice in the entire time I've known Benny. It's mainly because I only have a handful of memories of my father.

"But, why? I don't need him. I have your grandpa. What even made you want to find him?" I ask.

Benny sighs, then turns to face me.

"I just thought you should know," he says, his tone suddenly gentle. "You never talk about him. You only told me what your mom said about him. But she was never a real mom to you. I just think there could be more to the story, his story. I don't know…maybe this was a bad idea. I just know how much I miss my parents. And if there was a chance I could see them again, for just a split second, I would."

My jaw feels suddenly heavy. It may be what Benny wants, but I don't know yet if this is what I want.

"I, um, I don't know what to say," I quietly mutter, running my fingers through my hair.

Benny suddenly looks regretful. But I just don't know how to process this, especially when I never had any intention of finding what I already had.

"I'm sorry, Penny. Maybe this was a—"

"Stop!" My hand instinctively covers his lips. "Just don't talk for a second. Apologizing is the last thing you should be doing. This is, well, this is super sweet of you. I just don't know yet if I want to pursue this."

I remove my hand from his mouth, and he grabs my wrist with urgency. I watch Benny's eyes close; his head bow. He pulls my hand to his chest. The flush of heat feels suddenly overwhelming, but in the best way possible.

"Benny, I—"

"Shhh! I just need to hold on to you. Is it okay I do this?" he asks, his eyes now looking desperately into mine.

I nod, unable to say a word. His hands slowly weave into my fingers, sending shivers through every part of my being. Then I watch as one hand lets go, reaching towards the back of my head. Instinctively, I let my face fall into his chest as he pulls me in.

Leaving his embrace feels impossible. I don't understand what's happening, but I don't want this feeling to end.

All I've ever wanted to do is touch Benny McClain. But touching him like this always felt impossible. This is no ordinary hug. It's purely intimate.

I let my arms go tight around his waist. The tighter I squeeze around his body, the tighter he pulls me into his chest.

Then his fingers go under my shirt, sliding along the skin of my lower back. I reciprocate by slowly gliding my hands under the back of his shirt. My fingers slide along his waistline, my pinky lightly touching his ass.

His lips slowly begin to hover over my forehead. He's smelling my scalp, which sends more chills through my body. Then I feel the warmth of his lips as he kisses my forehead.

"Penny," he whispers, suddenly gasping for air.

I tilt my eyes up to his. His mesmerizing look down is fiery with need. It's a need so unexpected, and so utterly perfect.

"Yes, Benny," I barely whisper.

"Can I?"

The warmth of his hands cup both of my cheeks, taking control. All he wants are my lips. The same lips he tasted almost a decade ago in this very treehouse.

I lean up to his lips. The pressure is slow and delicate at first. Then our lips join, and we move slowly, tasting what feels forbidden. His tongue slowly slides into mine, tasting the tip of my own tongue.

Then his weight falls onto me, and our kissing becomes more fast-paced, deeper. I'm hungry to taste every inch of his lips, his tongue and mouth.

A moan escapes me as his lips move along my neck. I dig my hands into his scalp, pulling his lips tighter into my neck. His lips slowly slide down my collarbone as his hand slides under my shirt.

My own hands glide under his jeans, grasping onto his hard ass. Then my hips spread wide as I pull his weight tighter into the space between my legs.

His breathing becomes faster as he presses his hips into me. I bury my face in his neck to taste and smell every part of him. My hands begin exploring more of him, while he does the same to me.

When I reach into his jeans, I feel his body tense for a moment. But the need to touch him there is desperate. I feel his hardness, the tip already damp with desire. Then I feel his fingers slide into my panties, brushing delicately along the lips of my insides. His fingers brush along my clit making me want to scream with desire.

A door suddenly shuts outside.

"Fuck," Benny whispers.

*Oh my god! Oh my god!*

We both quickly adjust our clothing and our hair. We can hear the person outside climbing up the tree.

We take a seat back at the coffee table, pretending to be playing a board game as Jimmy appears.

"Grandpa needs to talk to you guys."

"Is he okay?" Benny asks.

Jimmy nods his head. His stare remains blank, but we both know his mind is in a hamster wheel. I wonder if he has some idea about what we were just doing.

A few minutes later, the three of us walk into the kitchen, where Ms. Green is sitting next to Dad. My mind and heart are still fluttering with desire, and I wonder if I'll be capable of holding a conversation. I'm praying Dad doesn't have some type of sixth sense about what's happening between me and Benny.

I give Benny a side glance and notice that his cheek and neck look extra pink. I'm suddenly grateful for my dark skin.

It's after 11, long after the time Ms. Green and Dad would both be asleep under their separate roofs.

"What're you two up too?" Dad asks.

*Oh nothing! Just making out and fondling my brother.*

"Just a little Scrabble," Benny calmly states, giving me a longer than usual side glance. "What's going on?"

"Well, Richard and I wanted to talk about something," Ms. Green says. "We feel you all deserve to be a part of this conversation."

That's when I notice Dad's hand resting on top of hers.

"It's a good thing we want to tell you all," Dad chimes in, looking suddenly nervous. "I was thinking it might be nice to have Clara live with us. We'd share a room so it wouldn't affect the setup we already have. I just think it'll be good to have her around more. She's good for all of us, and I really, really like her company."

Dad pauses, sharing a jovial smile with Ms. Green.

I've never seen a black woman blush. But Ms. Green appears to be blushing on the inside. It shows in her smile, which practically illuminates the room. It's clear she doesn't just like Grandpa. This is pure, unadulterated love.

Benny and I turn to look at each other. I want to look composed, with Dad and Ms. Green across from us, holding hands. But I can't stop from smiling. I'm almost giddy with laughter.

"Yeah, that's fine with me," Benny says.

"Me, too," I quickly chime in.

"What do you think, Jimmy?" Dad asks. "Are you okay with Ms. Green living with us?"

Jimmy's eyes are glued to their hands, resting together on the table. He lightly rocks back and forth in his chair.

"Is Ms. Green…your girlfriend?" Jimmy asks, looking confused.

"Um, I…" Ms. Green hesitates, shifting her glance to Dad.

"Yes, you can call it that, Jimmy," Grandpa calmly replies, still smiling at Ms. Green. "But she's also my best friend. She cares about all of us. She's incredibly kind. And she makes me happy. It's all an old man like me could ever dream of having—two times in my life."

A silence settles over all of us as Ms. Green's eyes become glossy with affection. Then a single tear rolls down her face as she gets up to hug Dad.

Later that night we all revel in the momentous day, replaying our favorite parts. But there are certain parts that Benny and I will keep confidential.

Once I head off to bed, a nervous excitement takes over my body. I smile at Benny as I close my bedroom door, and his own smile has my heart fluttering all over again.

I have so much to be thankful for, but there's one thing I'm most thankful for in this moment: Benny's room is right next to mine.

# CHAPTER SEVEN

## Benny

### *3 months later*

"How was your night, Penny?" I ask, feeling my grin stretch wide.

Looking at her curves, I recall how her body felt in my hands last night. It's taking enormous restraint to not drag her into the nearby orchard. I want so badly to touch every part I was touching last night when I snuck into her room.

"My night was pretty good. But I didn't sleep much," she giggles.

Her playful smirk and sassy tone have my heart racing. I glance down the dirt road we're walking along, but don't see a soul. I put my arm around Penny, leaning down for a quick taste of her lips. I keep kissing her until she playfully pushes me away.

"Contain yourself, Benny!" she shouts with a mischievous grin.

I can't get enough of Penny McClain. My need to touch her is like the need to breathe, and the need to kiss her is like my thirst to live.

Our relationship does have complications, mostly because I can't get enough of her. Most of the day she's my sister. But during the first twenty minutes of our walk to school each morning, and our "night cuddle time," as she calls it, are my favorite times.

Last night she was still on her period, so I wasn't able to pleasure her like we both wanted. But she gave me a blow job that felt so good I almost woke up the family.

We're still learning how to pleasure one another. Lately it's gotten even better because we're starting to let one another know what we like.

We've yet to go all the way. I get nervous when she brings up the topic because I've only done it once, and I didn't last very long.

It's not easy telling her we don't need to rush things, because time isn't on our side. I'll be graduating from high school in a few weeks, then moving out of the house a couple weeks later when football practice begins.

"How do you feel about us, Benny?" Penny asks, her tone suddenly careful.

"I feel great about us. I mean, there's things I'd change, if I could."

"Like what?" she eagerly asks.

I know the answer she wants. She wants our secret relationship to no longer be hidden. But we both know that's not possible—not in this town.

I take a long sigh. "You know what I want. I want you, and not this life of secrecy. I want to be with you and not worry about what's happening around me. That's what I want, but…." I pause to take a deep breath. "But I don't know how to do that without risking so much."

Looking into her beautiful brown eyes, I try to imagine what she's thinking. But Penny just remains silent, probably dreaming about the what ifs in her imagination.

But what if my hopes could be a reality, and not a dream? The only way is if we both just say, "Fuck it," and get the hell out of Dodge. But Dad isn't leaving, and neither is Ms. Green or Jimmy. They've all found a rhythm to this life of secrecy.

"What if there was a way?" Penny mutters.

"How?"

"What if one day we just get out of this place, maybe even this state, and start somewhere new? Not now, obviously, but maybe one day."

"I'd like that. I'd like that a lot, Penny."

The back of my hand brushes along her cheek. Her smile widens as I tuck a few strands of bangs behind her ear. Her eyes are lost in a trance as mine get further lost in her smile.

Every detail in her natural beauty has me enamored. The baby soft smoothness of her dark skin. Her hair in a flipped bob, curling up perfectly at the shoulder. And that's only the beginning blossoms of her beauty. It's what's on the inside that makes everything feel right in this upside-down world.

"Hey, come with me real quick," I say, dragging her by her hand to the orchard trees.

Once behind the trees, I kiss her, grabbing her ass as she lets out a satisfying moan. My hand goes under her panties, tracing along the crack of her ass.

We're lost in the moment like so many moments we share at night. But this time the feelings are heightened. We're not in the dark trying to be quiet. We're giving in to our desperate need to touch and feel each other.

A snickering from behind startles us.

"What was that?" Penny asks, burying her face in my chest.

"Hey you two! Get the fuck off my farm!" a man's voice screams.

We both head quickly back to the road. That's when we see him, heading right towards us through the trees.

It's Vern Manningham. He owns the Orchard Farm. I only know him because his son Ryan is the starting safety on our defense. He's never uttered a word to us in the ten years of walking down this road to school. And I rarely see him in the stands at football games.

"I see you two screwing around again on my property, I'll… Hey, you're Benny McClain. Aren't you?"

"I'm sorry sir, we'll get going. It'll never happen again," I say, pulling Penny by her arm to walk faster.

"It better not, son," he says, his voice lower. "What're you doing kissing up on some bitch nigger, anyways?"

I freeze, my fists clenched so hard I feel my arms shaking. I turn around as Penny starts tugging on my shoulder.

"Forget about it, Benny. We'll be late for school. Let's go!"

Her words don't register. Mr. Manningham flashes a smirk as I shake Penny off and charge at him like a bull. Penny screams and I stop, sliding along the dirt with my arm raised. He flinches.

"What did you call her! Say it again! Say it again! I dare you, motherfucker!"

I take a step closer, breathing hotly only inches from his face. He steps backwards, tripping on something and falling to the ground. Penny quickly steps between me and Vern.

"Benny! Go! He's not worth it! Please, Benny! You're better than this," her voice begs, on the brink of tears.

Vern Manningham just lays there like a beached whale, grabbing his lower back and grimacing in pain.

I lower my fist because Penny's right. This old, fat-ass piece of shit isn't worth it. Penny turns around to Vern. Then she shocks us both by extending her hand to him.

"Can I help you up, Mr. Manningham?" she calmly asks.

His grimace melts as a gust of wind kicks up. The cigarette falls from his mouth as dirt plumes all around us.

How does she do this, I wonder. This man is sick in the head, a known member of the Klan, a walking example of everything that's wrong with this town. I want to hurl insults at him; I want to punch him. But Penny's offering to help him up.

I stare at her, wondering how she keeps her rage at this town from getting the best of her. Maybe she does it because it's the only way she can protect me.

Vern says nothing, just looking at Penny like she's the scum of the earth.

Penny takes a long sigh as Vern slowly gets up on his own. She hands him his hat, which he practically slaps out of her hand.

"Sir, I'm not a bitch nigger," Penny calmly says, staring daggers. "My name is Penny McClain. I'm just a girl who knows better than you ever will. We're going to mind our business and walk to school. And you're not going to speak a word of what you saw in the orchard. You hear me. We'll mind our business, and you'll do the same. That'll be that."

And just like that, Penny walks away. I take one long last look at Vern Manningham, who's still glaring at Penny as she confidently walks away. Then he looks to me, flashing a mocking smirk while shaking his head.

"You make me sick, son," he says. Then he walks away.

I catch up to Penny as we continue our long walk to school. I apologize and try talking to her, but she tells me she just needs a little bit of space.

That night, around dinnertime, we sit down with Ms. Green and Grandpa to tell them what happened. We give them every last detail except for the one key detail they can't know about—*us*.

I say that we were just picking a couple oranges, and luckily they don't press on that detail. Still, I get the feeling Ms. Green knows something is up.

After dinner, I head into the living room to tackle my homework, and Penny goes up to the treehouse to do the same. We typically do our homework together, but I want to honor the space she needs.

I don't blame her for being upset. I shouldn't have lost my cool. Doing so only puts us more at risk.

Our family had a target on our back until I became a bonafide star on the football field. But I worry that we've upset someone with true clout in the Ku Klux Klan. The likelihood for revenge feels imminent.

There's no saying what could happen because none of us know Vern Manningham. The only person that knows him is Grandpa, but even the look on his face was extremely worried.

He and Ms. Green spend an unusually long time talking outside. They sit out there talking most evenings, usually for about ten minutes after dinner. But tonight, it's almost 10 p.m. and they've been out there for over an hour.

I feel terrible for lying to them about my relationship with Penny. And I know Penny is even more upset now that I've dragged her further into this lie. She's hardly been able to look at me all evening.

"Hey, I'm off to bed," Penny says, startling me.

"Oh, okay. Well, goodnight," I reply, my voice gentle, but unsure.

"Hey, um, for the next few nights I think it'll be best if you stay in your room. I kind of feel like they're on to us," she whispers.

"Oh, okay. If you think that's what's best, I understand," I lie.

She offers a fake smile, then turns away, heading for bed.

*Say something!*

"Hey Penny, wait," I call out, following her into the hallway.

She stops, turning around. She's wearing the pajamas that hug her hips in a way that drives me wild.

I'm suddenly tongue-tied. I want to take her worries away and make everything perfect in our world. But there's nothing I can say, because we have so little control over this situation.

I take a deep breath. "I just want you to know I'm sorry for how I handled things out there today. Not just at the Orchard Farm. And I understand why you need space from me. But, when you're ready, I just want you to know that I don't want space from you. Our world could crumble into a fiery hell, and it won't change how I feel about you."

Penny wipes at her eyes. "Okay," she whispers with pain in her voice. "I'm sorry, too."

The opening of the front door startles us both. Grandpa and Ms. Green walk into the living room.

"Goodnight, Benny," she says with trembling lips as she dashes into her room.

I want to follow her in and hold her like I do every night. I want to tell her that things will be okay and that one day we'll be together in peace. But they're all probably broken promises.

"You okay, Benny?" Ms. Green asks, walking past the hallway.

"Yeah, I'll be fine," I lie.

She turns around quickly, catching me off guard with a big hug. I feel her mouth lift up to my ear.

"Picking oranges, eh?" she whispers.

Ms. Green pulls back from our embrace and grabs me by my cheeks.

"You're a strong boy, Benny McClain. But now we have to be stronger up here."

She points at her head. Her stare sharpens, then she pats my chest and quietly walks to bed.

When her door shuts, I look up at the ceiling, squeezing my eyelids in frustration.

*It's time.*

Grandpa is puttering around in the kitchen. I head in there, feeling more nervous than ever.

"Grandpa, can we talk outside?" I barely mutter.

"Speak up, son. What did you say?" he asks, shutting the fridge.

"I have something I need to tell you."

"Well, go ahead. What do you got for me?"

We walk outside together, and I turn to face him. "I'm sorry."

"It's okay, we'll get this all worked out. Things will pass with Vern. He may be dangerous, but we're going to just lay low and be vigilant."

"No, Grandpa. It's not just that. I'm sorry for lying to you," I pause, trying to swallow the lump in my throat. "You see, Penny and I weren't picking oranges."

"I know," he calmly replies.

"You do?"

"Ms. Green and I have had our suspicions for the last couple months. But there's nothing wrong with having feelings. I mean, I'm not going to lie, it's not what I would've ever expected to happen between you two. It's just, um…"

Grandpa takes a long sigh. "It just can make things a bit complicated, for all of us. You know, even grandpas don't always know the answers to things. I can't even explain how I ended up with Ms. Green, especially after losing Madeline. But it's such a blessing having her in my life."

Grandpa pauses and steps closer to me. He puts his hand on my shoulder. "We just take it a day at a time and trust the good Lord to help guide us."

"So, you're not mad at me?" I ask, still trying to process what he's telling me.

"Mad at you, no," he shakes his head. "Penny may be your sister, but she's not your blood. And besides, there's not a kinder or more beautiful young woman on this earth than she. Her heart is bigger than the both of us. She's out of everyone's league. But then again, so are you. Frankly, I don't say it enough, but I'm just so damn proud of you all. And I don't know how you didn't beat the shit out of Vern," Grandpa chuckles.

My mouth falls open. Grandpa just uttered the first bad word I've ever heard him say. But somehow that's the least surprising thing he said.

"I don't understand. How are you not upset about this? I'm telling you I like her. And Grandpa, this feels like more than just liking her."

"Does it?"

I just nod, not knowing what else to say.

"Well, is that a bad thing?" Grandpa asks.

*I guess it's not.*

I shrug my shoulders. Feeling lost, I look deep into his eyes, hoping to find a sense of calm there. But all I notice is his furrowed brow. He's still worried, but about which part, I don't know. Or maybe it isn't worry, maybe it's just heartbreak. A heartbreak for letting go of a daughter, and a son.

"Listen up, Benny. Let's be real for a second. I'm okay with you liking Penny and wanting to spend extra time with her. But let's get two things straight. One, you'll be out of this house in a couple months. That's something the two of you need to discuss. And number two is important. There'll be no funny business under my roof. That's non-negotiable."

"Funny business," I mutter, clearing my throat.

"I see how you two look at each other. But not under my roof. She's still such a young girl. And she deserves to be treated with respect and patience."

I nod again at Grandpa, feeling my face flush with heat.

"Relax, Benny. You got your whole life ahead of you. Now get off to bed."

Once in bed, my eyes refuse to stay shut. I miss Penny's closeness at night. There's also too much to think about.

I'll be out of the house in a couple months and a full-fledged adult college student. My focus will be football. It'll be all about putting in the work to live out my dreams. Meanwhile, Penny will be alone in this town, with fewer protections and so much responsibility at home. The tradeoff doesn't seem fair. But there's one thing that would be more unfair than anything else.

*Breaking her heart. And mine too.*

# CHAPTER EIGHT

## Penny

"So, what are you going to get him?" Sarah asks, taking a bite of her sandwich.

The air outside the cafeteria feels stale and humid. It's the opposite of my insides, feeling like suppressed fireworks. I take a deep breath. My stomach is doing summersaults over Sarah's question. I'm nervous to tell her what I plan on giving Benny for his birthday.

"Just a card," I say, smirking.

Sarah raises her eyebrows. I feel my smirk widen.

"Oh my god!" she gasps, grasping my arm. She leans in closer. "The V-card," she whispers.

I quietly nod yes.

The rarely spoken topic has been a much bigger part of our conversations in the last couple months. I can't help it, Benny will be gone soon. It's something I want to experience with him before he goes.

Sarah's known of my feelings for Benny for quite some time. She's also the only friend who knows about our secret relationship. Outside of our family, the only other person who knows is Paul.

There's been good and bad parts about Dad and Ms. Green knowing. The good is we can be somewhat affectionate at home. We don't have to portray that friendly brother-sister relationship in front of them. He puts his arm around me when we snuggle on the couch, he holds my hand, and he's able to give me those lustful looks with his green eyes. On occasion we'll get caught kissing one another. Ms. Green doesn't seem to care. Grandpa on the other hand will playfully groan at us.

The bad part is our doors always have to stay wide open. If we're together in each other's room, one of the adults is constantly walking through the hallway to check on us. And our nighttime cuddle sessions are more difficult to pull off with Grandpa roaming the halls a couple times a night. But we've found different windows of time in the middle of the night where it's safe to fool around.

A few nights ago was utter bliss. Benny went down on me and used his fingers and his tongue at the same time. I experienced my first orgasm and screamed every ounce of pleasure into my pillow. It's a miracle no one heard.

Our obsession with each other's bodies has distracted us from the elephant in the room: how things will be once he goes off to college. I tried talking about it a couple nights ago, but we got side-tracked with touching each other.

Things have been surprisingly normal ever since the Manningham incident a few weeks ago. We've even walked by Vern a couple times on the way to school. He just acts like we don't exist.

The only difference this week has been Benny himself. He seems a lot more distant, especially over the past couple days.

"Tomorrow night will be the night," I quietly tell Sarah. "Dad and Ms. Green will be up in Tuscaloosa overnight to check in on Ms. Green's sister. She's sick. Benny's spending the night with Paul. I'll be across the street spending the night with Jimmy and Christine. We're both going to sneak out in the middle of the night to meet up in the treehouse."

"The treehouse?" Sarah asks, looking befuddled.

I shrug my shoulders. "It's special to us. It was the first place he ever kissed me."

"Are you sure you're ready?" Sarah asks, her tone careful, wearing a look of concern. I wonder if she feels like we're rushing things.

"I'm ready," I say, feeling confident.

"It's going to hurt. I mean, it did with me and Luke, but it'll get better with practice. And it may not last a long time. I guess it's hard for guys, early on."

I nod. Sarah has been very open with me about her relationship with her boyfriend, Luke.

"I'm excited for you, Penny. But are you sure this is what you want to do? Won't it just make you miss him more when he leaves? You know, I think the world of Benny. And I know he wouldn't pressure you into doing this if you don't feel ready."

Losing my virginity will change things. But I know it'll be worth it. Besides, the only pressure I'm feeling is coming from me, not from Benny. He's ready, but he's been very open about not rushing things.

"Trust me, Sarah. I know I'm ready."

Sarah's lips become a straight line of rigidness.

"What is it? You're telling me this is okay, but at the same time you're not. Just get it off your chest," I demand.

"Penny, I have no problem with you and Benny doing it. He's the best. But you guys need to be real about your situation when he leaves. I mean, you don't expect him to be loyal to you while he's away, do you? And he probably wouldn't expect the same from you. Just talk about it before you go through with this. Otherwise, the heartbreak's going to be worse when he leaves. I just think you owe that to each other."

I briefly ponder the idea of discussing our future tonight. But I know it'll ruin the moment. Maybe another day, but not tonight. I end up changing the subject because I know she's right.

After school, Sarah and I walk home with Paul and Benny. Benny's quiet, and obviously troubled by something. But he isn't saying what it is.

Once we're home, I ask him, but he just tells me not to worry. He seems like the old Benny.

Later that night, he and Grandpa make last-minute plans to go out to dinner. Ms. Green, Jimmy, and I have a quiet supper together. It's weird that we're not invited for dinner, but Ms. Green assures me that Dad just wants to spend more one-on-one time with Benny before he leaves.

It still feels like something fishy is going on.

The next day I decide to be cagey. I play the silent game all morning, saying as little as possible to Benny. It takes a while for him to notice.

"You okay?"

"I'm fine," I tersely reply.

"You don't seem fine."

"What were you and Dad up to last night? I know you guys didn't just go out for dinner. And you got home super-late for a school night."

I can see the tenseness in his jaw. Even his eyes take on a different shade of green. There's more honey-brown in them.

"Can I tell you tonight?" he asks.

I can tell he doesn't want to say anything in front of Paul and Sarah. I nod my head, but now I'm even more anxious.

Later that evening I'm able to sneak out. I wait in the treehouse for Benny to arrive. It's a couple minutes past eleven. He said he'd get here at about 11:30.

I start writing in my journal to slow my racing mind. My writing leads me down a path of looking at my life's chronology that led to today. It feels like a lot of happy miracles with plenty of tragedy sprinkled in.

I'm not ready to lose Benny in a few weeks. My life has been defined by loss. Yet, all these losses somehow led me to a new family, a family I feel truly blessed to have. But without Benny around, things will be much harder.

I hear Benny climbing up the treehouse ladder.

"Hey," he smiles, looking lighter and more relaxed.

I quickly dive into his open arms. My grasp feels secure and desperate. His hands go up and down my back, and I relax.

"I'm sorry I was so grumpy this morning. Are you okay?" I ask, leaning back with my arms still tightly wrapped around his waist.

"I'm good now. I've just had a lot on my mind the last few days," he explains.

"Are you nervous about tonight?" I ask.

"Yeah, but that's not what's been really going on. I need to tell you something…." Benny pauses to take a deep breath. Then we sit down together.

"I've been getting threats," he murmurs.

"Threats!"

"Yeah, they've been left on my truck at school a couple times this week. I would have told you earlier, but I didn't understand it at first. The first couple of threats were just notes saying 'We know.' Then I got another one a couple days ago with all of our names on it—Jimmy, you, Ms. Green and Grandpa. That one had some pretty bad stuff written about us."

"What did it say?" I ask, angrily. "Tell me!"

"Okay, just calm down. And please know it's all been handled. And I'm not going to repeat what was in that note because it's so vile. But I'll let you read it."

He hands me the paper from his back pocket. I slowly unfold it as my hand starts to tremble.

**We STILL know. Two nigger lovers = two bullets. See you soon!**

I keep reading the note even though it makes me want to vomit. Then I look below it seeing the names of every McClain, including myself and Clara Green. The one distinct difference is my name and Ms. Green's has a red line through it.

The goosebumps bubble up throughout my body. I'm angry and confused at the same time. I finally look up from the note. Benny appears unusually calm.

"We took care of it, Penny. Me and Grandpa did," he says, looking assured and confident.

"What? How?"

"We went to the Manningham farm. Me and Grandpa went there last night. There were others there. I think it was some type of Klan meeting. Even those Monroe assholes were there—brothers, dad, and all. Grandpa spoke to them. They agreed to a truce. Well, maybe that's not the word. They at least agreed to let us be."

"But how?"

Benny gives a nervous chuckle and shrugs his shoulders. "Well, Grandpa did all the talking. I was just there in case things went awry. I guess Grandpa and Vern have some type of history or back story. Grandpa wouldn't tell me what happened, but apparently Vern owes a great debt to Grandpa."

"I still don't understand. You're telling me you and Dad went to a Klan meeting. Like, what the fuck! Are you guys stupid or something?"

I let out a long sigh, shaking my head. "You guys could have gotten yourself killed!"

Benny's hands latch onto mine, and he gives me a smoldering look.

"I'm sorry I didn't tell you about last night. I swear we didn't know it was a Klan meeting. We just went to Vern's hoping to speak to him. Those assholes were just all there. But Grandpa wasn't fazed. He just stood up and spoke. He argued for privacy under our roof and the declaration of letting our family be as long as we keep things private. Then Mr. Manningham pulls Grandpa aside for a long private conversation. Then, a couple minutes later he declared the McClain's no enemy of the Klan. The others clearly weren't happy, but according to Grandpa what he says is what goes."

I see relief in Benny's face and posture. But I don't feel what he does.

"Okay, um, I just need to try and process all of this. It's a lot to take in."

I sigh, rubbing my eyes, and feel my breath trembling and my heart pounding. The only thing keeping me together is Benny's closeness.

"Do you really believe that everything is going to be okay, Benny?"

"I don't know. I didn't this morning. But after chatting with Grandpa again he seemed really confident. I think we just need to lay low for a while. Besides, it took a lot of guts for us to show up there last night. And I'm glad we did. They need to know we aren't scared of them."

"But Benny, what about the note? Do we know who was making the threats?"

"I don't know. Maybe the Monroes? I just think the only thing keeping us safe right now is Grandpa's good standing with Vern."

Benny chuckles nervously under his breath, shaking his head. "That crazy old geezer has too much faith in people, but somehow he and Vern have a history that saved us."

I close my eyes, trying to will Benny's confidence into me. His arms go tighter around my body, giving me hope.

I rest my head on his chest. The thudding of his heart becomes a relaxing tune. We share a long, silent embrace that helps calm my nerves.

After a while, Benny begins gliding his fingers delicately through my scalp. Then the back of his hand runs along my cheeks. It helps me level out and let go. The safety of his body and his touch is all I need.

It's dark in the treehouse. The only light is from the stars shining through the open window. Yet, even in the darkness I revel in the beauty of his green eyes, which appear to be glowing.

We start out softly kissing. Every touch of our lips is a release of pain and pressure. Inhibition slowly drifts away. The continuous tasting of his lips has me wanting more.

I don't know if tonight will be the night. But right now, the moment feels too perfect to stop. Moments like these shouldn't have an ending. It should be the beginning of something infinite.

My hand glides down to his zipper. I feel his body tense and his eyes flash wide.

"Are you sure?" he whispers, knowing I want something more.

"I am." I pause to take a deep, trembling breath. I've never felt so nervous and excited at the same time. I feel the sudden need to ask him something.

"Benny McClain, will you be my first?"

His head tilts back a couple more inches.

"Penny, can I tell you something first?" he whispers.

I nod, admiring his gorgeous face from up close.

"Penny, if we do, I just want you to know what you truly mean to me. You need to know that I don't love you like a brother loves his sister. You're something more than that—much more. I love everything about you. Who you are. How you make me feel. I just love you so much."

Benny's voice breaks. His eyes are damp. "And if we do this, we do this knowing that neither of us can promise what the future holds. I can't promise what we will be a few months or a few years from now. All I can promise is always loving this part of you."

Benny's hand slides under my shirt and over my heart. His hand feels warm, cradling the part he loves most.

My hand mimics his. I feel my vision go blurry with tears. All of the emotions in my head and heart finally make sense. I want to give this man my unrelenting love.

Benny is my protector. He's my best friend. But most importantly, he's no longer my brother. Tonight, he'll be the first, and hopefully the last man I ever make love to.

"I love you, too."

Once our clothes are off, I take Benny's weight onto me. The pressure from his naked skin lathered over mine is bliss. He's all mine. And I'm giving him every piece of me.

"Are you ready?" he calmly asks

"Yes," I whisper, my heart pounding.

I lower my hand to feel the warmth inside of me. I've never felt more wetness and lubrication. Benny begins brushing the tip of his penis along the lips of my insides. It lightly brushes up to my clit sending a shock wave of euphoria through every nerve ending in my body.

Then his erection lightly presses into my small bare opening. He lightly thrusts deeper into me until I let out a soft moan. Then he pulls it out, going back in one more time.

"Ow," I whisper. "Just go a little slower."

"I'm so sorry."

I shimmy my hips to be in a better receiving position. I'm not fazed by the pain because it feels perfectly right at the same time. He slowly thrusts his way back inside. This time he goes slower, sliding a little deeper than before. I feel my vagina barely wraps around the tip of his erection. Then he slowly begins driving it in and out of me.

The deeper he goes the more I feel the lips of my pussy melding over his shaft. It still hurts, but now it feels like nothing I've ever felt before. This is not his fingers or tongue inside of me. It's all of him—his engorged erection stretching my insides. It's the part of him that could create life in me. And while he knows to pull out, I fantasize on the what if. What if at the end he stays inside, filling me with his seed to create life. It's everything I'm not ready for, and everything I could ever want one day at the same time.

His lips fall back onto mine as the thrusting picks up pace. The need to have him deeper inside me becomes instinctual. My hands slap down on his perky butt. I grasp tightly around his ass, pulling him further into my warm insides.

His lips come off mine as the moaning explodes out of me. The intensity of the moment is overwhelming. It still hurts, but pleasure is now winning over pain. Having him inside me is too perfect. It feels wrong to be fucked by my brother. But tonight, he's not that. He's my best friend that I'm madly in love with.

*Oh fuck!*

"You heard that, right?" he whispers.

I nod frantically. "Yes."

Then we hear a door open. The sound is from beneath us. It's the familiar squeak of our back door.

"Go in the corner," Benny demands.

We both pull our clothes on as quickly as we can. I watch Benny crawl to the opening near the ladder and quietly peer over the edge. The longer he looks, the more terrified I feel. Eventually Benny crawls back over to me.

"Who is it?" I whisper.

"I don't know. But the back door window is broken. Maybe whoever did it got spooked. But I need to go down there and check it out."

"No. Are you crazy? We'll wait it out from up here. No one knows we're up here. Please, Benny," I beg, grabbing his hand. I can barely see his face through the darkness, but I know what he's thinking as he pulls loose from my grip.

"Whatever you do, stay here until I get back," he quietly demands.

Benny heads down the treehouse ladder. I quietly crawl to the window, peering down below. He walks to the back door, opening it slowly, then disappearing inside.

Seconds begin to feel like minutes. I hear nothing but deafening silence. My heart feels like it's about to explode.

Then I hear a thud—or at least, I think I do. The split-second noise is quiet and quick. Fear for my life has given way to an emotion that's even worse—helplessness.

# CHAPTER NINE

# Benny

The blackness feels infinite and inescapable. I'm weightless in the dark abyss, like I'm floating when I should be running. A warmth takes over, enveloping my body like a slow electrical shock. It's followed by a cold shiver and wetness all over.

The smell of wet Bermuda and the taste of metal are everywhere. Darkness slowly gives way to visions moving in and out. I see what I think are tree limbs and stars up above.

My body begins jerking as a tightness overtakes it. First, it's my arms. Then it's my chest and my lungs compressing inward.

Screams of panic bring the dark visions back. The disorientation fades to an orange glow reflecting off my truck. I think I'm waking up, but I have no control over my arms, or my body. The sounds of pain and begging carry on as I will myself to full consciousness.

"Benny, help me! Please! Somebody!"

The scream suddenly feels closer.

"Penny, Penny," I mutter, trying to scream. I begin coughing up blood. I'm gasping for air that I can't seem to find.

My breath slowly comes back. I finally realize my hands are bound behind me. I'm tied to a tree in my front yard. The glow off my truck gets brighter as embers rain from the sky.

"Jimmy, no!"

Then I hear it. The sound of fighting. The kind of fighting where flesh and bone meet with a thud. Penny's screaming for Jimmy to leave. I've never heard a more desperate plea of helpless panic.

The adrenalin to get free sends me into a manic rage. But I can't escape the ropes. They're too thick and too tightly wound around every part of my body.

I try everything. I blindly will my fingers into the knots around my wrist to pinch my way free. When that doesn't work I use my legs to push the rope into the bark. I slide it up and down to create friction. But everything is hopeless no matter how hard I try.

The screams of agony begin to die down. Meanwhile, the glow of more embers fly past me. I'm even more terrified of the madness behind me that I can't see.

Are they both trapped in the house? Are they being burned alive?

Then I hear another whimper for help from Penny. But this one sounds more like a last gasp.

"Ahhhhhhhhh!" I scream until my ear drums pop.

I finally feel my finger slide through a knot. It happens as I hear a truck peeling out in the distance.

Once my hands are free, I'm able to shimmy under and out of the rope that was around my chest. I stumble around the tree and instantly feel the blazing heat on my face. The entire house is engulfed in flames.

"Penny! Jimmy! Where are you guys!" I scream, stumbling toward the plume of smoke that used to be my front door.

I reach for the handle and burn my already bloody hand.

"Benny!" Penny screams back. "Help us!"

Her voice doesn't sound like it's in the house. It's more distant. I step back, stumbling over the weight of my own feet. I limp my way around to the backyard. Then I see her.

Penny's tied to the base of the tree that holds our treehouse. Her head is limp and hunched over her collarbone. Her head turns to me as I dive my arms around her.

"Are you okay?" I ask, running my hands along her body. Then I look into her face, covered in blood. One of her eyes is swollen shut. The fear in her face is overwhelming. She seems almost catatonic from the trauma.

"I'll be okay," she cries. "But Jimmy's hurt. He's hurt real…r-real bad," her voice sputters.

Penny nods behind me. Jimmy lays lifeless, face down in the grass.

I quickly untie all the ropes around Penny. The embers rain down as we go to Jimmy's lifeless body. I flip him over seeing a pool of blood pour out the top of his head. I take off my shirt to press it firmly into the wound. He's hurt bad, but he's still breathing.

"They kept hitting him with the butt of the gun. But he didn't stop fighting, Benny. He wouldn't stop fighting for me," Penny whimpers.

Penny helps me pull Jimmy up to a sitting position. He stays hunched over, mumbling unintelligible things.

"Jimmy, are you okay?"

His face is still a smear of blood and swollen bumps. There's gashes on the top of his head and below his right eye, creating a red waterfall pouring down his face.

"I p-protect her. I p-protect her. I p-protect Penny," he barely mutters the words.

We hear the fire truck in the distance. It's then I notice that one of the tree limbs has just caught fire on the treehouse above us.

I prop Jimmy on my shoulder as the three of us get out of the backyard. We stumble our way to the edge of the front yard, collapsing on the ground from exhaustion. Christine comes running out from across the street looking frantic with disbelief.

"I need towels or he's going to bleed to death!" I demand.

I have to scream the words two more times before it registers. Christine runs back into her house. Jimmy's head stays cradled in my arms. I press my blood-soaked shirt tighter into the top of his head as he groans in pain. Then I turn to Penny. She looks dazed and confused at her home burning away before her eyes.

"Are you sure you're okay, Penny?"

She turns back to me with her lips still trembling. Her face reflects the orange from the fire. It almost glows with her mix of tears and blood. She scoots closer to me, looking suddenly concerned by something else. She runs her hand along my forehead. It stings a little.

"You're hurt, Benny," she softly whispers.

I push her hand off of me. "You should have stayed in the treehouse! What were you thinking!" I shout as her body shudders to my outburst.

Penny says nothing, staring at me in shock. I can't think straight with all that's happened. My mind can only go to one place right now—*revenge*.

"Who did this. Was it Vern?" I frantically ask.

Penny shakes her head. "I don't think so," she whimpers, trying to catch her breath. "They were all wearing ski masks. One of them had curly blond hair. I think it was—"

"Monroe Twins?"

Penny nods her head up and down, still looking terrified. "There was also another one with a ski mask. He was the one with a gun. But he seemed older and frail. He's the one who kept hitting Jimmy with his shotgun. Then he put it to his head until a different smaller boy in a ski mask tackled him. He took the gun and they all ran away together when they heard the sirens."

"So wait, how many people were there?" I ask to clarify.

"I think there was four of them."

"Did they touch…" I pause, unable to utter such a horrifying question. But I have to know.

"Did they touch you, like, sexually?" I barely mutter.

"No," Penny quickly replies. "The brown-haired one punched me a few times. Then he and one of the other guys tied me up. Then he um, he whispered in my ear." Penny begins bawling, unable to utter another word.

I bow my head, feeling defeated by life. I let this happen to her and Jimmy. Grandpa and I should never have gone down to talk to Vern. There's no doubt in my mind it was the Monroes. The only part that doesn't make sense is why one of them would want to spare Jimmy.

The fire truck pulls up as Christine returns. She hands over the towels and helps tend to Jimmy as I get up. The paramedics quickly load him into the ambulance. Penny and Christine follow him into the back.

When the doors close, I can hear Penny screaming. She's begging me not to go. I have to drown out her voice of reason. This could be four against one, but I don't care. There'll be blood shed for what's been done here tonight.

I quickly hop into my truck. I floor it out of there noticing the flames turning into a mushroom cloud of smoke. The firemen douse everything with water, but it's too late. The last thing I notice is the treehouse in the back slowly becoming engulfed in flames.

I speed my way to Monroe farms in less than ten minutes. The back roads are all I take. I pull up to the back entrance of the farm. Once I'm about a quarter mile away I shut off the headlights. When I run out of tree cover, I hop out of my truck, silently shutting my door.

I jog up to the back of the house armed with only a wooden bat and my bloodied fists. Once I reach the stairs I tiptoe my way up to the backyard porch. I carefully peer around the window. The lights are on. There's commotion inside but I don't see anyone. It sounds like a couple people arguing on the second floor.

Then I hear footsteps coming around the side porch of the house. My breathing slows as my heart comes alive. My bat goes in the air, ready to break some legs. The anticipation grows as I inch closer to the corner they'll hopefully come around. Then I stumble a bit. The sound around the corner comes to a complete halt.

*Fuck!*

The sounds from inside the house grow louder. It sounds closer than before. I can't make out what they're saying. It's distracting as I wonder if they're still coming around this corner. I look back into the window still not seeing anyone.

Then the air is suddenly knocked out of me. My bat flies out of my hands as I crash into the ground. I roll over feeling a body wrestle over the top of me.

It's Terry Monroe. His hands go directly to my throat, strangling the life out of me. My hands instinctively go to his face as I try to hit and gouge his eyes out. Then I knee him in the balls, pushing him off. He gets up to stand right as I swing my fist directly into his face. The collision and force is so strong I watch him fly backwards and down the stairs. I follow him down the stairs wanting to do more damage to his face. But another body flies into my back sending both of us rolling down the stairs.

The air is knocked out of me, again. The blood dripping down my face is obstructing my vision. I try to get up but can't breathe. It feels like every rib on the left side of my body is shattered to pieces. Then I see John, the other twin, coming at my hunched-over body. It's then I notice the rock barely within my reach. I grab it and lunge towards him. The collision of rock to face is unlike any sound I've ever heard. It catches him perfectly across the cheek, likely knocking him out instantly.

Then everything goes black to a booming sound. The dark abyss is back, but this time the darkness feels permanent—like death.

# CHAPTER TEN

## Penny

### *3 weeks later*

The wait outside the courthouse is exhausting. Seconds feel like hours. Hours feel like days. The verdict will come down any moment now.

Dad is the only one allowed in the courthouse. I can only imagine how helpless he feels watching his grandson in an orange jumpsuit.

I look down at Ms. Green's hand, tightly holding mine. I'm mesmerized by the darkness of our skin. It's the unintended curse that brought all of this nightmare into our lives. It's also the curse that won't allow us in the courtroom to support Benny.

*Whites only.*

The worst part is Benny won't speak to anyone—not even me. They also don't allow children the opportunity to visit, much less black kids. My only way to communicate is through notes, which he's yet to reply too. I don't even know if he's reading them.

Benny is allowed one five-minute call per day from his cell. Yet we haven't even heard from him once. We don't even know if he's making any calls at all.

I know he's depressed. He just turned 18 in a jail cell. His football dreams are gone. He's probably terrified for his family. And the worst part, I know he blames me and Dad—probably himself too.

This all started when I let the McClains adopt me. I could have moved away with my aunt, but I fell in love with a boy and I found a dad. Things between me and Benny started to come to fruition. Then I messed it all up by kissing Benny in public. It was only a matter of time before the Klan did something to us.

There's only one sure feeling I have in the core of my soul. Benny McClain is not a murderer. He should've never gone to Monroe Farms that night. But he doesn't have it in him to kill another human being. There's too much good beneath all of those callous layers. It took me years to find his heart. Then I gave him all of mine, along with my virginity. But all of that feels meaningless now.

The story reported by the Monroe boys is that Benny went there and beat up the twins. Then he apparently wrestled the gun away from their dad and shot Terry Monroe in the head. The only witness to the incident was their father, Clarence Monroe. Apparently John Monroe was unconscious and the younger brother, Ricky, was inside the house.

Benny's given his testimony already. He claimed he was knocked unconscious about the time he heard a gun go off. He has no recollection after that point. But his claim is he never saw a gun—nor did he ever wrestle it away from their father.

Our family was not able to press charges against the Monroes due to insufficient evidence. It wouldn't have mattered anyway. The local police force is full of bigots just like the Monroes. And at the end of the day, we never saw their faces, even though I know it was the four of them.

Dad said yesterday things don't look promising. Benny is being tried for murder as an adult even though he was 17 on the date of the incident at Monroe Farms.

Dad hasn't been the same person since that night three weeks ago. His usually optimistic ways are now overtaken by guilt and moping.

Ms. Green has more faith in how things will play out. She believes that justice and truth will somehow reign supreme. I for one think she's delusional. Or maybe she's just terrified for Benny's future and placating herself by being strong for the rest of us.

At the end of the day, there's no silver lining, regardless of the verdict. We have no home. We're all living in Christine's tiny little house. We can't move into a new place until we get the fire insurance money and that could easily be many more months of waiting.

The only good news is that Jimmy is going to be okay. Physically, anyway. Mentally may be a different story. He's been home now for about two weeks. He doesn't talk as much, but every day I hug him and tell him how much I love him. He hugs me back, but it doesn't feel the same.

He broke three ribs in his fight to save my life. Then it took staples and 42 stitches to sew up his face and head. It's likely he'll wear those scars for the rest of his life.

The court doors swing open. We quickly jump to our feet. Dad's the first one out.

"What happened? Richard? Talk to us." Ms. Green begs, already hanging on Dad's arm.

Dad walks past me, looking visibly broken and pale.

He continues to ignore our pleas for the verdict until we get outside. He finally turns around and grabs both of us by a shoulder.

"It's, uh…." He takes a long sigh. Then he starts gnawing on his bottom lip. He's trying to find the words.

"How long?" Ms. Green asks.

"Ten to fifteen," Dad replies, looking like a deer in headlights.

"What? Ten to fifteen years? That's not possible!" I cry.

I hunch down over my knees, gasping for air. Dad and Ms. Green put their hands on my back, trying to soothe me.

I can't catch my breath, fighting the panic within.

"How could they do that? He's innocent, Dad. We all know it. He would never kill another person. Hurt them, yes. But he'd never kill them. I know it. I just know it. Not my Benny."

The next thing I know, I'm slowly waking up on the hot pavement. Dad helps me to the car after my fainting spell. I continue to cry, all the way home. Ms. Green tries holding me tight, but I barely feel her touch. Everything inside me is hollowed out.

Ten to fifteen years feels like a lifetime. I can't imagine the loneliness Benny will experience. The headspace he'll be in for all those days behind bars will scar him for life. He'll never be the same person. The hopes and dreams we shared in the treehouse will become what they were all along—just hopes and dreams.

----

Later that night, I go into Jimmy's room to tuck him into bed. He's been even more quiet after we told him that Benny will be gone a long time.

He's reading his favorite comic books that he's read a million times over. I don't want to disturb him. He's living in his happy reality where the superheroes are winning and the villains are losing. I wish I could believe in that reality.

"Hey," I whisper.

His eyes stay on his comic book, but I know he can hear me.

"I just wanted to say goodnight and tell you how much I love you," I say, trying to will the muscles in my face to smile a little.

His eyes glance up for a split second. Then they quickly flash back to his comic book.

I wish I could get in his head and understand what he's feeling. The look on his face all day long has been blank and void of any emotion. He's able to hide those feelings on the inside with ease.

Jimmy still has a hard time picking up on the emotions around him. He'll know something's wrong if I'm crying, but social cues and norms are still hard for him to decipher. It may make things easier for him, but I just want him to open up to me.

I take a seat on his bed. "Do you want to talk about Benny?" I ask, rubbing his shoulder lightly.

His eyes stay glued on his comic book. I can tell this is going nowhere so I start to get up.

"Three thousand, six hundred and fifty days," Jimmy says, his eyes still glued to his book.

"What? What are you talking about?"

He flips his comic book face down and stares up into my eyes.

"Or it will be 5,475 days," he calmly states.

"I don't understand, Jimmy."

Jimmy quietly sighs, picking up his comic book to keep reading. Then it hits me. He's done the math on how many days Benny will be in prison. I guess I shouldn't be surprised, since math is the subject Jimmy knows best.

"I get it, Jimmy. He'll be gone for a lot of days. But how does that make you feel?" I ask, leaning my eyes down to his level.

"Sad. But he'll be home soon enough," he plainly states.

"He'll eventually be home, but that's a lot of days. You know it's okay to—"

"Stop it!" he raises his voice. "Just stop it!"

I put my hand on his shoulder. He slaps it away.

"Ow, Jimmy! Why did you do that?"

"It's not a long time. It's not a long time. It's not a long time," he keeps repeating the same exact words. Each time it's progressively faster and his voice is becoming gruffer.

Jimmy's willing himself to believe that Benny will be back soon. Deep down he knows. But I'm not going to rain on his parade.

"You're right, Jimmy. You're right," I say, leaning back down to his eyes. "Benny will be home soon. But for now, we have to stick together. You, me, Dad, and Ms. Green. We all have to be strong. Can you do that?" I beg.

"I know, Penny." His eyes finally focus on me. "I can be strong like Benny," he whispers.

I give him a kiss on the head. Then I lean down to his ear. I whisper the same words I've whispered every night for the last three weeks.

"Thank you for saving my life. I love you so much—always remember that."

Back in my bed, I try to sleep. Eventually I get up and start writing in my journal. Then I write another letter to Benny. I've done at least one letter every day now.

When I still can't sleep, I head into the kitchen for some water. I'm startled by Dad and Ms. Green.

"Trouble sleeping?" Dad asks.

I nod my head. They're both sitting at the dining room table, sipping their tea. Seeing the two of them sit together in silence reminds me of the earlier days in their relationship. They'd just sit next to each other for hours saying very little. It's as if being together is all they need for reassurance.

"Come sit with us, Sweetheart?" Ms. Green asks, patting the chair next to her.

I take a seat, briefly noticing that Dad is staring hypnotically into his cup of tea. I bow my head and fidget with my hands in my lap. It's hard to see Dad in such pain. It's not something I'm used to.

"How's Jimmy holding up?" Ms. Green asks.

"He's okay. He did the math on how many days make up ten to fifteen years. And he thinks Benny will be home soon," I explain, letting out a nervous chuckle.

"How are you, Sweetheart?" Ms. Green asks, rubbing my shoulder.

I take a deep breath in. Then I summon the courage to look up into her brown eyes, still somehow full of hope.

"I'm okay. I just don't know what to do," I admit. "I just wish he'd write back to me. I just want to know how he's feeling. And that's probably stupid because I know how he's feeling. But I think if Benny would just start writing back to me, then maybe it would help him, just a little."

"Does it feel good to write to him?" Ms. Green asks.

"It does."

"Then don't stop doing it. Write him every single day if you need too. Right now, you need to follow your heart and your gut. We're all grieving. What works for each of us is going to be different. But I have faith. Benny is going to be okay. He's not dead. He's still living. Everything else will somehow work out in his favor. I just know it. This whole household is going to be okay. I don't know how, but…" She pauses, letting out a long sigh.

"Hey," she says, squeezing Dad's shoulder.

He clears his throat, looking startled by her touch. "Yeah, we'll be okay," Dad quietly mutters. He briefly looks up, forcing a fake smile that disappears in the blink of an eye. Then he goes back to staring aimlessly at his tea.

The despair in Dad's eyes is hard to see. It's a lifeless look, but there's more to his sadness.

I want to be strong for everyone. But I don't know how to take away the guilt he's feeling right now. I don't blame Dad, and I've told him many times over since the incident. He visited Vern to make peace, and he succeeded in a way at the time. Now, he feels like he only incited the Monroes even more.

When I can't take it any longer, I get up and walk behind him. My arms drape over his shoulders and around his chest. My head nuzzles into his neck for the comfort and security I desperately need. Then I lean my lips up to his ear.

"I'm really sad. And I need my dad. I need you to tell me things will be okay and actually mean it. Please, please, Daddy," I beg.

The only thing I can hear is his labored breathing. He remains silent, but I need him to say something. I need him to be my rock. I just want my dad back. But maybe Ms. Green is right. We all grieve differently.

Then I hear it. It's a whimper so faint and soft, like it's being suppressed, but found a way out through the cracks. The sound is so foreign because I've never heard a grown man whimper. Then it slowly evolves as he buries his face in my hair.

The crying comes on so suddenly I don't know what to do. My only response is the one that comes naturally. I cry with him. We hold on tighter to one another because we need each other's strength.

The night wears on like this. Sometimes it's just me crying and sometimes it's all three of us. We don't have an answer to the ways of the world. For now, crying is our only form of catharsis.

Eventually I head to bed at around 2 a.m. I'm still lost on what the future holds for the McClain household. But at least I have a compass on how to live without Benny in my life. And the way to do it is by keeping him present. There's only one way to do that.

*I'll write, every single day.*

# CHAPTER ELEVEN

# 1966

## *One Year Later*

Letter #365

Dear Benny,

I received word yesterday that my mother passed away due to liver failure. She literally drank herself to death.

I should be sad about not having my biological mother, but I'm not. I'm glad she's gone. Besides, Ms. Green is every bit the mother I could ever dream of.

I hope you are doing okay. We're all really frustrated. You can choose to not call us or not meet with us for your court-granted monthly visit. But you have to at least write back to me. I need to know you're okay. I'm begging you!

I will never stop writing you, Benny McClain. You're still my best friend and the boy I fell in love with in a treehouse. And I still need you in my life in some capacity.

Things have changed a lot in the last year. Our new house is out in the boondocks. It's about 40 miles outside of

Birmingham in the forest. We're starting to feel safe out here since very few people even know where we live now. Dad and Ms. Green grow a lot of the food we eat in the garden out back, which means we very rarely drive into town. The only hard part about living in the middle of nowhere is only being able to see Sarah twice a week.

I only have to go to school two days a week now. It's because of the situation I've been trying to tell you about when we come to the prison once a month to see you. This new situation is life-changing and something even bigger than you not being here. Hopefully the next time we come you'll agree to meet with us.

I wish you could see your brother. He's able to attend a new high school for people like him. Ms. Green found it for him. It's 60 minutes away from our house, but she and Dad drive Jimmy there three times a week. The teachers are able to harness his intelligence and let it grow organically in a way that best fits him. He's continuing to excel in mathematics. But it's way more than just academic growth. He's learning about emotional intelligence too. Whenever you see him next, I know you'll be blown away by his growth into manhood. It's such a blessing to witness.

There's something else I need to get off my chest. Every night I close my eyes for bed, my mind only goes to one place—the treehouse. It's the one place where I truly feel connected with you. And it's still the one place I feel safe and disconnected from all the noise in the world. I miss being up there with you so much it hurts. Even though we all live a secluded life now, it's still not the same.

Yesterday I dreamt of being with you in the old treehouse. You were dressed in your football uniform. You had just won the National Championship of college football. We all had a party in that treehouse—me, you, Dad, Ms. Green, Jimmy, Paul, and Sarah. Then the treehouse got hot and smoky. I woke up in a pool of sweat.

I still have flashbacks to that night. They're less frequent, but I still don't know how to get rid of them. But at least I have people I can talk to here. Do you?

You must be lonely. I worry for the health of your mind. It's not good to hold it in, especially with where you're living.

Is it guilt? Is it stubbornness? What is it, Benny? You still need us. We will always need you. No one here is mad at you or thinks less of you. And no one here sees you as a convict or murderer. You're still the same Benny. You just have to find yourself again! You have to stay strong!

I remember you as a person with a heart bigger than any other human being on earth. I reminisce about a man who fell in love with a girl he wasn't supposed to love. But I don't regret my feelings for you. And time and distance won't take those feelings away—*ever*!

I just want the old Benny back. Whether it's the one who loves me as a brother, or the one who loves me like you did that one night in the treehouse. I'll just take whatever pieces of you I can get.

Please write back!

Love always, Penny

## *One Year Later*

Letter #730

Dear Benny,

Happy 20th Birthday. I've given up on asking you to write me back. Ms. Green told me the other night that maybe I should take a break from writing you every day. She also said that it's okay to move on and live my own life. It's what I've been doing anyways, or at least I'm trying to.

I still don't see the harm in missing you a little. And it helps writing you. But maybe I'm being delusional in pretending you're reading my letters.

I still have bad dreams. But lately it's imagining you in solitary confinement. In the one last night you were starving yourself to death and whittling away into a Benny I couldn't recognize. I wish I could just stop from dreaming ever again. It's rarely anything good.

But here are some good things going on. Paul is starting at Left Tackle for Eastern Alabama University. It's a big deal since he had to red shirt his freshman year. According to Sarah he's one of the top offensive linemen in the entire nation. She tells me that he believes he can go pro. I know you'd be so proud of him.

I'm also about to be a high school graduate in a couple weeks. Me and Sarah have been accepted into the Teacher Preparation Program. I'm not sure what grade I want to teach. But I know I'd love to one day teach people like Jimmy. It's something I'd be good at and it's something that will bring me happiness.

The junior college is about an hour-and-a-half away from our new house so I'm looking at moving away from Dad and Ms. Green. It'll be hard to leave them, but I know it's for the best. I've even told them that I've thought about having Jimmy live with me. He helps me a lot with things now. It's still something we're discussing. But I think it would be good for Jimmy and me. We both need each other in ways you wouldn't be able to understand.

Dad and Ms. Green have been doing better lately. There are still times where I see that desolate look in their eyes because they miss you. But I'm so glad they have each other. I even saw them kiss the other day. Jimmy made a vomit noise and I choked on my soda from laughing so hard. I wish you could've been there.

Since you won't tell me how you're doing, I'll at least tell you what I'm hoping for. I hope you have friends in prison or at least a counselor to talk to. But more than anything, I'm hoping you're reading my letters and smiling. Even if it's a smile for a split second, it would mean the world to me.

I miss the way your eyes looked when you smiled. They glistened like a lake sparkling from those first moments of tranquil sunrise. I call it the treehouse smile. It was in all of those perfect moments we shared together as young teens. You weren't my annoying older brother on those days. You were the man that I was and still am madly in love with.

It sounds crazy to fantasize over eyes, but it's what I do all the time. The vision won't go away. I want to stare into you and let you stare back into me with time completely frozen. That's what I want to dream about. Those are the moments I want to re-live.

I miss you so much! Please write back!

Love always, Penny.

## *Six Months Later*

Dear Penny,

Hopefully this letter finds you. I'll make this brief and simple. PLEASE STOP WRITING ME LETTERS! I'M A LOW LIFE MURDERER. DON'T EVER FORGET WHO I AM.

I'm not deserving of a letter after all the mistakes and pain I've brought to the McClain family. Every single letter you've sent is unopened and sent to one place—THE TRASH CAN!

The only advice I would give is to change your name back to Jones. You don't deserve to be a McClain, and you never did. Everything that happened after your adoption was a curse we should have saw coming.

And you only made things worse by coming down from the treehouse that night. If you just stayed up there none of this would've happened. Why did you have to be so fucking stubborn?

Please know that I won't ever forgive myself. It's just impossible when you're rotting away in a cell each day. I did something stupid and as a result I'm no longer there for you. And that is unforgivable.

This is my last communication with you. Just move on, and please be safe.

Benny

# CHAPTER TWELVE

## Penny

## *1968*

### *One Year Later*

The sweat streaming from his wrinkly, angry face has me laughing to myself. I'm doing my best to help him, but it's not easy.

Dad is almost 80 now. We're both trying to load a brand-new queen-size mattress and box spring into his truck. The old man was too stubborn to ask for help, even though the attendant offered twice.

"There, I got it," Dad groans, trying to smile while catching his breath. He lets out a long sigh and straightens out his posture.

"You okay?"

He's trying not to grimace, but I can tell his lower back is aching.

"Oh, I'm fine. I'm just so happy I can help you with all this stuff."

Dad's smile wilts the slightest bit. He's worried about what the future holds.

We both hop into the truck. We're two people carrying lots of heavy emotions. It's weird feeling happy, sad, and vehemently angry all at the same time. But I can't help it. Some days I just don't know how to process it all without a good cry.

Dad's hand squeezes my shoulder, startling me from my reverie.

"How are you doing, Sweetheart?" he asks.

"I'm okay."

"Penny, it's okay to be nervous. Hell, I don't know how Ms. Green and I will empty nest without you and your brother around. But I don't want you to worry about us. You hear me, Sweetheart?"

"I hear you, Dad," I say quietly.

"Good, because I'm proud of you for wanting to share this journey with Jimmy. You all are going to be one big happy family up there. And on days you need us, we'll be there at the drop of a hat. I mean that. We'll always be there."

"I know, Dad."

"Besides Penny, it's good to be off on your own. It's how you learn to take on this world. And you're ready. I couldn't be more proud of you."

"Thanks, Dad."

He's such a sweet man. I don't know why I deserve to be loved so well by him. But it's more than the love I get from Dad. Ms. Green is basically a mother to me. I still only call her Ms. Green, but she's been there for me through so much over the last couple years. She understands my feelings for Benny better than anyone.

Then there's Jimmy. In my eyes, he's a fully independent 19-year-old man now. It may be an adjustment moving out with me, but I'm used to Jimmy and all of his quirks.

Either way, there's no turning back now. I'll be moved out in about a month and I'll be starting my first semester of junior college in six weeks. Grandpa said it best. It's time to take on the world. The only problem is, my world still feels lonely.

"Hey, I got an idea," Dad announces in a chipper tone. "How about we grab a sundae before we head back home? It'll be just like old times."

I'm hesitant because it's something we very rarely do in this town since leaving Birmingham. But I agree because I can tell it'll make Dad happy.

Driving to the ice cream parlor, I see a lot more black people out and about in the streets of Birmingham. It has me wondering if things may be changing a bit. There's still plenty of signs about segregation, but there's a lot more of my people walking side by side with white folks.

There's a lot of change going on in the world nowadays. They're calling it the Civil Rights Movement. Dad seems to think my world will look vastly different by the time we make it into the next decade. I don't fully believe him, but I like that he has hope that the 1970's will be better than the 1960's have been.

While we're eating our sundaes, Dad becomes quiet. There's not a lot for us to say. We're both going to miss living with each other. We both still miss Benny. And we're both nervous for all the changes that await our future. There's parts that are exciting, but for the most part it just feels like a swirl of emotion too uncertain to articulate.

"Can I ask you a question, Sweetheart? It's something that may upset you, but I'm just curious."

I nod my head. "Sure."

"Do you still write to Benny?"

"No."

"When did you stop?" he asks.

"About a year ago. He wrote me, telling me to change my last name and never write him again. He said he hasn't read a single one of my letters."

The pain in my chest suddenly feels suffocating. It's like I'm reading his spiteful letter all over again for the first time. My breathing goes shallow. I close my eyes, hoping to stop the tears.

Luckily, the tears never come. I'm able to fight them off using my pure hatred of Benny. He's just an evil person now. It's been years since he's spoken a single word to any of us. Then he has the gall to write something so heartless to me. There's no denying I miss him, but I miss the old him. As far as I'm concerned, he's dead to me.

"I'm sorry he wrote those things to you. But I don't think he truly believes it. I know I've told you before, but adopting you was—"

"I know, Dad," I interrupt in a bitchy tone. "I know it was his idea to adopt me. But I don't care. Fuck Benny!"

Dad lets out a long sigh. He doesn't like when we use foul language. But he lets me be.

"Can I ask you one more thing?" Dad asks, his tone still on edge.

I nod, taking another frustrated breath.

Dad's hand grasps mine. His eyes are filled with worry. "Does he know?"

I feel the air leave my lungs as the panic sets in.

"No," I mutter, trying to catch my breath. "And we're never going to tell him. You understand? He doesn't need to know. And he definitely doesn't deserve to know. Okay?" I raise my voice.

Grandpa bites his bottom lip like he's wanting to say more.

This is a topic I try avoiding with Ms. Green and Dad. They bring it up because they care. However, they don't understand the depths of my pain. No one can unless they walked through these last couple years in my shoes.

"Can I tell you a story?" he asks.

I groan right away. "Is this another life lesson?"

"No. It's a sad story, but a true one. Hear me out. My son Chip, Benny's dad, grew up hating my guts. He had every right to. I wasn't always the best father. It's because I worked too much and when I was around, I was always bossing him around. I was trying to teach what my dad taught: tough love. And do you want to know how many times I told him I loved him? Go on, take a guess?"

I shake my head, shrugging my shoulders.

"One time," he whispers. "Can you believe it? *One…goddamn…time.*"

Dad lightly pounds the table with his fist. He bows his head down, shaking it in regret. Then he looks up, taking a deep breath, trying to sniffle the tears away. But it's too late. They're already trickling down his face. "You see, when he and his wife got in the car accident, she died instantly. But he was still alive when I got to the hospital. I got there with Madeline, and we held his hand, looking at his lifeless, pale, bloodied up body. I squeezed his hand, willing him back to consciousness, but there was nothing," Dad whimpers.

"Oh, Dad!" I cry, coming around the table to hold him.

"I'm not done," he says, his voice quivering. "I leaned down to his bloody ear and whispered that I loved him so much. I told him I'd be a better dad to Benny and Jimmy. Then I said I'm sorry. And I begged him to forgive me. Then the miracle of all miracles occurred. His hand squeezed back with every last bit of life he had in him. And then he was gone…forever."

We cry together, handing each other napkins in the tiny confines of our booth.

"Why are you telling me this now?" I ask.

"It's simple. I tell Benny, you, and Jimmy I love you every single day. No matter what you guys do to disappoint me. It doesn't matter. You all were born with hearts of gold. When Chip squeezed back that day, I knew he had forgiven me. But with forgiveness comes great responsibility. It means I have to do better this time around. And I know I'm not perfect. But neither is Benny, or any of us. Just give it time. You can hate him all you want to, but give it time. Because hanging on to hatred is no way to live. It's the poison that rots the soul. And it's no way to leave this world."

Dad's words carry a weight I don't feel ready to unpack. I want to tell him how it feels good to hate Benny. It sounds crazy to think that way, but it's what's keeping me together for some odd reason. Besides, even if Benny wants to be forgiven, he'll have to earn it. I've wasted too many letters on him and too many long nights worrying about him. I'm done.

"I'm sorry for getting all emotional," Dad says, taking a long, deep breath.

"It's okay, Dad. Can I tell you something I've never told you before?" I ask.

"Of course."

"Did you know that Benny tried finding my real dad?"

"He did?"

Dad's look of shock stuns me. I don't even know why I'm telling him this for the first time. After all, Richard McClain is the only father I'll ever need.

"Yeah, it was a few years back. Apparently he was living up in the Boston area. I don't know if he's still there or somewhere close by. But Benny was trying to find him for me as a birthday present. He said that he never got to know his real father. And he thought it would be important for me to meet him and learn about his story."

"Is that something you want to do, Penny?"

"No. I already have my dad. But who knows, maybe one day."

"Well, if you ever want to look into that, please know I support you," Dad smiles.

Neither of us has much more to say after such a heavy conversation. But it feels okay to just sit in silence, shoulder to shoulder with the man who takes pride in being my father.

Deep down I don't want to live each day full of hatred for Benny. But maybe finding the path towards that journey will come in due time.

When Dad heads to the bathroom, I stare aimlessly out the window, thinking about my future. There's so much new that awaits me. And I feel the need to embrace that while at the same time letting go of Benny. Even when he gets out of prison in a few years there's no telling if he'll want anything to do with us. Maybe the best I can do for my family is to let him go for good.

I notice a small crowd of people gathering across the street. I can see the people begin to wave frantically and shout at others. Then I see a lifeless body on the ground at their feet.

I run outside to see if I can help. I bust through the crowd of people and see the  lifeless man, flat on his stomach with his face turned sideways in a pool of blood.

"What happened to him?"

"He collapsed!" one of the women shouts. "His son just ran inside to call emergency services. Oh my Lord, is he alive?"

*Don't panic!*

I hear Ms. Green's voice in my mind. It's like she's calmly whispering the words in my ear. A former nurse, she's trained us all in giving CPR.

I go to one knee and feel for a pulse on his wrist. I don't feel anything. Then I do the same reaching around to the front of his neck to confirm there's still no pulse. Still feeling nothing, I try flipping the man on his back. His dead weight makes it almost impossible, but I finally get it. Then my body shudders at the bloody ghost staring back.

I immediately flash back to that night, under the treehouse.

"Oh god, I can't," I whisper to myself, staring away from the man's face.

I feel like I have to vomit. It has nothing to do with seeing a man who's lifeless. It has everything to do with who the man is.

*I can't do this.*

Someone screams for a doctor or nurse. I could wait here and do nothing until help arrives. Or I can try to revive a person more vile and evil than the devil himself.

"What's this nigger going to do?" the scream comes from behind me. I turn to see a white woman gritting her teeth like I'm grossing her out with my very existence.

She doesn't know I could potentially help bring this man back to life. She's more worried about a black woman touching an old, wrinkly, bigoted white man.

She puts her hand on my shoulder. "Get away nigger!" she screams in my face.

The reflex comes out of nowhere. My open hand slaps right across the face of this racist bitch. It feels like heaven.

She steps backwards, holding her hand to her face.

"Don't touch me, you crazy bitch!" I scream. "I can help this man. Unless you can help him, don't fucking touch me again!"

I turn back to Clarence Monroe's lifeless body. The last time I saw this man he was pounding away at Jimmy's skull with his shotgun. The moment is so real, but I must erase it from my mind if I'm going to do this.

My hands pound into his chest as I count to 30, calling the numbers out loud. I try to not look at his face. Each time I pump his chest, it's with anger. When I finally reach 30, I fear what has to come next. But I can't hesitate. I lean my mouth down to his for two full breaths. The smell of tobacco and old-man breath almost makes me vomit.

The rhythm of another 30 chest compressions and two breaths becomes a rigorous routine. His body becomes more pale and lifeless the harder I work. But I keep going. I have no choice. I wasn't raised to not help others. It's not who I am.

"Hey, I think he's breathing!" a man shouts.

I quickly lean my ear down to his chest, hearing a slow thud. Then I feel the same beating pulse on his wrist and neck. The color in his face is coming back. Everyone around me starts snickering loudly as the ambulance pulls up.

"She saved him! She saved him!" The people around me keep shouting.

I get up to take a step backwards as the paramedics take over. Then I bump into a young man's chest. I turn around to see a face I instantly recognize. The young man looks at me like he's seen a ghost. Then he shoves me out of the way to lean down to his father.

"You're going to be okay, Dad," Ricky Monroe says.

Clarence Monroe's eyes begin to flutter open. I turn away quickly. The last thing I want is him knowing I saved his life. Besides, people sick in the head like him don't deserve another second in this world. I only did it because that bitch behind me pissed me off. Or at least that's what I'm telling myself.

"What's going on here?" Dad asks, startling me from behind.

"It's nothing," I reply. "We need to go."

I try walking away, but a police officer stops us both. He's big and scary looking, but ends up being surprisingly nice. He just wants a quick story on what I witnessed. I don't have much to say other than helping to revive the old man.

When he lets us go, I realize that Dad doesn't know that I just performed CPR on Clarence Monroe. He just knows that I helped someone. If he found out who I'd saved, I have no idea how he'd react.

The rest of the day feels really eerie. Dad and Ms. Green keep telling me how proud they are of me. I fake my appreciation for their gratitude while my insides stew.

The night wears on and I continue to feel less proud of what I've done. It just feels impossible that on the one rare day we are in town, I run into Clarence and Ricky Monroe, the two men who probably know the real truth of what happened on that night.

"You okay in there?" Jimmy asks.

It's my second time vomiting in the last 15 minutes. Each time I imagine tasting the nicotine and wretched bad breath of that man.

"I'm okay!" I yell back. "It's just a little stomach bug."

I'm so worried that I'll wake everyone in the house. The last thing I need is another night of restless sleep, getting up every couple hours.

After flushing the toilet, I open the door to Jimmy holding a bowl of soup like a waiter presenting a meal. I can't say no to his worried face.

"Oh, Jimmy. Thank you so much. You're such a sweetie. I'm going to save it for tomorrow."

"Why are you sick, Penny? What's wrong with you?" Jimmy asks, looking deeply concerned. It's like he knows something's up.

We both flinch when the doorbell rings. Dad is quickly in the hallway with his bat in his hand. It's well past 10 p.m. and we very rarely have visitors, especially this late.

The four of us quickly head to the front door.

"Stay back!" Dad barks at us.

He slowly peers behind the curtain.

"What the fuck!" Dad shouts.

"Who is it?" Ms. Green asks.

"That fucking Ricky Monroe kid! Stay back, I'll scare him off," Dad says, his face getting redder by the second.

"Wait! Wait! Stop, Dad!" I scream, lunging into his body before he opens the door.

"What, Penny?

"I know why he's here, Dad. Just wait a second. The person I did CPR on was…." I pause. I can't say the name out loud. It hurts too much.

"Tell me, Penny. Come on," Dad begs.

My mouth can't move. It feels impossible to utter that last name in this house. Then Dad sighs, reaching for the doorknob again.

"It was Clarence Monroe!" I finally shout. "I think I may have saved his life today. I didn't want to. I'm so sorry. The one person in the world we all want dead and I tried to save his life. I'm so sorry," I beg for his forgiveness, hanging on to his shirt collar.

The living room becomes silent. Dad looks away. The disappointment in his face is like ripping my heart out of my chest. I look around, seeing only shocked expressions on the faces of Jimmy and Ms. Green. They don't know what to say, and neither do I. Then Jimmy runs into his room, slamming the door shut.

Dad continues to look away. Ms. Green walks over to me, grabbing me by my hands. "It's okay, Penny. You did the right thing."

"No she didn't! Are you all crazy!" Dad shouts. Then he reaches for the doorknob. But as the door swings open, Ms. Green quickly slams it shut.

"What are you doing, Richard? You going to go out there and kill the boy! Are you crazy!" she hysterically shouts, her face vibrating inches from his. "We don't even know what happened that night. We may never know. But going out there and doing something stupid is only going to bring on more pain, to you and everyone. I'm done with that. We'll go out there and see why the boy is here. Then we'll ask him to leave and never show his face here again!"

"But—"

"No buts!" she interrupts. "Let's go!"

The three of us walk outside. Ms. Green leads the way. Standing a good ten yards from the door is Ricky Monroe. He's not as big as his brothers. His hands are buried deep in his pockets. His posture is hunched like he's unsure about why he's here.

"What do you want?" Dad tersely demands.

"I, um…" He clears his throat. "I need to talk to all of you."

"You got one minute, or my dad's going to beat the shit out of you," I calmly say even though my heart beats like a machine gun.

"This may take more than a minute, but you need to hear this," he says, taking three steps closer with his hands raising up in surrender.

Dad raises his bat in the air the slightest bit. The tension in the air is palpable.

Nothing makes sense. Me saving his dad's life. Him being at our house in the middle of the night. I mean, what does he want from us? He's already taken the most precious thing from us all.

*Our Benny! My Benny!*

# CHAPTER THIRTEEN

# Benny

## *2 weeks later*

The sound of pumping weights is the best part of my day. It's the way the metal and iron rhythmically ring with each rep. It's the only music I've known for the past few years.

Every ounce of anger and resentment goes into each one of my reps. All of it is pent-up regret and pain that leaves my body for 90 minutes every day. It's the only bliss I have left in my life.

It's a weird thing, getting used to being in prison. Everything is so structured, from the minute I eat, to the minute I shit and piss. There's rarely anything out of the ordinary anymore.

The good part is I no longer have to deal with shit. I got into scuff-ups with other inmates during my first couple months in Montgomery Penitentiary. But after winning my last couple fights, I've become off limits. No one has the balls to mess with me. I'm stronger than anyone here and I like how others are scared of me.

I have no friends in here, only acquaintances. All I do is work out, read, study, do my woodworking, and sleep. It's like clockwork, going through each day.

I'm still not used to the boredom I feel on a daily basis. However, it's the bed I made for myself by killing another man.

"You're headed up to the courthouse tomorrow. You hear me, Benny?" the guard shouts from outside the door.

"No, thanks," I calmly reply. I go back to my pushups and sit-ups. When I finish my set, I sit back up. "Are you serious?"

"Ten a.m. tomorrow. You have no choice. You're going. It's the judge's orders," the guard calmly states.

I lay in bed that night, wide awake. My brain won't shut up. My routine is being thrown off tomorrow and I don't like it one bit.

I still have about six years left to go in here. Why the hell would I be going before a judge?

The weird part is what has me most worried about tomorrow: seeing them again. I couldn't bear seeing the pity and disappointment in their faces.

I'm sure they still miss me. But the reality is I miss them more. And who knows how things will be if I get released in six years? Grandpa could easily be dead. Ms. Green is a few years younger than Grandpa, but she could be dead, too.

Penny will be off changing the world. She'll be the best teacher there ever was. I just hope she's living her best life and not worrying about me anymore. I'm sure she's pissed off about the one letter I sent to her. But I had to do it. She would have never stopped writing me.

I wonder what will happen with Jimmy's life, too. Who knows if he'll ever be able to live independently? He was making such progress before I left. There's no telling the direction his life is headed with me no longer in it. But I'm glad he has Penny to look after him.

Paul writes every couple of months. He told me a while back they bought a new house with the fire insurance money, out in the boondocks. He said it's about an hour long drive from our old house. He and Sarah try to visit them when they can to see how everyone's doing. I haven't gotten a letter from Paul in the last few months, but I know he's focused on football. I'm happy for him.

----

The next day I take a long bus ride to the eastern part of Montgomery. I'm struck by the beauty of the endless rows of cornfields. I suddenly yearn to be free like a bird.

Once we get to the courthouse I, chained at the ankles, shimmy walk my way through endless hallways. I'm led by a guard into a small, stagnant room. All the walls are bright white and completely empty of decoration. There's only a small round table and a couple chairs.

I take a seat with two security guards standing behind me.

"Can you guys at least tell me why I'm here?" I ask.

"We don't know, Benny. Just shut up and wait for your lawyer," one of them barks back.

Moments later a short, bald man wearing a cheap suit and carrying a brief case walks in. He smiles at me like we're best friends. I want to flip him off, but I also don't want to get hit in the back of the head.

"I'm Mr. Chapman. I'm your lawyer," he says, extending his hand to me. "Do you know why I'm here?"

I just stare at his hand, refusing to shake it. If this guy is anything like my last lawyer, I'd much rather spit on it.

"Nope. And I don't care. I just want to get back to my cell, take a nap, and then get to my workouts."

"Do you not know who I am?"

"Fuck you," I calmly say.

The blow to the side of my face doesn't surprise me.

"Ow! Fuck!" I groan.

"Show this man some respect. He's here to help, you dumb fuck," the guard says.

"You didn't need to do that, mister," the guy in the suit says. "Benny, listen to me. My son's name is Tony. Tony Chapman played tight end with you when you guys won the state title for Westchester a couple years ago. Do you remember Tony?"

"Of course I remember him," I admit, trying to wipe the blood on my shoulder. "But what does he have to do with any of this?"

"You're right. He has nothing to do with me being here. I just thought you may remember me. Anyway, I was hired by your grandfather. I'm here because Ricky Monroe is going to re-testify before the judge today. You're going to do the same."

"I'm not doing shit. Don't you remember? I'm a fucking murderer!" I shout, gritting my teeth.

"No. You're not. Don't say that. All you need to do is testify to what you remember on the night Terry Monroe was killed. Just tell the truth. The same truth you testified to almost four years ago. Ricky Monroe will give his testimony as well."

I shake my head in utter disbelief. None of this makes a shred of sense. The last thing I want to do is re-live the night I've tried so hard to forget. I may have no recollection of shooting someone, but if given the opportunity I know I'd do it if I could. Besides, I've accepted the fact that I'm a murderer. It's my identity now.

"Listen to me, Benny. This testimony and court injunction is all voluntary. This was Ricky Monroe's idea."

Mr. Chapman stops to slide his chair closer to me. Then he leans towards me, glaring. "You're going to want to hear what he has to say about that night his brother died. Trust me, son."

"You're wrong. I'm not going through with this. You don't understand. I killed someone. And I can't walk into a courtroom with that asshole. Especially if my grandpa is going to be there. I don't want to see him or any of my family."

I'm sick just imagining the situation.

"Listen to me!" Mr. Chapman shouts, banging his open hand on the table. "Do you want to possibly get out of this hell hole? Or do you want to be here till you're practically 30? It's your fucking choice!"

I sigh, looking at the shackles around my wrists and ankles. Of course I want to get out of here. But I don't believe this man in the least. Even if he is Tony Chapman's dad. I made my peace a long time ago that I'd be here a long time. And I'm too much of a wimp to get out there and re-testify.

"If I do give another testimony, who would be there?" I ask.

"It'll be me and you. Ricky Monroe and his lawyer. The judge and the bailiffs. And whatever family members want to be there. Whites only, of course," Mr. Chapman explains, clearing his throat.

"So my grandpa will probably be there?"

"Yes. Maybe Jimmy too."

"Oh my god," I sigh.

I bow my head down as I try to catch my breath. The ache in my chest is as strong as it was the day I was sentenced to prison.

I have no faith in my own innocence. Why would a Monroe testimony change what's already happened? I've accepted what I am, even if my memory is linked to some blurry version of reality.

*But what if?*

"If I do it, I don't want to see them. Is that possible?" I ask.

"Well, I can't make them not come. But you can bow your head down and just avoid looking towards the back part of the room. But I can't promise what you will or won't see when you step in there."

I take a long, deep breath, knowing I'll regret whatever I decide today. But I have to give this a shot.

"Okay. I'll do it. When do we start? I want to get this over with."

"It happens today. All you have to do is sign the paperwork that you give consent to re-testify. Then we'll head into the courtroom in about an hour or so."

Mr. Chapman slides the paperwork across the table, handing me a pen. I fill out all the forms. After he leaves, I find myself sitting alone in my familiar silence.

Time passes by slowly. There's no clock in this tiny room, but it feels like I've been in here for hours. Then a knock on the door startles me.

"It's time!" someone shouts from outside my door.

The guards lead me through more hallways. We stop at a large double door that I figure leads into the courtroom. I take a deep breath as the guards grab my arms on each side and guide me into the room. I keep my head bowed down.

Once inside, I feel a large draft of cold air. I notice as the carpet turns into hardwood. Then I feel my calves touch a chair. I take a seat, still refusing to look up.

"Please rise for the honorable Judge McCarthy!" someone announces.

I stand up, looking straight ahead for the first time, seeing only the judge. I refuse to look behind me, knowing who's probably here today. Everyone takes a seat when the judge sits down.

"We're here today for the injunction filed in the case of Monroe versus Benjamin McClain. I've spent the last few days reviewing the evidence behind this case as well as the prior verdict. Now, Mr. Chapman, your turn," the judge says, gesturing to my attorney.

"Yes. Your Honor, we're here today because a witness who was a minor at the time of this alleged murder would like to re-testify. He's an adult now. It's my belief that this testimony will prove my client's innocence in the murder of Terry Monroe. I'd like to call this witness to the stand, Your Honor."

Judge McCarthy puts on his reading glasses and shuffles through some papers. "You may, Mr. Chapman. The court calls Ricky Monroe to the stand."

I look down again at the shackles around my wrists. Then I look up once he's up on the stand. He's much taller than I remember. His hair is bushier and longer. He's read his rights, then he begins to offer his testimony.

He goes over the night that he, his dad, and his brothers came to our house. He recalls waiting in the car and then coming out to the backyard when he heard people scream.

"I saw my dad with a gun to the head of Jimmy McClain," Ricky says, taking a deep breath. "I don't think he was going to pull the trigger. I honestly thought he was just trying to scare him. That was my dad's goal, scare them and hurt them a little. It was all with the hope to scare the McClains out of Birmingham. But I saw his finger go over the trigger and I tackled him. I wrestled the gun away and then we sped out of there as their house was burning down."

"And who burned down the house?" Mr. Chapman asks.

"I honestly didn't see who started the fire. But I'm sure it was my brothers and my father. My job was to just stay in the car and get us out of there once everyone finished the job," Ricky explains, letting out a long, slow breath. "Then we got back home. Dad and Terry were upset with me. John was, too. They were all worried someone may have seen us leave the house. Then a couple minutes later me and Dad heard some commotion in the backyard. We looked out the second story window and saw Terry on the ground. He was trying to get up while John and Benny were fighting. Dad told me to stay put, and I did, at first. But after a few seconds I went downstairs. I didn't go outside. I was too scared. But I pulled back the drapes to look outside. That's when I saw Dad hit Benny from behind with the butt of his gun. He hit him perfectly in the back of his head. But right as he hit him in the head…the gun—" Ricky stops talking. His face goes pale.

I watch as his lips start to tremble. Then he wipes his eyes. He looks so pathetic up there, sniffling back tears. I want to scream at him to finish his story. I've waited over a thousand days for the real truth.

"Please continue, Mr. Monroe," Mr. Chapman calmly requests.

"Well, my brother Terry was getting up behind my dad. And when Dad swung the gun at Benny I think he accidentally pulled the trigger. And that was it. All I saw was smoke fly from the gun right as my brother's head, and chunks of blood fly out of it," Ricky says, his eyes looking lost in trauma.

All I hear next is a loud exhale from behind. Or maybe it was a moan of disgust. Either way I feel the presence of those I love. I want so badly to turn around, but I still can't.

The pressure in my chest slowly dissipates. The weight I've felt for so long starts to drift away. Then my body starts to tingle all over. Maybe it's adrenalin. Either way, I'm not sure what I should be feeling, other than shock.

I've spent so much time over the last three-plus years believing that I really did kill Terry Monroe, even though I testified otherwise. I just figured that when I got knocked out I probably didn't remember what happened. But my reality has been false all along. I truly did not kill another human being. I wanted to that night, but I didn't do it.

That piece of shit, Clarence Monroe, killed his own son. And he knows it.

"And what did you do when you witnessed this?" Mr. Chapman asks, his tone gentler.

Ricky's eyes go suddenly wide with fear. It's like he's vividly reliving the moments in his head.

"I was standing near the couch, I think," he pauses to clear his throat. "I didn't know what to do. But I grabbed the closest pillow, pulled it over my face, and screamed as loud as I could. And I kept screaming until Dad came in the house. He asked if I saw what happened. I was too scared to speak a word, but I think he knew. I couldn't even look him in the eyes. Then he told me that Benny shot Terry in the head. He kept repeating those words, almost thinking he could brainwash me, which he did. Then it must've been seconds later when the cops pulled up. They asked what happened and I just told them I heard commotion out back then a single gunshot. And that was it. I lied. Benny McClain is innocent. He may have hurt my brothers. But my dad is the one that pulled the trigger. He hated the McClains so much. He despised how they would mix."

"What do you mean, mix?" Mr. Chapman asks, taking a few steps closer to Ricky.

"Well, he didn't like how they took in those two black girls into their home. Then there was a rumor of the Grandpa having a romantic relationship. Then when he found out that Benny and Penny were together, he lost it. He wanted the whole family to disappear from our town, forever."

Ricky turns to me. His eyes are still wet, and his lips part and quiver. He wants to say something, but he can't. Instead, he just stares at me with despair.

Every hair on my body stands tall. I don't know whether to hate this person's guts, forgive him, or fight the urge to kill him. He and his dad have stolen so much from me and my family. And he's lived with this secret for so long. But then it hits me.

*Guilt!*

Guilt is an emotion I know far too well. It can tear us down from inside. Ricky Monroe was a kid when all of this happened. He still looks like a kid, but this experience has clearly aged him. He's forever scarred, just like me.

"Is there anything else you'd like to say?" Mr. Chapman asks.

"Yes," Ricky says, rising to stand from his seat. "I want to apologize to the McClain family, Benny especially. I don't deserve their forgiveness. I never will. But I am sorry. I'm truly sorry. And they may never believe me. But I believe my dad is sorry, too. He may never say it, and he may never forgive me for what I've done today. But I had to do this. I couldn't live any longer knowing there's an innocent man behind bars. A man with a courageous hero for a sister."

*Hero?*

Mr. Chapman lets Ricky off the stand. I'm given no time to process his words as I'm quickly called up to give my testimony.

I walk up there in what feels like slow motion. When I turn to sit down, I slowly look up. There's only one person I know present in the back: Grandpa.

His hair is shorter than I remember. Or maybe there's just less of it. His stare is void of emotion. I don't know what to think, because he still looks like his jolly old self.

After I'm read my rights, Mr. Chapman wastes no time getting started.

"I'm handing the defendant four pages of transcribed testimony from about four years ago. I'm going to have him read it aloud. Go ahead, Mr. McClain," he says, gesturing for me to get started.

I read through it word by word, stumbling over my speech at the hard parts. But I get through it.

"And do you still attest to the testimony you gave almost four years ago?" Mr. Chapman asks.

"I do."

The cross examination from the other lawyer has me go through everything again regarding that night. My memory is still surprisingly sharp. I go through every detail and provide extra details when pressed by the lawyer. Then the judge announces a short recess to meet one-on-one with the lawyers.

Both of the lawyers are still worried about John and Clarence Monroe. Apparently John is overseas and not able to be located so his testimony can be given. Clarence isn't well enough to testify. He had a heart attack a couple weeks ago. Then he got sent back into the hospital a few days ago when he found out Ricky was going to re-testify.

Meanwhile, I'm escorted back to the same depressing little room. Sitting with the guards, I can't help but feel different. I don't know if I'll be getting out today, a couple of weeks, or if this could get dragged on longer. But I can't deny what my gut tells me: There's a major change on the horizon.

I should be excited, but I'm not. I'm more terrified now than ever. I'm not ready to just start living like a free man with my family. I'd rather not have them be a part of my life for a while.

Ricky's testimony today changes many things. But it doesn't change the fact that I sought out this fight through revenge. Grandpa told me many times over, from a young age, that revenge is a never-ending cycle. But my stubborn ass didn't want to listen.

I was nothing more than a fool that night. A fool who went to Monroe Farms with the hope of killing or seriously hurting people. I was an absolute monster. And while it never happened, it can't take away the pain and anguish I brought to my family. All of these days since my incarceration have been torture for everyone involved, even the Monroes.

My innocence will only make me a free man sooner. But my innocence will not make anything easier. Soon I'll be faced with my new life, and I'm nowhere close to ready.

# CHAPTER FOURTEEN

## Benny

"Are you sure we're on the right road?" the cab driver asks.

"I'm sure of it," I lie.

The truth is I've never been here. This may be the only time I ever come here. I look at the directions that Paul mailed to me. His note says two miles down the dirt road. It's the right road, but it feels like we're driving into the middle of a forest. This house must really be out in the middle of nowhere.

Then I see it. It's nothing like I was expecting. It's a little bigger than our old house. It has a beautiful wrap-around porch. The front of it is an A-frame design with three medium-sized windows. I don't see my truck at first. Then we pull around the dirt driveway and I breathe a sigh of relief when I see it parked under a tree.

I get out of the car, knowing I have to make this quick. All I need is my car keys—that's it!

I made it very clear in my letter to Grandpa that I'd be coming by today to pick up my keys. He should know it's my only purpose for coming home. I don't want anything to do with him.

I give three loud knocks on the door. Then I take a deep breath.

Ms. Green opens the door.

"Hi, Benny," she says, looking worried.

"Ms. Green," I reply, nodding my head. "I'm just here to grab my keys."

"I know. Are you sure you don't want to come in?" she politely asks.

"I'm sure."

I have no reason to be mad at Ms. Green. But I know if I set foot inside the house it'll be impossible to avoid Grandpa. I'm surprised he's not the one who answered the door, to interrogate me or give me more meaningless life lessons for the future. His lessons of kindness, forgiveness and showing restraint have only brought more darkness to our family. I may be at fault for a lot of things, but I share that fault with Grandpa.

It only takes a few seconds for Ms. Green to come back to the door with my keys. She opens the screen door to hand them over, then she stops, pulling the keys from my grasp.

"I just have to get something off my chest, then I'll let you be," she calmly says.

I look away, huffing out a raspy exhale.

"Hear me out, Benny. You can be mad at him all you want. But he didn't tell you to go to Monroe Farms that night. He still feels terrible and responsible for a lot of things. But hating him and avoiding him until he's dead will be the biggest regret of your life."

"You done talking?" I bark back.

"And the second thing. It's simple. Go see her and Jimmy. There are some things you have to see with your own eyes. Do you hear me, Benny McClain?"

"I will. Just not right now. I need to get some things straightened out with my life first. Can I just have my keys?" I beg.

Ms. Green hands over the keys, still looking perturbed. "Just don't wait too long. Good things pass by too quick in our lives. Some things you can't get back."

I walk around the house to my truck feeling the need to get out of this place as fast as possible. I climb in wondering why I'm being such an asshole to Ms. Green. She's never done a thing to me. But she's with my grandpa. It's guilt by association. And I know she believes he has no culpability in what's happened.

Nevertheless, I can't get over the urgency in her voice. She acted like seeing Penny and Jimmy was a life-or-death thing. But it's not. They know I'm out of prison. I'm sure Grandpa even mentioned me coming here today. If they wanted to find me, they could have come here today. Or they can come to Paul's place.

I jump into my truck, start it up, and peel out past the house. Then I have no choice but to slam on my brakes—standing in my way is the crazy old man. The dirt plumes around Grandpa. He doesn't even blink. He just raises his arms high in the air like he's surrendering.

I quickly wind down the window and lean my head out. "Get the fuck out of my way! I told you I came here for one fucking reason! Now move before I run your old ass over!"

He ignores me. Then he calmly walks up to my hood, placing both hands on it. "Just shut it off for one minute!" he yells over my revving engine.

I turn off the car because I know the old man is stubborn like a bull. He walks up to my door looking annoyed.

"It's good to see you too," he says with a sarcastic smirk. "I'll be quick. You need to go see your sister—"

"I know. I know," I interrupt him. "Ms. Green told me. I need to go see her and Jimmy. Like I told Ms. Green, I'll do it, but not now."

I want to let him have it. Then I want him to say he's sorry for going to Vern's place. Why can't he just admit it? Why can't he just take some of the blame? He doesn't need to take all of it, just a piece of it, to help relieve my own guilt.

"Son, what the hell are you going to do right now? Tell me what's more important than seeing your sister and your brother. Look, I know she hates your guts, but who cares. Grow a pair and drive down there," he says handing over a piece of paper. It looks like an address.

I refuse to grab it. He tosses the sheet of paper into the window of my truck.

"I'm not going there. I'm going up to Eastern Alabama University to live with Paul. I'm going to get me a job and find my life again. Maybe take a couple of college classes too. I'll go see them when I have my shit together."

I turn and glare at him. I want him to feel my rage. "Don't you pretend you know what it's like to waste so many days rotting in a cell. You don't know what that does to a man. I can't just suddenly get out of prison and be the same big brother. I'm fucked in the head. I'm no good to anyone right now."

I put my keys in the ignition.

"Wait, wait, wait!" Grandpa shouts, grabbing my shoulder before I turn the key. "I know you're mad at me. And maybe everything was my fault. I'm not perfect, you know. I'm still trying to do my best. But listen. You're an adult now, Benny. You can do as you want. And I don't blame you for all that's happened. I don't want you blaming yourself, either. You didn't kill that boy. Forgiveness is everything and more, Benny McClain. Don't you ever forget that lesson. And don't forget that I'll never stop loving you like my own son, no matter what."

"I'm not your son," I coldly reply. "Your son died in a car accident. As far as I'm concerned, you're dead to me, too."

I start the car, noticing the lifeless look in his eyes. Then I peel out, leaving him in a cloud of dust.

I don't care if I'm being a spiteful asshole. He's talking about forgiveness, about "maybe" being at fault. I was there the night he went to Vern's house. He shared too much about our family. His honesty burnt down our house and almost got Penny and

Jimmy killed. It incited everything that went down at Monroe Farms. He's as culpable as me.

I'll heed their advice and one day see Jimmy and Penny. But not now. And I'll never forgive him for setting in motion the tragedy we lived through.

# CHAPTER FIFTEEN

## Benny

*One year later*

"What time is she coming up here?" I ask.

"She just said sometime in the afternoon," Paul replies. "Don't worry, Benny. She knows the drill."

My only deal with having Paul's little sister staying with us is to keep my family drama off the table. Speaking a word of it is not an option, and Paul's already agreed to it. I don't want to hear about why I still haven't gone to see Jimmy and Penny. And I especially don't want to hear a word about Grandpa.

Sarah is visiting her brother because she and her cousins are going to watch the game tomorrow night. Eastern Alabama is taking on the University of Alabama. It's their in-state rival and a game that could determine if Eastern Alabama can play for a national championship.

"Did you look at the blitz schemes and packages I wrote out for you?" I ask.

"I did."

"What about the packages where they rush seven? You know that outside linebacker is crazy quick off the edge."

"I know, Benny. I got it all down. Frontwards and backwards, believe me, I'm ready for the game."

"What about the—" I stop.

Paul starts laughing. "You know, Benny, you might as well just become our offensive coordinator if you can't make the team. You know more than that dumb-ass assistant coach."

"Tell that to the NCAA," I sigh.

The NCAA Compliance Committee is made up of ten jackasses—at least that's the nickname we have for them. These guys hold my dreams in their hands. They only know me as a paper application that's applied for reinstatement in NCAA Athletics every three months for the past year. I only have one more year of college football eligibility now. If they don't reinstate me this next time around, I have no chance of playing football in college or the pros.

"Do you know when you'll hear back next?" Paul asks.

"They'll send a letter back sometime this month letting me know if I'm in or not. This is my last chance."

All I can do from here is hope and pray. I'm a little more hopeful I could get approved this time around. My application for reinstatement was boosted heavily by Brett Kitchen. He's the head coach for Easter Alabama.

I've been playing on the team's practice squad for the past six months, thanks to Paul talking the coach into giving me a chance.

Right now, there are ways I'm a part of the team, but also not. I don't get to suit up on game days and I'm not even given a jersey. But I've done my best at being an asset to the team. I go to film study whenever I'm not working my construction job. I mentor the quarterbacks on the team. Lately I've also been working with the offensive linemen on blitz pick-up and effective audibling at the line of scrimmage. I've even volunteered my time in coaching a youth team for the local Boys and Girls Club. I couldn't be doing more to get back out there.

Being on the practice squad has its ups and downs. My main job is to run the opposing team's offense in practice each week and test out our defense. I've been shredding them all week, which is a good thing in helping me stand out, but also proof that our defense has major holes.

The worst part is I can't be on the sidelines during game day. It makes me feel like I'm on the team the other six days, but when it counts most, I'm parking my butt in the stands.

Nevertheless, I've gained a lot of respect from the players who suit up every week. It feels good that they already trust my intentions in helping the team. It's like I'm a pseudo coach on the team in some ways.

Coach Kitchen helped me put together my last application for reinstatement. His letter of recommendation and the calls he's made to his resources will hopefully pay off this time around. If it does get approved, it means I only have one year to live out my dream of playing college football and maybe making it to the pros.

"I don't get it, Benny," Paul says, shaking his head. "You were proven innocent in a court of law. What else is left to prove?"

I shrug my shoulders. "I think it's the optics of it all, man. I got in a fight and as a result someone died. They don't care that it's an accident. And they don't care that it was someone else who pulled the trigger. Besides, I wasn't proven innocent. They just reduced the charges to second degree assault. The NCAA doesn't like blemishes like that on people's records."

"I still say it's bullshit," Paul says, slapping my throwing shoulder. "Because you still got it, my man. I swear Coach got a hard-on the other day, watching you sling it 70 yards down the field," Paul smiles, mimicking the touchdown pass I made.

Later that night, I return home from work after a long day. I had practice in the morning, then class until 2 p.m., followed by a full shift at the construction site. The second I crack the door, I hear arguing coming from Paul's room.

"I'm home!" I shout, hoping they can hear me.

Paul's bedroom door swings open. Sarah trudges right past me, as if I don't even exist.

"Hi, Sarah," I say, glancing over my shoulder. "Good to see you, too."

"Fuck you, Benny! You selfish piece of shit! Fuck you!"

She slams the front door.

"What was that all about?" I ask Paul.

He just looks at me with a dumbfounded stare.

"No, seriously. What did I do?" I ask.

Paul shakes his head. "What did you do? It's more like what you didn't do."

He heads into the kitchen, looking as perturbed as his sister. I don't get it. He knows the rules. What is this bullshit?

I follow him. "What the fuck is going on?"

"Everything, Benny. Everything is going on. And you are just living in your tiny-ass world."

"What's that supposed to mean?" I ask, fuming to his cryptic words.

"I promised you we wouldn't talk about your family shit. So what do you want me to say?" Paul says, stepping closer.

His eyes are wide with anger. It's like he wants to hit me, which makes no sense. He was in such a happy mood this morning.

Paul has about 100 pounds on me and six inches of height. I wouldn't stand a chance, but it doesn't matter. I'd never fight my best friend.

"Fine! The promise is off the table. Just spit it out, Paul."

"You don't understand. I can't do that. But I can give you an ultimatum. So, I'm telling you right now. You have until Christmas to go visit Penny and Jimmy. If you don't, I'm kicking your lame ass out onto the streets."

I start chuckling. He can't be serious. But his look of rage says otherwise.

Paul's given me my space on this topic for quite some time. Why all of a sudden is it do-or-die?

"I don't get it. Is someone dying?" I finally ask.

"No one's dying, Benny. But here's the thing!"

Paul pokes me in the chest.

"You are a fucking sissy. Yeah, you may be getting your life together. But you got some shit you need to straighten out at home. I can't tell you what's really going on because she won't let me. But you need to go home and see it with your own fucking eyes."

"I'm not doing that, Paul. I'm not—"

"Man, fuck you! I don't want to hear this not-ready bullshit. You were in prison for almost four years. Now you've been out of there for over a year. I gave you your space to get your head right. But I'm done! You hear me! Done, motherfucker! If you don't go home by Christmas your sorry ass is living on the streets! You hear me?"

Paul's eyes look like they're going to pop out of his head. I don't know what he and his sister were arguing about, but this is bullshit.

"Fuck this!" I shout, bumping his shoulder as I head out the front door.

The second I'm outside the apartment I hear crying down the hall.

*Oh fuck!*

I turn right to avoid Sarah even though I need to go left. After a few steps I freeze in my tracks. I can avoid this and deal with Paul's grumpy ass. Or I can get to the bottom of what's really going on.

The closer I get to her the more her crying becomes hysterical. I sit down next to her, letting her cry it out before I say a word. After a couple minutes, I seize my opening.

"Can you please tell me what's going on?" I ask.

Sarah begins chuckling, looking at me like I'm stupid.

"You want to know what's going on. Of all people…*you*," she says with a bitter tone, shaking her head. "That's fucking hilarious."

"Yeah, I don't know shit. Did something happen between you and Paul?"

"No, he just doesn't like me keeping secrets from him."

"So you kept something secret from him?" I ask.

"Yes."

"And now you're both upset because of this secret. Right?"

Sarah just nods her head while rubbing her eyes. I feel like this is still going nowhere.

"Can you maybe give me a clue to what's going on. Please?" I beg.

Sarah sighs, shaking her head side-to-side. Then she starts to get up.

I reach for her shoulder to stop her. "Come on—"

"Don't you fucking touch me!" Sarah begins wagging her finger. "No. You are a cowardly piece of shit! Our family is going to have nothing to do with you until you right this wrong."

"But I don't know what's going on. Just tell me something, please!"

Sarah shakes her head, mocking me with a fake smile. "I'll tell you what you can do, Benny. Do you know where your Grandpa lives?"

"Yes."

"Go up there and see your family. Penny and Jimmy are up there visiting them at least once a month. You do that and maybe one day me and Paul will forgive you."

"I, uh—" I pause in defeat, feeling helpless.

I don't owe Sarah and Paul anything. And I have no clue why they're all of sudden up in my family business.

"I just can't," I finally mutter.

"That's what I thought. I'm out of here. I thought I could stay one night under the same roof as you, but there's no way. You're just despicable. Penny was right."

She stands and glares at me as she heads down the hallway and quickly out the exit.

I don't know what to do, so I just sit there. Digging my fingers into my scalp, I contemplate pulling out my hair. It's never been on the radar to go home so soon. It's partly me avoiding what I don't want to face. I know this. But I can't deny how two people I consider family looked at me today like I was the worst person on earth.

Going home was going to happen at some point. I just assumed it would be when my grandpa passed away and I was forced to go back. But there's too much mystery surrounding the events of today. I may not want to go home, but I have to.

# CHAPTER SIXTEEN

## Benny

*Christmas Eve*

I'm here, but this doesn't feel like home. There's no treehouse out back. There's no neighbors to play with. There's a front yard, but no grass. Just dirt and endless pine trees everywhere. It reminds me more of a campsite than an actual home.

The only person I'm excited to see is Jimmy. And I'm a little bit excited to see Penny. Okay, maybe I'm really excited to see her. It's just an odd feeling when I know she probably doesn't want me in her life after my last letter. But I can't blame her for that when it was all my doing.

I walk up to the front porch, where Grandpa and Ms. Green are sitting outside with their arms around each other.

"Surprise," I announce in a monotone voice.

They both stand up, looking unsure of what to say.

"Can I head in and grab some water?" I ask.

"Of course," Ms. Green says, her smile looking slightly confused. "Actually, let me get you something to drink. How about a lemonade?"

I keep my eyes only focused on Ms. Green. "Water will be fine, thanks."

Ms. Green heads inside.

"Where's your stuff?" Grandpa asks.

"It's in the truck. I have a mattress back there, too," I calmly explain.

It takes a second for Grandpa to understand what I'm telling him.

"Oh, okay. Are you sure you don't want to sleep inside? The rooms are all taken but the couch folds out into a bed. It's no trouble."

"No, thanks. If you're sleeping inside, then I'd rather just sleep in my truck. I'm only here for one reason. And it's not you." I head inside admiring how cold my tone felt and how good it feels to be an asshole to Grandpa.

"Wait, Benny," Grandpa calls out. "Why are you here?"

"Apparently there's something I need to see. I'm here to see it. Don't worry, I'm not ruining Christmas. Just here to see Jimmy and Penny. I'll probably head back later today or tomorrow."

"Jimmy's out back!" Grandpa hollers.

Ms. Green hands me a glass of water.

"I'm really glad you're here," she says, looking relieved.

"Oh, yeah. Well, that makes one of us," I murmur.

I walk past her towards the back of the house. I feel her following me close behind.

"Benny!" she hollers.

"Yeah."

"I mean it, Benny. I'm really glad you're here. I could care less if you don't want to be here."

"Well, it'll probably just be a day or two."

Ms. Green steps in front of me, and I'm suddenly frozen by the look she's giving me. She pats my shoulder and chuckles under her breath. "Oh, I think you'll stick around a little bit longer."

She quickly walks away. I can hear her softly chuckling to herself. "Go say hi to your brother! Penny will be back in an hour!" she hollers, heading to the front porch to rejoin Grandpa.

I reach out to open the door to the backyard and stop. The last time I saw my brother, he was mostly unconscious, bleeding out of his head. I wasn't sure if he was going to live that night.

Paul told me a long time ago that Jimmy made a full recovery. He's even given me snippets of how well he's been doing with Penny's help. I know the two of them were living with each other for a while, and that Jimmy even has a good-paying job. But other than that, I know very little about the past few years of his life.

I head outside. As I walk up to Jimmy, I can sense he knows it's me walking up from behind him.

He's sitting on the tire swing reading. It looks like one of his old comic books.

"Hey," I say.

Jimmy ignores me, so I walk around him.

"Hey, how are you?" I ask.

Jimmy glances up briefly, then goes back to reading. I can't believe he's a 21-year-old grown man.

His green collared shirt is tightly tucked in, and his brown hair is neatly combed over into a side-part. He looks so grown up and mature.

He clearly doesn't want to talk yet. I'm not going to force him to. I settle on just taking a seat next to him.

I guess I'll just do all of the talking. It reminds me of when he was really little. He didn't start talking until he was six, so there were quite a few years where my conversing with him was just a monologue.

"I want to hear what you've been up to for the past few years. I've heard some stuff, but I'd like to hear from you. That is...." I pause to clear my throat. There's still a nervous energy in the air. "When you're ready, Jimmy. No rush."

A breeze kicks up. I watch as his eyes take quick glances at me every few seconds. I can tell he's no longer reading.

"I'll tell you a little about what I've been up too. You can listen or just keep reading. I won't care either way."

I let out a long sigh. "I became a master carpenter in prison. They actually teach you things if you want to learn. I got real good at it. I feel like I can build almost anything now. It's what I do now as my part-time job. I'm also taking a couple classes up at Eastern Alabama. But you want to hear the best part, Jimmy? I'll tell you. I'm playing football again. I'm on the practice squad team. It doesn't mean I play for the school yet. But I'm hoping next year I can be out there. I feel like I still got a lot of good years left in me. Paul says I'm throwing the ball better than I ever have."

I glance at Jimmy whose now fully engaged.

"You want to play catch?" Jimmy asks, his voice raspy and deep. I don't even recognize it at first.

"Um, yeah. I'd love to. Does Grandpa have a football around here?"

"Wait," Jimmy says, running inside.

He comes back seconds later with a football.

His first throw to me hits me right in the chest. I throw it back and he easily catches it. Each time he throws me the ball it gets successively harder. I do the same to him as we start to back up.

"Where did that arm come from?" I ask, giving him a wink.

"I learned from you," he says, ambivalent to my sarcasm.

I chuckle to myself. Jimmy never played sports when he was younger. He would have. It just was never offered for people like him. It was a shame. Instead, he just parked his butt in the stands, watching his brother compete through most of his childhood.

"How's Penny doing?" I ask.

"Bad."

I watch as his facial features change the slightest bit. He was never good at showing emotion, so it's hard to decipher what he's thinking.

"Why?" I ask.

"Because Patrick's dead," he plainly states like it's written on my forehead.

"Oh. I'm sorry to hear that."

I want to ask who Patrick is. I imagine he'll tell me. But maybe it's better I have this conversation with Penny.

Nevertheless, my mind runs wild with possibilities. It's the different possibilities that suddenly make me feel nauseous— really nauseous!

*What's happening?*

"Give me a second, Jimmy," I say, raising my hand for a timeout.

I go kneel down next to the closest tree. I look up seeing the perfect opening 15 feet up. I imagine our old treehouse. Then I imagine another man with Penny. The imagery quickly becomes vivid and sexual in nature. Then I can't hold it back any longer.

I vomit up everything I ate this morning. It keeps coming until I find myself gagging.

Then I feel it. A hand rubbing the center of my back. I wipe my face with my forearm as I stand up. Jimmy's wearing a deeply concerned expression I've never seen from him. It touches something inside me I wasn't expecting to feel so suddenly. The tears pour out quickly as I dive into Jimmy's arms.

Jimmy says nothing. He just matches the strength of my desperate hug.

"Are you okay, Benny?" he whispers.

I finally let go and crack a smile.

"I'm okay."

"I thought you didn't know Patrick," Jimmy says.

"I don't know him. I was crying because I miss you. And I'm just sorry I've been gone for so long. You don't have to, but maybe one day you can forgive me for all of that."

Jimmy's face quickly becomes a scowl. His eyes widen with anger. He takes two steps back like he's suddenly allergic to my presence.

"I hate you," he says in a cold tone, leaving me speechless.

I hear commotion inside the house. Jimmy turns from me to walk back inside. Once he walks in I hear cheering from inside the house.

I don't know what I did for Jimmy to suddenly tell me he hates me. But I guess I can't blame him. I hate myself, too.

"What! What!" someone screams from inside the house. The sound of agony comes from an eerily familiar voice.

"Marcus! Don't go out there!" Penny screams.

I watch as the back door swings open. A little boy wearing blue overalls, his hair in an afro, stares at me from across the backyard. His head tilts at an angle. The look of unbridled confusion has us both in awe.

Maybe I'm finally seeing what everyone wants me to see with my own two eyes.

# CHAPTER SEVENTEEN

# Penny

I take two steps outside, quickly snatch up Marcus, and dart back into the house. I carry him on my hip, trying to rush out the front door. Ms. Green quickly steps between me and the front door.

"Stop!" she shouts, holding her hand out. "You're not leaving, Penny," she calmly says.

"Oh, the hell I'm not. You need to move. I'm not spending Christmas with that asshole!"

"Asshole?" Marcus mumbles.

"Don't say that, Sweetheart. But that man is an asshole."

I look down at Marcus's confused face. I can't believe what I just told my own son.

"I want my daddy," Marcus whines, heading into a full-on meltdown.

"Oh, Honey," I sigh, going down on one knee. My hand glides along his wet cheeks. "I told you before, Dad isn't coming home anymore. He's not coming back, my love. I know it's hard to understand. But you won't ever see your daddy again. I'm so sorry," I cry with my baby in my arms.

I look across the room, squeezing Marcus tighter. Sitting on the coffee table is a copper urn. It's all that's left of the person he calls Dad.

"He said he'd only be around a little while," Dad says. "Don't you think it'll be good to let him know what's going on?"

"I already tried. Can you just make him leave? I can't sleep under the same roof as him. This weekend is supposed to be about Patrick—not that asshole!"

"You won't have to," Ms. Green says. "He's probably leaving later today. And if he does stay the night, he's already volunteered to sleep outside in the bed of his truck. You and Jimmy can have your own separate rooms like usual."

"But I don't understand. Why is he here?"

Ms. Green backs away from the front door, kneeling at my side with her hand running along my back.

"Honey, you know why he's here. It's time."

"No, no, no. Not tonight. I'm only here for Christmas with my family and to celebrate Patrick's life. Benny's not family anymore. That's the only reason I'm here. He'll just ruin everything. That's all he's ever done to our family."

"That's not fair, Penny," Dad chimes in.

"What? Why are you defending him, Dad? He hates you more than anyone else."

"I hate him more," Jimmy calmly says, strolling his way into the living room. When Marcus notices his only uncle, his tears melt away. He runs into Jimmy's arms.

"Freeze tag?" Jimmy asks.

Marcus starts bobbing up and down with excitement. Then he darts his way to the front door while Jimmy chases him down. The two of them are like two peas in a pod. They always have been.

I'm still irate, but thankful Marcus is out in the front yard. He doesn't need to see what may be coming for Benny.

"Just go talk to him, Penny. He didn't come to see me or your dad. Heck, he still won't give your dad the time of day. He said he's only here to see you and Jimmy. So go on. Get it over with," Ms. Green nods.

*Fuck this!*

I stand up tall, puffing out my chest and balling up my fists. Years of anger bubble to the surface as I march towards the back door.

"Penny, just—"

"Let them work it out, Richard!" Ms. Green raises her voice to interrupt Dad.

I swing the door open, swiftly walking straight to Benny. I'm a woman on a mission. He looks the same, despite a more muscular frame and lots of facial hair.

"Hey," he quietly says.

I run right at him. My fist cocks back, swinging with all my strength at his face. His arm goes up to block the first blow, but he doesn't see my left fist coming. It connects with his nose, making a loud cracking noise. I keep swinging at his head with every ounce of hatred from the last few years.

Finally, his hands grab both my wrists.

"Let go!" I scream into his face.

"Stop it, Penny!" he shouts over my grunting noises. "Please. Don't do this. What's wrong? I don't know what's going on. Paul and Sarah told me to come see you!"

His hands wrap tighter around my wrists. I try to punch him, but he's too strong. I feel my anger melting away. Then I see my opening. I pull his hands into my body and yank my knee up into his groin. The connection with his balls sends him instantly to the ground, rolling in agony.

"Ow! Fuck, Penny!"

I collapse to the ground. I try catching my breath, but it's hard because I can't stop laughing. It felt so good to hit him. I could die a happy woman today.

Once I catch my breath, I turn around to head inside. The second I close the door I notice everyone hovering near the window. They were definitely spectators for the ass-whooping I just gave Benny.

"How did that feel?" Grandpa asks, fighting back a smirk.

I let out a sigh of relief. "You have no idea."

Ms. Green walks out of the kitchen, chuckling. "You two are still in love," she jokes.

I make a gagging noise as I wash my hands. The hand I punched Benny with is already swelling up.

I glance outside to see Benny trying to stand up straight. He's looking more like a man with a stick up his ass. Watching him suffer makes me feel good. Maybe a little too good.

*What am I doing?*

"Fuck," I mumble to myself.

I grab an ice pack from the freezer. Then I write down a quick note and tape it to the ice pack. I open the door and chuck it at Benny's face. He catches it in the nick of time. Then I slam the door shut.

Benny reads my note aloud. "Give me an hour to cool down and I'll give you ten minutes of my time. Then you can get the fuck out of here."

"Thanks for the ice!" he yells back. "Maybe you can tell me why you want to beat the shit out of me!"

Ms. Green and Jimmy agree to look after Marcus for the next couple hours while Dad takes a nap. Meanwhile, I head out to the front porch for some fresh air and a chance to write in my journal.

This day was already going to be emotional enough. It was supposed to be about Patrick, not Benny. I just don't understand why he's here. I mean, deep down I think I know. But at the end of the day, I don't want him around me or Marcus.

Our family was happy when we found out he was innocent and getting out of prison early. But I can't forgive him for how he's treated all of us for the past few years. Especially after he got out of prison. It's one thing to abandon me. I've accepted that reality, based on his last letter. But having nothing to do with Jimmy, Dad, and Ms. Green was the last straw. They all love him so much and would welcome him back with open arms. But he can't see that. He's close-minded and selfish. I guess he prefers to wallow in his own guilt and anger at life.

I'm not ready to give him a chance at being welcomed into my new family. And I don't feel at all ready telling him about all that's changed in the past few years, especially certain things I know he's not ready to handle.

The longer I stay outside, the better I feel. Sweating feels good. I'm like a cat, looking for a patch of sunlight. I keep moving my chair until I find myself getting a little too close to the side of the house. I don't want Benny to see me. But then I hear him.

I quickly grab my book and pretend I'm reading as he walks to his truck. He grabs a book and lays down in the bed of his truck.

I let out a long sigh, knowing I need to get this over with. I trudge over to him.

"Please don't kill me," he mockingly says, not moving his eyes from his book.

"How are your balls feeling?" I ask, hoping he sees the smirk on my face.

"Luckily, it wasn't a direct hit," he says. "I think I'll still be able to have kids one day."

"You ready to talk?" I ask, trying to summon some courage.

"Are you going to try and beat the shit out of me again?"

I chuckle under my breath. Then I begin laughing for no reason.

"You think this is funny, don't you?" he asks, sitting up.

"Yep. It's very funny. And I'm not sorry for hitting you," I say in my bitchiest tone.

I start walking away. "You coming?"

Benny hops out of his truck, jogging to catch up to me.

"If it makes you feel better, I'm pretty sure I broke my hand when I hit you," I admit.

"Really?"

"Yeah, I can't move it."

Benny grabs my arm, pulling me to a stop.

"I'm fine, Benny. It's no big deal. Besides, it was worth it."

Benny chuckles to himself, running his fingers along my knuckles.

"Oh, shit! You got a sixth knuckle right here," he says, prodding the most tender parts of my hand.

"Ow! That hurts!" I whine.

"Stay here. I'll be right back."

Benny runs back to his truck, grabbing the same ice pack I gave to him earlier.

"It's still pretty cold," he says, handing it over.

"Was this—"

"Oh my god, Penny. I didn't put it directly on my dick. I promise, there's no cooties."

"Fine," I give in, grabbing the ice pack.

We begin walking in complete silence. The further we get the more the silence grows louder. It's just a matter of who will blink first.

The problem is I don't know where to start with him. There's so much he still doesn't know about me. And there's little I know regarding the last few years of his life. Regardless, there's things he's definitely not ready to hear. At least not today.

Eventually, the silence between us becomes too much.

"Why are you here, Benny? What do you want from us?"

Benny cracks a smile and shakes his head. "I'm hoping you could tell me. Sarah and Paul gave me an ultimatum. That's why I'm here."

I stop walking and grab his arm. "Wait. What did they tell you?"

"Not a whole lot. It was more Paul's ultimatum. Sarah just hates my guts. But they basically said I need to make things right on the home front. They mentioned there's some things I need to see with my own eyes. That's about it. Paul was threatening to kick my ass to the streets if I didn't come here. So...."

Benny pauses as I let go of his wrist. "There's also the fact that you have a son. I guess that's pretty big news."

"Yeah, that's pretty big news," I admit, swallowing hard. "Anything else you noticed or heard?"

"Yeah. I was talking with Jimmy. He said that Patrick is dead. Who the fuck is this Patrick guy?"

The second Benny says Patrick's name, I slap him across the face.

"Fuck, Penny! Really?"

Benny groans. I don't know why I just hit him. He doesn't even know what he's saying. But I guess that's his fault.

I don't regret hitting him a third time. He says Patrick's name like he's a disposable piece of shit. But the only disposable person is the selfish asshole still wincing from my slap.

"You can't just say his name like that," I raise my voice, feeling my chest tighten.

"I'm sorry. I just don't know who he is. Is that Marcus's dad?"

My mouth hangs open. I nod my head up and down slowly, feeling a swirl of emotions.

"I'm sorry, Penny. I didn't know. I swear," Benny says in a remorseful tone.

I feel the muscles twitching in my arm. It's taking every last ounce of restraint to not hit him again.

"I know you didn't know. You couldn't open up one letter. I mean, are you fucking serious? You're rotting away in a cell. I pour my heart into almost 1,000 letters, and you can't open one. Not one!" I scream in his face.

"It's not that easy, Penny."

"Easy? You want to talk about what's been easy. You don't know what I've been through the last few years. It would've been hell if we didn't find Patrick. And it's all because you stopped caring. My whole life, you were there to protect me. Then you mess up one night and just say 'Fuck you, Penny!' And I get it. Your emotions got the best of you that night. But did you not think we would forgive you? I mean, don't you know? We all wanted to do what you did to those Monroe pieces of shit. I'm jealous you got to pound their heads in. But one bad night doesn't mean you can just say 'Fuck you' to your family and then come back here with your tail between your legs. They may forgive you, but I won't. So fuck you, Benny McClain!"

I can barely catch my breath, while Benny just gives me a wide-eyed look. I wish he would say something. But maybe he realizes his words mean nothing to me. Furthermore, any apology he gives would be coming too late.

I turn around and start walking back to the house. He follows at my side but gives me some space. It reminds me of the thousands of times we walked to school together. I felt safe on those days. He also made my heart swell with affection once upon a time—until he irreparably broke it.

"Can I just say one thing?" he quietly asks.

I ignore his question because I don't care. Whatever his one thing is, it already feels meaningless.

"I'm sorry, Penny. But I didn't completely ignore your letters. I didn't put them in the trash either. I lied. I kept them— every last one of them. I was just too much of a coward to ever read them."

"Then why not take our phone calls or come see us? We submitted the paperwork every month to try and meet with you in prison. And every time you refused our visits," I complain, feeling my throat tighten with emotion.

*Keep it together, Penny. Don't let him see you cry.*

"It's not that I didn't want to see you guys. I just felt ashamed. You see, for a while there I actually believed I killed someone. That's crazy, right? I get knocked unconscious, then people label me a murderer. Then I start to believe it. Being proven innocent didn't change me. I still feel so ashamed for the person I am. And if I saw you guys in person during that time, I wouldn't even know what to say."

I take a deep, quivering breath, trying to understand what he's said. I can't relate to what he's been through, just as he can't understand what I've been through. We're at an impasse.

"I just wanted to see you. That's all. I missed you so much. I just needed you," I admit.

"I know," he quickly replies.

I want to regret what I said about missing him. But the words have already left my body. And they came from a place I swore to never show him again—my heart.

I want to be strong and stand up against him. But I'm also tired of being so angry. Maybe he's tired of being angry too.

"When did your husband die?"

My heart instantly aches over that one word: husband.

"About three months ago."

"I'm really sorry, Penny," Benny says, running his hand along his cheek, a nervous habit of his that I'd forgotten about.

We're both quiet for a moment. This time I'm okay with the silence.

"Do you mind if I ask what happened?" he finally asks.

I take a deep breath, trying to gather my thoughts. This isn't what I want to be talking about. But I can't ignore his question.

"Vietnam. He didn't want to go. But he got drafted," I quickly explain.

"How are you raising Marcus? I mean, now that it's just you."

"I have help."

"Grandpa and Ms. Green?" he asks.

"A little. They come down once a month to help out. But mainly Jimmy."

"Really?"

I nod my head, then I let out a nervous chuckle. "Your brother has really come into his own over the past few years. He's so smart, so talented. He can do anything he wants. But he's best at being an uncle. When I moved away for college he moved with me. We still live together. He has a job. He cooks. He cleans. He takes care of himself, and others too. And he's become even better at communicating and understanding the emotions around him."

"Wow. That's great. But you know why he's like that, don't you?" Benny asks, flashing a smile.

"What do you mean?"

"Penny, almost everything good in him is from you. You've always looked at him like he's gold. And now he feels that way. You've instilled belief in him, and you've been an incredible sister to him. I appreciate it more than you'll ever know. You may not see it like that, but I do."

"Maybe," I mutter, trying to deflect his complement.

I want to tell him how much Ms. Green and Dad have done, too. But he knows that already. He's just too pissed off at Dad to say anything good about him. But deep down, he knows.

Furthermore, Benny did so much when he was around in our lives. Most of what I learned when it comes to compassion for Jimmy came from him.

Eventually we get back to the house.

"Thanks for the ice pack," I say, handing it back.

"Sorry for getting my dick cooties on your hand," he jokes.

I try to not giggle, but it happens anyway.

"Is this the part where I say sorry for kneeing you in the balls? Or punching you in the nose and slapping you in the face?" I ask with a smirk.

"Nope," he replies with a stoic look. "I deserved it. And a lot more, too."

"Mommy!" Marcus screeches with excitement, diving into my legs.

I pick him up, burying kisses in his neck and face until he's laughing hysterically. "Oh my god! I love you so much!"

I rock him up and down until I see him look away from Benny and bury his head in my neck.

"I don't like that man, Mommy," he whines.

"Oh yeah, Honey? Why is that?"

"Jimmy doesn't like him, so neither do I," Marcus says, giving his best pouting face.

"I'm sorry Jimmy doesn't like me," Benny says, hunching down to Marcus's eye level. "I've made some mistakes. But hopefully Jimmy will forgive me. For now I'm going to let you guys enjoy your Christmas. But it was nice meeting you, Marcus."

Benny gives me a quick wave and a sad smile.

*Let him go!*

I take a deep breath, fighting the urge to call Benny back. I know the easy way out is to let him go. But I can't do it.

*Fuck!*

"Benny, stop!"

I put Marcus down and walk up to his truck before he gets in.

"You don't have to leave," I sigh.

"Yeah, I do."

He opens up the door. I quickly slam it shut.

"Where are you going? It's Christmas Eve. You have something better to do?"

"Penny, I uh…" Benny bows his head, letting out an exasperated breath. I watch as his fingers dig through his scalp. Then he looks up to me with longing and pain in those majestic green eyes. "I just can't be here right now. And I know most of you guys don't want me here either. Heck, I didn't want to come here in the first place. I thought the next time I'd be around was when Grandpa dies. And that's fucked up, and wrong. I'm sorry, but I have to go."

His truck revs up. My thoughts are a mess. I want him out of my life, but at the same time I know I can't let him go—not until he knows.

"Wait!" I yell, grabbing onto his door. "Marcus, go run inside."

I wait for Marcus to reach the front porch, then turn to look back into Benny's eyes. The pain I see there reflects my own suffering. We are so similar.

"Penny, I—"

"Just shut the car off!" I demand, interrupting whatever excuse he was going to offer.

I take a deep breath as the sound of the engine dies down. "I need your help. I can't believe I'm actually saying this. But I need you to stay until tomorrow. Come on. You owe me, Benny."

"You need my help?" His eyebrows go up. "I mean, um, okay. What do you need me to do?"

"The main reason I'm here, aside from Christmas, is tomorrow we're going to be saying goodbye to Patrick. It's kind of a celebration of his life. I want Marcus there for it, but he's too young to understand. And I was going to have Ms. Green look after him, but I know she wants to be a part of this. I just need you to look after him tomorrow afternoon for a couple hours. Can you do that?"

"You want me to babysit…your son?" he asks through gritted teeth.

I nod my head slowly. This already feels like the worst idea I've ever had.

"I've never babysat…" Benny pauses, taking a long sigh. "I mean, of course I'll do it. What time do you want me back tomorrow?"

"No. You're not driving back a couple hours only to turn around and drive back here tomorrow. That is, unless you have somewhere else you need to be for Christmas."

Benny starts to softly chuckle. "Well, to be honest, I guess that would be silly. But I'm not spending the night or eating dinner with that man."

I roll my eyes, huffing out an exhale. He's so annoying.

"Really?"

"Yeah. I'll stay and help you. But I need to keep my space from him. I don't want anything to do with Grandpa."

"Fine," I mutter.

"Look, Penny. It's better this way for everyone. I got food, water and everything I need to sleep in the bed of my truck. It'll be like I'm camping. We'll stay out of each other's way, avoiding any family drama. You'll get your Christmas with your family and your time to say goodbye to Patrick. It's a win-win."

"Fine. Whatever you say, Benny."

He should at least come inside and sleep on the pull-out couch. But I'm not going to argue with him. Benny's the most stubborn human being I know.

I head inside. The day has been nothing but ridiculous and unexpected. I drove out here this morning in a swirl of emotions. Now I don't know what to think.

Having Benny here today is just bad timing. Letting him watch Marcus is even crazier. I clearly don't know what I'm doing. But the worst part is I can't tell him what's really going on here. All I can hope for is he finds out on his own.

# CHAPTER EIGHTEEN

## Benny

"Fuck off!" I shout at Grandpa.

I keep my eyes on my book, taking another bite of my peanut butter and jelly sandwich. I don't look up because he doesn't deserve the time of day. Then I hear the front door close.

*Thank god!*

Grandpa's invitation to come inside and eat dinner is not an option. It may look silly, me eating out here alone in the dark. But I got used to being by myself when I was in prison. Besides, laying in the bed of my truck seeing a billion stars through the trees is quite the upgrade from my cell.

The only shitty part is the temperature dropping fast. I find myself putting on another layer as I climb into my sleeping bag. I put my book down to give the battery life in my flashlight a break. My mind starts to wander as I tip my nose to the sky.

I still can't believe all that's happened in one day. Penny tried beating the shit out of me. I find out she's a mom. She *had* a husband. And now Jimmy is the main male influence for little Marcus.

What makes no sense is why Penny wants my help. She clearly wants nothing to do with me. Yet, she wants me to look after her son. Even when she asked for help, it felt like she instantly regretted the request.

Besides, I've never babysat anyone in my life other than my siblings. I don't even know what I'll do to keep the kid entertained for a couple hours.

The exploding sound over my head startles the living shit out of me. I go flat as a pancake, covering my head. It was no doubt a gunshot.

The explosion happens again. "Benny! I know you're out there!" Ms. Green shouts. "You got ten seconds to get your ass inside for supper!"

I peek over the edge of my truck bed. There, with a shotgun on her shoulder, is 70-year-old Ms. Green. I didn't even know she knew how to shoot a gun. Then I watch as the barrel shifts in my direction.

"You all are fucking crazy!" I shout, putting my hands in the air.

Ms. Green starts counting down. I know she wouldn't shoot me. But I'm not about to let her lose her mind.

"Okay I'm coming." I jump out of my truck and jog up the front porch. She lowers her gun, then pulls the screen door open for me, flashing a smile.

I take the empty seat between Marcus and Jimmy and directly across from Penny. I let out a long sigh because I know dinner is about to get real interesting.

Then the scent hits my nostrils. My mouth starts to water. The way the steam comes off each plate of food is the most beautiful thing on earth. There's turkey, mashed potatoes, gravy, macaroni, collard greens, and my favorite: green bean casserole.

There's no one on earth who makes a better green bean casserole then Penny. Every day I ate the slop they served in prison, I imagined how good it would be to taste her casserole again.

I eye the casserole sitting at the opposite end of the table. It's directly in front of Grandpa. *Fuck!*

"Dad!" Penny shouts across the table. "Pass the casserole down for Benny."

I serve myself while watching Ms. Green clean the barrel of her gun. Then she places it up in the closet. She takes a seat next to Grandpa, looking like she just came in from trimming her rose bushes. Grandpa puts his hand over hers. "Good lord, I love you, Sweetheart," he says, smiling at her with admiration.

Jimmy starts laughing out of nowhere. Then Penny joins in, trying to stifle it, but she can't. It's a matter of seconds before everyone but me is laughing. I don't know if I crack a smile or not, but I just start shaking my head at how ludicrous this all is.

During dinner the small talk is sparse. It's mostly people complimenting the food or talking to Marcus about Santa Claus.

I can't help but notice how Marcus keeps looking at me. I try to keep my eyes on my food. But it's impossible not to notice how curious he is.

His eyes are so big and emotive, like his mother's. His denim overalls remind me of a kid who works on a farm. And his fro has so much volume and life in it.

He continues to stare.

"Do you need something, Buddy?" I ask, my mouth still full of casserole.

His eyes grow wider. Then his tiny hand delicately gestures for me to come closer. I hesitate, feeling Penny's glare from across the table. I lean down, turning my ear to listen.

"What's an asshole?" he delicately whispers.

The food shoots out of my mouth as I cough, choking on my food. I get up from the table, heading to the sink, laughing.

When I come back, I realize that Penny is wiping away at her shirt.

"Did I—" I stop, realizing I just spewed food across the table. It was a direct hit on the one person I didn't need to piss off.

"Thanks, Benny," she complains, gritting her teeth. "Marcus, Honey. What did you just say to Benny?"

I watch out of the corner of my eye. Marcus crosses his arms while shaking his head.

"Marcus!" Penny raises her voice.

"He asked if I liked the green bean casserole," I chime in, smirking at Marcus. "And what I meant to say is this is the best green bean casserole I've ever eaten. Seriously, Penny. It's really good."

Marcus starts to giggle. We both ignore Penny's loud sigh and eye roll, digging back into our food.

"Benny," Ms. Green says. "We heard through the grapevine that you are playing for the practice squad. I think it's great that you're out playing on the football field again."

She's smiling at me even though she was just pointing her shotgun at me a few minutes ago and whizzing bullets over my head.

"What's a practice squad?" Penny asks.

"It's mostly non-scholarship players that practice with the starters to help them get ready for game day," I explain.

"Do you still play with lucky number 13?" Jimmy asks.

"Well, they don't give practice squad players numbers or actual jerseys. We don't even suit up on game day or get on the sidelines. We're just practice players."

"So, what you're really saying is you're not good enough. Isn't that right, Benny?" Penny chimes in with an accusatory tone.

It's obvious she's trying to needle me. "That's not true. I could start for them right now. They just won't let me."

"Why? Is it because you're a *felon*?" Penny asks.

It feels like she just spit the word felon in my face. I want to stand up for myself, but I know this is just her form of revenge.

"Can you pass the collard greens?" I ask Ms. Green.

"That's it, isn't it? They don't let...*felons* play. Do they, Benny?" Penny raises her voice, giving me her best fuck-you smirk.

"That's enough, Penny!" Grandpa shouts, startling all of us.

"You don't need to defend me, Richard," I bark back at Grandpa, glaring in his direction. He looks away, trying to pretend that my calling him by his first name isn't an insult. But I know it pissed him off.

I throw my napkin on my plate. "I lost my appetite."

I get up to walk out the door. Then I hear Penny mutter something else under her breath.

I can't fight the urge any longer. I turn around. "What did you say?"

"I said 'Good.' You got a problem with that?" Penny asks.

I close my eyes, trying to swallow the pain. There's nothing I want more than to explode on everyone and get the hell out of here. But I can't. At least not yet. There's something bigger going on here, I just know it.

I take a deep breath. "Thanks for dinner, Ms. Green. And thank you for not shooting me. This has been a lovely Christmas Eve dinner. Oh, and Penny," I pause to clear my throat. "Marcus asked me what an asshole is. Should I tell him it's Benny McClain, or should I tell him it's the hole between his butt cheeks? I'll let you decide, since you're the mom. Good night, everyone."

I slam the door on my way out.

----

The next morning I go on a long run to blow off some steam and to warm up after freezing my ass off for most of the night. At some point in the middle of the night, someone threw a comforter on top of me. I didn't see who did it, but I think I know.

During my run I get to admire a beautiful sunrise. The way the light cracks through the openings in the forest is invigorating. It feels almost symbolic the way the sunlight appears and disappears through the trees.

My life is nothing but flashes of light with overwhelming darkness. The darkness is what I know best. Living in it makes it easier to wallow in self-pity. I've gotten really good at that.

It's weird how my mood changes. When I'm on the football field or exercising, things just become clearer in my mind.

The reality is Penny has every right to hate me. Jimmy has every right, too. Grandpa should hate me for all I've become, but he doesn't. That's the most annoying part. I can tell he's still willing to mend things with me. But it still bugs the hell out of me that he tried to defend me last night.

Penny was right. I'm a convicted felon. I know it doesn't define the person I am. But it's my truth that I need to own up to. I'll never be able to right my wrongs, but maybe I can come close. I'm guessing that's why Paul and Sarah want me down here.

When I get back from my run there's a note on my truck. It looks like Ms. Green's handwriting.

**Benny,**

**You can pay your rent by chopping up all the firewood on the east side of the house. The axe is in the shed. Patrick's eulogy is at 2. We'll pack snacks for you and Marcus. Thanks a bunch.**

**– Ms. Green**

I was going to do my calisthenics but chopping wood may actually be a better workout.

When I pull around the side of the house I notice three stacks of uncut wood, stacked about six feet in the air with an abundance of pine.

Each time I explode the wood in two it makes the most gratifying sound. After about 20 minutes I'm able to get through one pile. I take my shirt off because the gust of wind feels good on my wet skin. A couple minutes later I go to the hose because I'm out of water. I turn the nozzle but nothing comes out.

*Fuck!*

I don't want to go inside. They're probably still opening presents. But I also don't want to die of dehydration.

The front door of the house opens into the living room, but I think the back door can get me into the kitchen unseen.

I sneak into the kitchen undetected. After filling up my bottle with ice and water I dart back around the corner, taking one last glance behind as I bump into Penny, dousing her in ice and water.

"Fuck!" she yells.

"I'm so sorry, Penny."

I'm frozen looking at Penny's post-shower attire. She's wearing only a towel that's tightly wrapped over the top of her breasts. They're breasts I've seen before, but they're also different.

*Stop staring!*

I run to grab a kitchen towel and hurry back to her. I quickly lean down to wipe up the water and pick up the ice cubes.

"What are you doing in here? Just get out!" she yells, snatching the towel out of my hands.

I raise my hands in the air like I'm under arrest. "I'm sorry. I just came in for water. I swear."

"I got it. Just go back outside. I'll bring you water."

"O-kay," I stutter, still frozen in shock.

"Benny! Your fucking ice is stuck in between my breasts! Now get out!"

I bolt out of the house having never felt more embarrassed. I've seen what Penny looks like naked. But she's older and even more developed than I remembered. Her curves are much more voluptuous. It's impossible to not fantasize about what's underneath that towel.

Then my fantasies quickly evaporate. I see him coming around the side of the house.

"Don't worry, I won't talk to you," Grandpa says, splitting a log with his axe.

I stand frozen, not knowing what to say. He's telling me this, but I know he's full of shit.

"Come on, Benny. This wood ain't going to cut itself."

"Don't you need to be inside opening presents with your family?" I ask.

"Nope. Marcus woke us all up at six. We've already opened everything and eaten breakfast. I'm just going to try and get through one of these piles to help you out."

The nonchalance in his tone has my insides boiling.

"I didn't ask for your help. I also didn't ask for you to throw a blanket over me in the middle of the night. I wasn't even cold," I lie.

Grandpa smiles and splits another log. "Penny did that. That wasn't me. And I don't care if you didn't ask for my help. It has to get done either way. You just do your thing and I'll do mine. We don't have to talk. Unless you want to."

I get back to splitting wood. I pick up my pace because I can't stand to be near the man. After a while, I notice that Grandpa is grunting and groaning each time he swings his axe.

"Dad, what are you doing out here?" Penny calls, coming around the corner. "You're too—oh, never mind. Here's your water, Benny. If you spill this one the closest river is near the Georgia state line."

Grandpa laughs, and I shoot him a glare that he ignores.

"Thanks, Penny."

When Penny heads inside I decide the silence between us is too annoying.

"Aren't you too old for this?" I ask, trying to get under his skin.

"Probably," he sighs, rubbing his lower back. "So, Paul told me—"

"I'm not listening!"

"I don't care," Grandpa replies. "Anyway. Paul told me you applied for reinstatement into NCAA Athletics. I hope you don't mind, but I have some alumni friends who work up there. I made a few calls. Don't know if it'll make a difference, but we'll see."

*That's it!*

"I didn't ask for your help!" I shout, slamming the axe down inches from his feet. "In case you haven't noticed, your track record for helping me isn't very good!"

"You might be right. But it doesn't mean I won't help you in doing what you love. That's part of my job in helping to raise you. And that job never ends."

"Was it part of your job to start a war?" I ask.

"What do you mean by that?"

"It means—you know what? Never mind," I sigh.

"You know, things changed when you went to prison. And I don't just mean Penny having a baby. I've made my peace with the Monroes. So did Penny. We all got the hate out of our hearts. It's not something you can live with."

I close my eyes, biting so hard on my tongue I can taste metal. He's trying to get me talking. I can't take the bait. Asking me to forgive certain people feels wrong. The Monroes are the vilest people imaginable.

"One last thing, Benny," Grandpa calls out as I look away from him. "Emotions are blossoms from the roots of love. Don't you forget that. And don't you forget that everyone has a story. We just need to be willing to listen. It takes willingness, Benny. That's how I got the hate out of me. And I'm sorry. I tried helping the night we went to Vern's. And I know I made things worse. That's my fault, Son."

I take a deep breath, trying to ignore everything he just said. Then I glance behind me as he walks back into the house. I still want more of an apology. But more than anything, I want an explanation.

*"Everyone has a story?"*

# CHAPTER NINETEEN

# Benny

"The snacks are in the backpack along with two water bottles and all of his favorite toys," Penny says. "And remember, we'll only need a couple hours so you guys need to be back by four. I'm calling the cops if you're a minute late. And he hasn't eaten lunch yet, so he'll get moody if you guys don't eat in the next hour."

"Moody?"

"Yeah, grouchy. Why are you smirking at me like that?"

"Oh, nothing. I just remember how moody you'd get on your period when you didn't eat on time."

"Mommy, what's a period?" Marcus asks, appearing out of nowhere.

Penny kneels down, running her hand along Marcus's cheek. Her smile is loving, but also worried. "I'm sure Benny would love to explain that to you on your walk, Sweetheart," she says, smirking up at me.

"It's punctuation. They'll teach you that in school. We ready?" I ask, hoping to avoid a talk on menstruation.

Penny pulls Marcus up into a hug. His feet dangle as they squeeze each other. She whispers something in his ear that makes him giggle, then puts him down.

"Okay. You guys are all set," Penny says.

"Don't worry, Penny. We'll eat the first random berries we find in the woods. We'll feed our food to the first bear we run into. We'll go cliff diving, and we'll be back at midnight," I explain with my best sarcastic grin.

"Very funny, Benny. Please take good care of him."

"I will. You have my word." I hold my hand out to Marcus. "You ready to go exploring with me?" I ask, raising my voice to sound more excited.

"I guess so," Marcus mumbles, taking my hand. I take one last glance behind me. Penny wipes at her eyes. I know she's emotional because of the eulogy, but there's something else that's worrying her.

After five minutes of walking I'm already exhausted. It has nothing to do with the hike and everything to do with my mental exhaustion.

I don't know how old he is. My best guess is maybe four years old. But I've never been bombarded with so many random questions and thoughts.

"If we find a bear, what would you do?" he asks.

"I'd turn the other direction and calmly walk away."

"Why?"

"I don't want to upset it. The mommy bears and daddy bears usually won't bother humans unless they think their children are in danger."

"I don't have a daddy anymore," he painfully replies.

I feel my throat lock up.

"I know, Buddy. But you have so many people who love you. It's like you have lots of daddies and mommies now."

My reply feels lackluster. I swallow back the despair, clearing my throat. I don't know what to say.

"Do you have a Daddy?" Marcus asks.

"No."

"Why not?"

"My mom and dad died in a car accident when I was younger. I was raised by your great grandpa. And I guess you can say by Ms. Green, too."

"So, you didn't get a new mommy and daddy?"

"No, not really."

We're both quiet for a while. All we hear is cracking twigs beneath our feet. It's relaxing being in the woods, but I can feel Marcus's mind racing.

He begins to cry.

I quickly kneel down in front of him and put my hands on his shoulders. "What's going on? You'll be okay, Bud. Do you need your mommy?"

He shakes his head, crying harder. I don't know what to do, so I hug him. He hugs me back, tight and strong for such a little guy.

I hold him in my arms, not knowing what else to do, as his tears soak my shirt. After a while, I rub his back and tell him he'll be okay.

It takes a while, but eventually his tears run dry. He tilts his head back to look into my eyes. "I don't like not having a daddy," he admits, eyes still pink and damp.

This poor boy doesn't deserve this. And I don't know what to tell him, other than the only truth I know.

"I didn't like it either. But your mommy is the greatest person on earth. She's like a superhero. She can do everything that a daddy can do, and more. She loves you so much. And right now it's okay to be sad. It's a good thing to miss someone. But you have to be strong for her, too. Because this is really hard for her. Can you do that?"

"Why are your eyes wet? Are you crying?" Marcus asks, touching my face.

"It's okay to cry, right?"

"Yeah, but you don't know my daddy, or my mommy."

"You're right. I don't know your daddy. But I do know your mommy. We grew up together. We used to be good friends. It's complicated to explain, but she's a part of my family too."

Marcus looks confused. I don't know what else to say, so I change the subject.

"Are you ready to eat lunch?" I ask.

Marcus nods his head. We find the first big boulder we see and take a seat.

It's nice to get a break from the questions and just sit amongst the whistling trees. I watch the little guy stuff his face, and when he's done there's streaks of peanut butter and jelly along his cheeks. I grab the napkins Penny packed and have him wipe his own face. He misses all the important spots, so I start wiping at his cheeks.

He starts to giggle for no reason.

"What's so funny?"

"You got food on your face, too," he says, still giggling. "Here, I'll wipe your face, Benny."

Marcus licks his napkin and mops at my face. I don't know whether to laugh, or tell him to stop, but I do neither. Instead, I stare into his beautiful brown eyes, feeling a profound connection to him.

Penny may not consider me family, but she entrusts me to look after her son on a day with more importance than any other. That means something.

It occurs to me that this little boy is going to need all the help he can get. Whether Penny accepts me as her brother or not suddenly feels irrelevant, because this little boy and I have bonded.

There's no way I can't help. Doing something for Penny and Marcus, whether it be small or big, suddenly feels like the most important thing in the world.

"Did your mom ever tell you how she came up with the name Marcus?" I ask.

"No. I never asked her. Do you know?"

Penny's brother floods my thoughts. The visions of playing catch with him in my backyard every day, rain or shine, are still vivid.

"I think I know. It was your mom's brother's name. He died a long time ago. He was one of my best friends growing up. Your Uncle Marcus was funny, kind, and he was always taking care of your mom. It's what big brothers do."

Marcus looks deep in thought.

"So he's like Uncle Jimmy?"

"Oh, yes. He was great, just like your Uncle Jimmy is."

"Why did he have to die, too?" Marcus asks.

I scoot over closer to Marcus until our shoulders are touching. "I don't know. But I sure miss Uncle Marcus. When I think of him, I try to not think about him not being here. Instead, I try to remember all the happy things I did with him. Maybe that's something you can try with your dad. What's your happiest memory of him?"

Marcus takes a long sip from his juice box, then looks up at the sky. "Oh! Oh! I remember!" he shouts, grabbing my arm. "One time Dad took me camping with Uncle Jimmy. And we had these things called mores."

"You mean, s'mores," I say, enunciating the "s" sound.

"Yeah, those sticky things. Then we went fishing. I caught six fish!" he proudly announces, holding up six fingers.

"Wow! Six fish. That sure is something. You must be a good fisherman."

"Can I tell you a secret, Benny?" Marcus asks.

"Of course."

Marcus leans close even though we're alone in the woods. "Me and Dad climbed lots of trees," he whispers, his hand covering the side of his mouth. "I'm not supposed to tell Mommy because she would have thought it was too dangerous. But me and Daddy did it without her knowing."

I start laughing on the inside at the irony of his secret. Penny climbed more than her share of trees in her childhood.

"That sounds fun. I loved climbing trees when I was your age. And don't worry, your secret is safe with me," I say, pretending to zip my lips. "Can I tell you a secret?"

Marcus nods his head.

"When me and your mom were young, we climbed trees all of the time. Our parents didn't mind it. We did it so much that one day Great Grandpa built us a treehouse. It was the most beautiful, red treehouse. All the neighbors were jealous. And you want to know who played there the most?"

"Benny?"

"No, no, no," I laugh to myself. "It was your mom. Your mom loved that treehouse more than anything in the world. It made her so happy. She would go up there every single day of her life if she could."

Marcus's eyes light up like it's Christmas morning again.

Meanwhile, I'm lost in my own treehouse reverie. I will my mind to only think about the perfect memories made over the years in that treehouse.

"Can you take me to this treehouse?" he asks.

"Um, I don't think so. It's not there anymore. But maybe one day someone can build a new one for you."

"Really?" his voice goes high.

"Well, let's not get to far ahead of ourselves. But maybe one day I can do it for you."

The clouds above are getting darker. It's getting close to the time Penny wanted us back.

Our conversation carries on with Marcus's imagination going wild. He's no longer worried about his dad, at least for now. Instead, he's talking about only one thing: his dream treehouse.

# CHAPTER TWENTY

## Penny

The ashes sprinkle out of the urn. Each piece of Patrick flows away, following the slight breeze in the air. My heart aches as I watch him spill over the earth. The ache is compounded by the look of distraught on Jimmy's face.

There's still a solidarity between him and this forest. He loved being outdoors. His bliss was being here with Jimmy and Marcus.

People aren't supposed to die at 22 years of age, especially someone as good as Patrick. I couldn't get many words out during my eulogy. I know I'll never meet a kinder, more loving soul than him.

Patrick has very little family, none of whom were able to make it today. He only has an older brother in Phoenix and some cousins up in Portland.

Having only me, Jimmy, Ms. Green and Dad here today makes my heart ache. My family is always changing. The numbers always dwindling away like Patrick's ashes.

I'm having a hard time processing my own despair. Without Marcus here today, I let myself wallow into the depths of my pain. The hurt feels different today. It feels oddly good to finally be vulnerable.

Ms. Green keeps telling me that this is a part of grief. She also keeps encouraging Jimmy and me to let it out.

Her speech about Patrick was so heartfelt. It was more than just the sweet things she said about him. She talked about loss, mentioning her late husband, Jonathan, who she lost to cancer. It was the first time she's ever mentioned his name in front of everyone. She shared how her grief has made her a stronger person and how love is infinite.

Dad didn't want to talk. I was a little surprised, given how fond he always was of Patrick. Instead, he held my hand while I spoke. Dad didn't need to give a speech. His support and tears are all I needed on this day.

Once the last sprinkle of ash hits the ground, we begin making our way back to the house. Dad and Ms. Green walk at my side, their arms intertwined around each of mine, like crutches keeping me upright. We're all still crying a little.

Once back at the house, there's about a half-hour until Benny and Marcus return. It'll be good to have these extra minutes to collect my thoughts before going back to Mom duty.

Outside, Jimmy is sitting by himself at the edge of the stairs. I take a seat next to him. He's staring straight ahead, lost in his own thoughts. It's hard to tell what's going through that unique brain of his.

"I don't know how to cry," he finally says.

"That's okay. We all show our emotions in different ways," I reply, putting my arm around his shoulders.

"No, Penny. I mean I don't know how to cry," he says, still not looking at me. "I feel it on the inside. But I don't know how to make it come out."

"Hey," I say, turning his face to mine. "You don't need to shed tears to cry. I know you were crying on the inside. We've all been doing that. And I know how much you miss him. We all know what Patrick meant to you. Please don't feel like you let any of us down by not crying. Is that what's bothering you?"

Jimmy begins to scratch his head with both hands, rocking back and forth the slightest bit.

"Can you give me a hug, Jimmy?"

Jimmy quickly embraces me in a desperate hug. I've had so many hugs today, but this is by far the best one. He may not know how to cry, but he knows how to show love. It's all I need as I grieve with my brother.

Jimmy and I don't share blood relations or skin color. But that's irrelevant. I just get him, and he gets me. More importantly, Jimmy's always been at my side in one way or the other. Our bond is inseparable, and our love is infinite.

----

"What time is it, Dad?"

My foot is tapping. My heart is pounding, and the rain is coming down harder now.

"Don't worry, Sweetheart. It's only 4:05," Dad says, trying to reassure me.

I don't need reassurance. These last few minutes have felt like hours. I can't believe I did this. Benny hasn't earned shit for trust. What was I thinking?

Then I see them both. Bobbing up and down through the trees, like two kangaroos, happy as can be, unfazed by the downpour that has them soaked to the bone.

When they reach the front steps, I'm still steaming.

"Sorry we're late," Benny says, ignoring my look of contempt. "Marcus got one hell of a gash on both knees. But man is he tough,"

He walks right past me, Marcus still holding his hand. "Thanks for the Band-Aids. They came in handy."

"Benny, come back here!" I shout, suddenly out of breath. "Marcus, go inside with Ms. Green."

Benny walks up to me with a look of complete innocence.

*Oh! He's so annoying!*

"What did I say, Benny? A minute late and I'm calling the cops. You're fucking five minutes late!" I shout.

"You're right, Penny. And I'm sorry, I really am. We uh, we got to climbing trees and he scraped his knees up pretty good. I swear we would have been on time, or probably early, if that hadn't happened. But you're right, it's totally my fault."

His look is so apologetic I just want to punch it off his face. But I've already gotten out most of my anger.

"Marcus knows he's not allowed to climb trees. But I mean, what are you thinking? You were in charge. I mean he's only…" I stop myself, not wanting to say anything more. Then I trudge into the house, slamming the front door.

It's a matter of seconds before Marcus is grabbing my hand and jumping up and down. He's recounting his day with Benny, second by second, with more energy than a brand-new puppy. It's hard to follow because he's talking so fast.

He's so happy I don't know what to think. I want him to tell me it was the worst experience of his life and that he never wants to see Benny again. It would give me the out I desperately need. But it's clearly the opposite. Benny's his new shiny toy.

I'm startled by the knocking at the front door. Dad walks with me and Marcus as I open the door.

"Hey," Benny calmly says. "I just wanted to say goodbye. To you and Marcus, that is."

"Benny, don't go!" Marcus shouts, grabbing his hand to pull him in the house.

Benny kneels in front of Marcus. "Ah, buddy. I'm sorry. You see, I came here without an invitation and that was rude of me. But hopefully I'll see you some time soon."

"Are you sure you don't want to stick around another night?" Dad asks.

"I'm sure. But Penny, can I talk to you in private?" He nods for me to come outside.

I close the door behind me, taking a deep breath as we walk to the edge of the stairs.

"What's your plan with Marcus?" he asks.

I'm confused by his question, and instantly defensive. "What do you mean?"

Benny runs his hands through his hair. "I just, I'm worried for you. The boy doesn't have a dad. And I know he has Jimmy around, but—"

Benny lets out a long sigh. Why is he suddenly so worried about us? He hasn't given two shits about our family for years.

"Benny, I think it's time for you to go."

"But I don't want to leave," he says. "I mean, I need to leave, to get back to some important things. But I don't want to leave you guys after what's happened to your husband. I'm sure you need help, right?"

I want so badly to just say "Fuck you." But I can't. It's especially hard when he seems genuinely concerned. It reminds me of the old Benny I once knew.

"So, you don't want any extra help with Marcus?" His question couldn't be more tentative.

"Why do you care? You haven't cared about any of us for years. Why now?"

My question is a challenge because I know his reply will be a bunch of bullshit. I just don't know how to trust him anymore. That bond disappeared years ago when he shunned all of us.

"Look, I know I've fucked up with us, with all of us. And that's something I have to live with. I figure the only way I can get your forgiveness is through my actions. And I know you're too stubborn to admit it. But you're scared. And you need help. I really enjoyed my time with Marcus. He's a great kid who would benefit from more male influence. This is something I want to do. Maybe you can give me part of a day once a week to be with him. Maybe we can try it out on a trial basis. What do you think?"

I look away for a moment to collect my thoughts. "Fuck," I mutter under my breath.

Why does he have to be so sincere in the moments where I need him to be the old, detached Benny?

There's no denying I need help. Hell if I know how I'll even survive tomorrow. The problem is I'm at an emotional standstill. My gut says to knee Benny in the balls one more time for good measure, then watch him limp to the car and drive out of my life for good. But my heart sees the old Benny I loved, the one that would do anything to protect me from harm. That version of Benny was the first person I ever loved with all of my heart. He saved me from a life of abuse and taught me true compassion and how to embrace difference. That version of Benny is everything I want Marcus to grow up idolizing.

But without trust, there's no guarantees.

"Maybe we can try something out," I say, unsure of where I'm going with this. "Like, one day a week maybe you can come see him. And we'll see how it goes."

Benny's smile grows wide. "I'd like that. I'd like that a lot, Penny. Thank you."

"But let me be clear about something. If you fuck up once, we're done. There's no second chances this time around. You got that?"

"Of course."

We quickly exchange numbers as the rain comes down harder. Part of me wants him to wait it out for safety reasons. But Dad beats me to the punch.

"Benny, I really think you should stay," Dad chimes in, appearing at the doorway. "There's some low-lying areas on the way out of here. They're not safe."

Benny quickly turns his back to Dad. "If I need to, I'll pull aside."

"Benny!" I call out as he jogs to his truck.

He stops with his hand on the door handle. The water strikes his chiseled build like an impenetrable statue. He patiently waits, looking so gorgeous in his soaked to the skin white shirt that hugs every muscle to perfection.

"Please be careful," I finally say, unable to hide the worry in my voice.

Benny nods his head, cracking the quickest smile before climbing into his truck. He drives away with one last wave.

Dad puts his arm around my shoulders. He looks down on me with a smirk. "Don't worry, Penny. He'll be back sooner than you think."

# CHAPTER TWENTY-ONE

## Benny

The rapids rush through the wash as the rain picks up. There's no way through it, even with my truck. I shake my head, still in disbelief that I can't go home. I'm supposed to hear back any day now about my reinstatement. I also need to be back at work in a few days.

My options are limited. I can find another way out of here, or crash in my truck. But sleeping in a bucket seat through the bitter cold sounds like a nightmare.

Then I see Grandpa's truck in the rearview mirror. He hops out with his umbrella and walks up to the side of my truck.

I crank my window down while muttering every expletive I know in my head. "I know. I know. You were right. You knew this wash would be flooded, didn't you?"

"It's the only way out, Benny. Looks like you're stuck with us for at least another night. You need to hurry back because supper is in an hour. And don't even think about sleeping in your truck. Ms. Green wants me to tell you that she's already reloaded her shotgun. You're sleeping on the fold-out couch tonight."

Grandpa quickly walks back to his truck. He knows I'm still not in the mood to talk to him.

Once back at the house, Ms. Green puts me to work peeling potatoes and boiling them in water. The whole time I'm working, Marcus keeps poking his head around the corner, playing his own version of peek-a-boo. Every couple of minutes I sneak up on him to scare him. He runs away laughing every time.

After a while, I change my approach.

"Hey, Marcus. You want to help me mash these potatoes?"

He eagerly nods his head, hopping his way into the kitchen. I stand behind him, giving him directions on how to mash as I mix in the butter and cream. At first it's a huge mess. But little by little, he's starting to get it.

"Wow, Buddy. You're really good at this." My compliments cause him to smile; he's so proud of himself. "Is this your first time cooking?"

I feel his posture hunch as he ignores my question.

"He cooked with his Daddy quite a bit," Penny chimes in from behind. "He's also Mommy's little helper whenever I need him."

The phone rings as we start working on the salad together.

"Benny, it's for you," Grandpa says.

Everyone stares at me. I'm just as shocked to be getting a call in this house.

"Sir, what's your name again?" Grandpa asks. His eyebrows raise up in curiosity. "Okay, he's right here. Benny, it's Coach Kitchen."

I'm immediately nervous. Coach has never even called me on my own phone.

I grab the phone and stretch the cord as far as it'll go. I want some privacy.

"Hello, sir. I mean Coach," I stumble over my words, feeling out of breath.

"Hey, Benny," Coach says in his deep southern drawl. "I just heard back from the NCAA Compliance Committee. Are you ready for the ruling?"

I close my eyes knowing this is my last chance. If they say no, my football career is likely over for good.

"Yes, sir."

"It was a six to four vote. You're officially eligible to suit up and play next season."

I close my eyes, feeling the tears come. I wipe them away quickly when I notice Penny walking past.

I take two deep breaths because I'm still unable to speak.

"Benny! Are you there, Son?"

"I'm here. I'm here, Coach. I'm sorry, I just can't tell you what this means to me. Thank you so much. This is everything I've ever wanted."

"You're welcome, Son. I haven't seen many of these things go through. But apparently, they told me your application was the most comprehensive one they've ever seen."

"I don't understand. It was ten pages with three letters of recommendation."

Coach begins chuckling. "Son, there were some people working behind the scenes. You had every starter write you a recommendation. Even your grandpa and grandmother submitted letters on your behalf. I'd say in all, your final application was a little over fifty pages. Most of those were letters from your teammates. You've meant a lot to this team in your short time here. The hours you've put into the gym, the film room, and in helping others has paid off. You've earned this, Benny."

Being proud isn't something I'm used to. The last time I felt this way was years ago, being carried off the field as a state champion. At the time it felt like my football career was just beginning to blossom. I was on top of the world at 17.

*Second chances are possible!*

This time around will be different. I need to stay humble.

"Thank you, Coach."

"There's one other thing, Benny. I've already spoken with the coaching staff. We'd like to also offer you a partial athletic scholarship. We'd give you a full scholarship but all of those have gone to our four and five-star recruits. But with what's left in the budget we'd like to offer it to you. It's not a whole lot, but it'll help. What do you say?"

I'm paralyzed by the news. "I uh, I don't know what to say, Coach. But thank you. Thank you so much. You have no idea how hard I'm going to work to earn my stripes."

"Well, you're welcome. You have a good rest of your Christmas. Voluntary workouts start in five weeks and spring practice begins March 1st. We'll see you soon. Take care, Benny."

Coach hangs up as I try to get control of my breath. I want to scream at the top of my lungs.

"What was that all about?" Grandpa asks as I hang up the phone.

"Oh, just some stuff about practice starting up in about a month," I lie.

"Whatever you say, Benny," Grandpa says. He knows that call was something more.

During dinner I keep the news to myself. I don't feel comfortable with all the attention this could bring to me. Still, I wish I could at least tell Penny and Jimmy.

Meanwhile, Marcus is sitting next to me again. It feels like he's looking at me more than his food, which he's barely picked at.

"Marcus, Honey. I need you to eat your peas," Penny says.

"But Mommy, I don't like them," he groans, bowing his head.

"Marcus," Penny raises her voice.

"But Mommy, Benny didn't eat any peas."

This kid doesn't miss a thing. The problem is I hate peas. It's the one vegetable I can't stand. The texture, the aftertaste, all of it makes me want to vomit.

Penny's eyebrows raise from across the table. I know what her look is saying: *Eat the fucking peas!*

"Oh, I guess I forgot to eat my vegetables," I say, reluctantly scooping a spoonful onto my plate.

"Here, Bud. Let's eat them at the same time. They're so good," I say, hoping I sound sincere.

My stomach does somersaults as I shovel peas into my mouth. Chewing through them is painful. Swallowing them feels impossible, but I do it anyway.

It becomes a game for Marcus as he tries to eat them faster than me. Thirty seconds later, our plates are clean. There's still some left in my mouth as I swallow my last bite. When it's all swallowed it feels like the peas are bouncing off my insides like it's a trampoline.

"You don't like peas, do you, Benny?" Marcus asks.

I ignore his question, feeling clammy all over. Then I can't wait any longer. I bolt to the bathroom. I flip on the light just in time as the peas start shooting out of me. When I'm finally done, my throat is still burning, but I feel better.

I make my way back to the dinner table, noticing the smirks from everyone, especially Penny.

"Tell us about your walk today, boys?" Ms. Green asks to change the subject.

Marcus launches into a second-by-second rundown of our hike.

"And then we climbed trees and talked about treehouses. Benny said he'd try to build me one. Then we talked about Mommy's brother and um, yeah, that's about it. Then we hopped all the way home in the rain. It was the best trip ever."

I glance around the table noticing everyone's curious looks.

"So, Benny promised to build you a treehouse?" Penny repeats the words in disbelief.

"Well, not exactly. I said maybe one day," I clarify.

"Benny, how would you even know how to build a treehouse?" Penny challenges.

"I could do it. When I was in prison I got trained in carpentry. I'm even working part-time in construction. I can build pretty much anything."

I feel like I'm boasting to everyone, but it's the truth. I know I'm fully capable.

"What's prison?" Marcus curiously asks. "Is that like jail?"

"Um, well, not exactly. Prison's a little more serious," I reply.

"What did you do?"

*Fuck!*

I swallow back the bile returning to my throat. His curiosity has gotten the best of me.

"He did nothing wrong, Marcus," Grandpa's voice roars from across the table. "He made a couple mistakes, but he only did it because he was trying to protect your mom and his family. Benny has more courage than most. Maybe too much courage at times. But that's who my grandson is. And that's all you need to know about that."

A silence settles over the table.

"How about dessert?" Ms. Green finally says to break the ice.

----

Later that night I'm getting ready for bed. Ms. Green helps me fold out the mattress from inside the couch.

"It's a bit springy, but it'll be better than sitting in your truck all night. Besides, we all miss having you around," she says, giving my shoulder a quick squeeze.

She heads off to bed.

"Hey, Ms. Green," I call out. She turns around at the edge of the hallway. "Thank you."

"You're welcome, Benny. You're *always welcome.*"

She flashes another bright smile, holding her gaze on me like a magnet.

"Did he mean what he said at the table?" I ask.

"What do you think?"

"With him, I don't know what to think anymore," I admit.

"Well, your grandpa loves you. And he'll never stop loving you, just like the rest of us. Good night, Benny."

"Good night."

I lay in bed but can't stop squirming. My brain is overloaded with so many thoughts and questions.

I can see the clock next to the window moving in slow motion. The stars shine through, lighting up the living room with an odd glow for the middle of the night. There must be a full moon out there.

The next thing I know a thick comforter is thrown over my body like a parachute. It startles me a bit.

"Penny?"

"I just don't want you getting too cold in the night. Dad is so cheap with his gas bill. Good night," she says, rushing back toward her bedroom.

"Hey, wait," I call back.

"What?"

"I can't sleep. You mind chatting with me for a bit?" I ask.

Penny sighs, then continues down the hallway. I hear the bedroom door shut.

*Oh, well. At least I tried.*

Seconds later her door opens again. She paces around my bed, sitting across from me on the coffee table. Her own blanket is wrapped snugly around her body, but she's still shivering.

"Are you still cold?" I ask.

"I'm always cold, Benny. What do you want to talk about?"

I quickly stand up, taking the comforter she gave me and wrapping it over her.

"I gave this to you. What're you doing?" she complains, shrugging off the blanket.

"Oh, don't be difficult. I was perfectly comfy with my two sheets. You clearly need it more than I do."

She relaxes, and I sit back down across from her, suddenly unsure of what I want to talk about.

"So," she says, nervously fidgeting.

My mind is blank. My hesitation is making her even more agitated.

"How are you doing?" I finally ask.

"Really, Benny?"

"Yeah, you're right. I'm sorry," I mutter, feeling like anything I say is the wrong thing.

I take a deep breath, trying to find something worth saying. "I'm sure today was hard with the eulogy."

"It was. I mean, I knew it would be, but I'm glad it's over with. Patrick is comfortable with where he is now."

"Yeah, Marcus told me how much he loved camping with Patrick. He said his favorite memory was climbing trees with his dad, but I'm not supposed to tell you that part."

"It's okay, I already know. That boy couldn't keep a secret if his life depended on it."

I slide myself closer to the edge of the bed. My legs hang over the edge, just inches across from Penny's legs. She's avoiding my eyes.

"Penny. Look at me," I demand.

She continues gazing at the floor. Then I hear the first sniffle. I lift her chin and look into her eyes.

"Hey, it's okay. You can cry in front of me. I know you miss him. And I know I don't know him, but he sounds like a wonderful, honorable man. And I can tell he made you happy. Just knowing you were happy, and found someone while I was gone, makes me happy. It's all you've ever deserved. I mean that."

She covers her face with both hands, trying to muffle her crying.

I want to hug her, but I don't know how she'll respond. But she's crying so hard, it feels like I have no choice.

My arms wrap tightly around her. Penny doesn't fight it. Instead, she cries harder, wrapping her arms tightly around me.

I bury my face in her hair and rub her back, just like I used to do. I whisper over and over again how sorry I am. There's nothing else for me to do or say. It's all I can give her in this dark moment.

Time goes on. I have no intention of letting go until she's ready. The closeness with her also feels good in so many different, yet familiar ways.

"Thank you," she finally says, pulling away from our embrace.

I grab her hand with both of mine. "What can I do for you?"

"That's the problem, I don't know. Jimmy's just—"

She sighs, taking a couple deep breaths. "I just don't know what I'm doing. Everyone is so good to me, but I'm just lost. I don't even know what I'm doing tomorrow."

"How about you do nothing?"

"What do you mean?

"Well, you should do something. But you need to also just let yourself be sad. Stop fighting it. Who cares if Marcus sees you crying? You don't think he's crying on the inside every day, too?"

Penny blows her nose. I don't know what else I can say. We've both lost people in our life. Words can only do so much. Actions is what she really needs.

"Let's build a treehouse!" I blurt the words out of nowhere. *What am I saying?*

Penny starts laughing. "You're crazy, Benny. I don't need a treehouse."

"Come on. Maybe it'll be fun to be outside and just break a sweat. Marcus already has the tree picked out. Grandpa already has all the tools.  All we would need is the lumber. I'd be happy to run into town tomorrow and buy it."

"You're really serious, aren't you?"

She still doesn't believe me. I don't even know if I believe me at this point.

"Well, we'd have to get started soon. I've got to be back at work in a few days. But we could easily get it built in a couple days."

Penny stares at me with a look I can't decipher. But she's right. It's a terrible idea. I know how to build a house, but without a stable foundation or knowledge of the trees around here, it'll be much harder to pull this off.

"Deal," she says, extending her hand to mine. "But on one condition. You have to let Dad help us out."

*Fuck!*

"And if I don't?"

"I'm not bending on this, Benny," she says, raising her eyebrows. "And you're going to be the one asking for his help. I'm not doing it."

I look away.

"Fuck," I mutter under my breath, shaking my head. "Okay, you have a deal."

I extend my hand. Penny squeezes it tightly with the hint of a smirk on her face.

"One other thing, Benny. Who were you on the phone with earlier? Was that really your coach?"

"It was."

"What's he doing calling you over holiday break?" she asks.

"He was calling to tell me I've been re-admitted," I say, trying to sound casual.

Penny just squints her eyes.

"It means I can play football again. I only have one more year of eligibility, but I'm on the team. They even gave me a partial athletic scholarship."

"Really!" she shrieks.

I nod my head, no longer able to hide my smile.

"Oh, Benny. I'm so happy for you," she cries, diving at me with a hug that knocks the air out of me.

Then it happens. I lose my balance on the edge of the bed, and we tumble right over the side, our arms stuck around each other.

We hit the ground with a thud. My body is pinned on top of hers, my mouth resting inches above her lips. Time freezes for a brief moment before she quickly slides out from underneath me.

We both stand up, staring aimlessly past one another, speechless with embarrassment.

"Good night, Benny," she says, avoiding my eyes as she bolts to the hallway.

"Good night, Penny," I barely mutter back.

Her door shuts. My body falls flat onto the bed. I stare at the ceiling as my mind comes alive. It was only a second of laying on top of Penny, but it felt so good.

It's hard to understand how I feel. There's only one thing that feels true. It's where both of our minds went in that moment of intimate proximity.

*The old treehouse.*

# CHAPTER TWENTY-TWO

## Penny

"I need ten more nails that look like this one," Benny says, holding up the nail to Marcus.

Marcus tightens his tool belt, then marches back to the shed.

It's cute seeing the two of them interact. Benny's anointed Marcus the foreman of the job. It basically means that Benny directs him to go inside and get things for him every couple minutes. Marcus is loving his role in the construction process. At this point he'd probably go fetch fresh deer shit if Benny asked.

"What're you laughing about?" Benny asks me.

"Oh, nothing. He just loves taking orders from you. It's cute seeing the both of you interact."

Marcus runs back with a handful of nails. I cringe, praying he doesn't trip over his own feet like he does most days. He makes it to Benny safely, holding his hand out for Benny to assess the nails.

"You did great," Benny says, patting his shoulder. "But I think your great grandpa just doesn't have everything we need.

That's okay, I need to run to the hardware store anyways. I'll be back in an hour."

I look at Dad, wincing with concern.

"It's okay," Dad assures me. "I drove out there a couple hours ago. The wash has completely dried up. It's only a couple inches. He'll be fine."

"Can I come?" Marcus asks. "Please, please, please."

He's flashing his most manipulative smile. I give Benny a look, unsure if he wants company.

"I don't mind," he shrugs. "It would probably help to have the foreman of the job help pick out the supplies. But only if it's okay with Mom."

I nod my head as Marcus starts jumping for joy. "Just get back before supper. You hear me, Benny?"

Benny gives me a thumbs up. The two of them walk side by side to his truck. I watch as Marcus reaches for Benny's hand.

Seeing the two of them, hand in hand, has my heart overflowing. It's more than just the small act of affection. It's that Marcus sees the best parts of Benny. The ones I could never forget.

The second they drive off, I get back to sawing up the lumber that Dad's already marked and measured. When I'm done, he brings me another load.

"Thanks. Can I ask you something, Dad?"

"Of course, Sweetheart."

"How did Benny ask for your help on the treehouse?"

Dad starts laughing.

"You really want to know?" he asks as he catches his breath. "He said, 'Richard, your great grandson wants a treehouse. I need your fucking help, old man.' There might have been a 'please' mixed in, but those are the parts I remember."

"Oh my god." I shake my head. "I guess I shouldn't be surprised. But I still don't understand. Why is he being such an asshole to you?"

Dad rubs his neck with a grimace. "He's got every right to be upset with me. I haven't been perfect. You know that. But everything I do for you kids is done with the best of intentions. And Benny doesn't understand my intent yet. But he will. Just give him some time. He's a smart young man."

"Have you told him what you did?" I ask. "You know, with the Monroes and all."

"I haven't. Not yet, but I will when the time is right. Have you told him what you did for the Monroes?" he asks.

I nod my head no. I'm still unsure how to broach that subject.

"What about the other thing?" Dad asks.

I nod again. I'm disgusted about the one thing I shouldn't be withholding from Benny.

"You can't wait on that, Penny. He needs to know."

"I know," I mutter, turning my attention to my sawing.

Each time I get through a new log, I get angrier. I'm angry because I did tell Benny. It was written in the letters that went unread for years.

I want to understand where he's coming from, but it's still hard. It's especially hard after seeing how quickly he's bonded with Marcus. I just feel like he needs to make the effort. He needs to ask the right questions and learn about all I've been through when he was away.

"I'm going to head in," Dad mumbles, giving me a funny look.

"You okay?" I ask.

Dad nods his head, pointing to the door as he mumbles something under his breath. I think he said something about water.

I get back to sawing. Then I notice how Dad is walking more slowly, without his usual energy. He just looks so frail. I decide to follow him inside.

"Where's Dad?" I ask Ms. Green.

"Bathroom, why?"

"Oh, nothing. I just wanted to make sure he was okay. Can I help with supper?"

"Yeah, chop up that broccoli for me, Darling. I'm going to go check on him."

While I chop broccoli, I can hear Ms. Green knocking on the bathroom door. Her hollering and pounding gets louder. I'm suddenly tense.

I hurry into the hallway and begin pounding on the door and shouting for Dad. I keep jiggling the knob, but he's locked it from the inside.

"Fuck!" I shout, running outside to grab a screwdriver.

Once I'm back inside, I watch as Ms. Green jams her shoulder against the door, which cracks open. Inside, we see Dad on his back, mumbling words we can't understand. He's clearly conscious but disoriented.

I hear the truck pulling up in the front yard. "Benny! Benny! Help us!" I scream as Ms. Green tries to assess what's going on.

"Oh my Lord, Penny. I think he's had a stroke. We need to get him to a hospital!"

I don't know what to do. Neither of us is strong enough to carry Dad. Then Benny rushes in with Marcus right behind him. I swoop Marcus into my arms before he can enter the bathroom, then run into the kitchen and dial 911. There's commotion and panic everywhere. I can barely breathe.

The only part I comprehend is Ms. Green yelling for me to have the paramedics meet us at Cherry Hill Road. It's a halfway point into town and probably our only shot at getting Dad the quickest help possible.

Everything else passes in a blur: Marcus screaming for his great grandpa. Ms. Green crying, begging for Dad to live. Jimmy, holding his hands over his ears to muffle the screams from every direction. And Benny, running through the house with 200 pounds of dead weight on his back.

*I can't lose the only true parent I've ever had. I can't lose my dad.*

# CHAPTER TWENTY-THREE

## Penny

The past seven days have invited a whirlwind of emotions. The first 48 hours were full of numbness and sleepless nights. Ms. Green and I held Dad's hand for every second we could be with him. It was hard seeing him unconscious with so many tubes and wires sticking into him.

But things have gotten better over the last few days. On the third day, Dad was more often awake, and on the fourth day the doctors gave an official name to what had happened: an ischemic stroke. It basically means there was a blockage in an artery that supplies blood to the brain. If we didn't get him help as quickly as we had, he could have died.

Over the last three or four days, Dad has become more conscious and communicative. The doctors are optimistic, but we all know the road to recovery with be long and arduous.

The plan is that Dad will come home in about a week. We'll then have weekly visits with occupational, physical and speech therapists. He'll be wheelchair-bound for the next couple months. His ability to talk right now is limited, but the doctors believe that it'll slowly improve with therapy.

We're each dealing with the stroke in our own way. Jimmy's refusing to talk about it. Marcus has no idea what's really going on. And Ms. Green is telling us that Dad will be "good as new" in a few months. I want to believe in her optimism, but I also know that Dad is creeping up on 80 years old.

The real question is how Ms. Green will take care of him. She's worked in healthcare most of her life, but she's also 70 years old. The therapists suggested an in-home nurse for the first few weeks to help him with bathing and other essentials. I tried telling Ms. Green I'd stick around longer to help out, but she said she can take care of him herself.

The past couple days have taken on a similar routine. Benny has begun building a wheelchair ramp for the house, with help from Marcus and Jimmy, then he comes to relieve me and Ms. Green around lunch time. He stays with Dad for about three hours until Ms. Green comes back. It's just the two of them during that time. I can't help but wonder what it's like to be a fly on the wall with Benny and his grandpa.

When I hear Benny come in behind me, I know it's time to go home. I want to go see how Marcus is doing, but it kills me every time I leave Dad's side. Even though he's on the mend, I worry that every time I leave it could be the last time I see him.

"How's he doing?" Benny asks.

"He's just napping. He's talking a little bit better today. He also wrote down some terrible jokes to tell Marcus later tonight."

"Oh, yeah. I bet he'll have Marcus in stitches," Benny sarcastically replies. "But how are you doing?"

I can't find the words. I settle on shrugging my shoulders and forcing a fake smile across my face.

"I know. But do you want some good news?" Benny eagerly asks.

"Sure."

"The ramp is all done. Now, when you see Marcus he's going to take all of the credit for the design and the construction. But all he did was ask a billion questions and fetch water and snacks for me and Jimmy. Anyway, it's a sturdy ramp. It should make things a lot easier when Grandpa gets home."

"That's great news. Thank you." I smile at Benny. He seems proud that he can help.

I take a deep breath, then I lean down to kiss Dad on the head. "I'll see you tomorrow," I whisper in his ear. "I love you so much. Always remember that."

Dad smiles a little, then goes back to sleep. On my way out, I give Benny a quick wave.

"Hey, before you leave, I think we should talk about what the plan is when Grandpa goes home," he says.

"What do you mean?"

"Well, we both know that Ms. Green can't do everything to take care of him."

"I know. Marcus and I will stay back. Jimmy's got work next week, so he'll probably head back. But he'll be fine on his own as long as he sticks to his daily routine."

Benny gives me a peculiar look.

"What about school? Don't your classes start up in two weeks?"

"I'll just take the semester off. I figure I can make up most of the credits over summer. It shouldn't delay graduation or getting my teacher credentials. But why do you care?"

Benny let's out a loud, huffing breath, shaking his head.

"I care because I care about you guys. And I know what you're going to say, so just give it a rest. I already know I fucked up, but this is my time to make things right. You go off to school and I'll stay back to take care of Grandpa for the next couple months."

"No!" I shout.

My reply came out harsh, but I don't care.

"What do you mean, no?"

"I mean no, Benny!" I shout again. "You have football practice. This is your last shot. It's your dream. And we both know it can't wait another year. My situation buys me plenty of time. Yours doesn't. So no, and that's my final answer."

"Well, suit yourself. Because I'm staying, and you're going back. You've done enough, Penny. Let me do this, please."

His demeanor quickly shifts from anger to desperation. He wants this more than anything, and I get it. But I want to be with Dad, plain and simple. He needs me to make sure he's given the best care.

It's not that I just owe it to him as his daughter. It's much bigger than that. Grandpa's given me a second chance at life. He's saved me in so many ways. Perhaps Benny feels the same way.

"Benny, who are you doing this for? Dad? Me? Jimmy? Ms. Green?"

Benny scoots his chair so close our knees are touching. Then he grabs both of my hands.

"Listen, Penny. It's for all of you. When Grandpa had the stroke, all the anger I had for him vanished. Every last bit of it was gone in the blink of an eye. It was so weird, because all I've known lately is hating him. And I realized as he's gotten better that I have no choice but to make things right with him. If I don't do it now, then I'm no good to the rest of you. Because you're all my family, including Marcus. And more importantly, you've always been *my* Penny McClain."

Benny continues to stare into me with so much conviction and determination. Everything he just said strikes the right chords in my heart, especially his final three words.

I lean back to catch my breath, letting go of his hands. He can't force us away from Dad, but maybe he can compromise.

"How about this. We both stick around the first month. And after that, you head off for spring practice," I say, hoping I sound confident.

Benny digs his hands through his hair, mulling over my suggestion.

"And what happens with you after a month?" Benny finally asks.

"We'll see. Maybe I go back to school. Or maybe I talk to my teachers and salvage my semester from afar. Or maybe I just get back to it in the summertime. But at least with my plan we all win. Because I'm not leaving Dad's side. Not until we know he's getting better."

"But, what if he doesn't, Penny? I mean, he's a tough old fart. But what if?"

"Just don't even think that," I quickly reply. "He's going to be okay. Together, we'll make him strong again."

Benny gets up and begins to pace back and forth in Dad's tiny hospital room. I'm hoping he'll follow my plan. I need the reassurance. Having him giving up on his dream just isn't an option.

He takes a seat by Dad. "Fine. We'll do it together. But only for one month. Then you're going back to school, and I'll head up north for spring practice. But we're going to hire help after that. There's just no way you can take care of Grandpa and look after Marcus at the same time."

I want to contradict him, but I don't. Besides, this is a fair compromise for both of us.

"Okay. Goodnight, Benny."

I walk out of the hospital with my head held a bit higher than usual. It's a rarity to win an argument with the most stubborn boy on earth. Well, I guess he's not a boy anymore. He's acting like a man. He's a man that gave me back my last name today. And a man that sees me in a way I hope to better understand.

*"My Penny McClain."*

# CHAPTER TWENTY-FOUR

## Penny

Someone is knocking on my door.

"Come in," I whisper.

The door slowly opens to reveal the silhouette of a man. My room is still pitch dark. All I see is the large, familiar outline of his body. He walks to the edge of the bed, sitting on his knees and grasping my feet.

"What are you doing?" I whisper.

"Shh," he whispers back.

His hands dig into my feet. Then he slowly glides the pressure along my calves. Then his massage turns into a tickle along my legs, relaxing and erotic as his fingers brush over my skin.

He suddenly yanks me by my feet to the edge of the bed. My legs hang over the side, and I spread them wide by his face.

"May I?" he asks, gliding his hands up the sides of my hips.

I eagerly nod my head, unable to utter a word.

His fingers loop under the side of my panties. The heat inside of me feels unrelenting. I want every bit of touch and taste he can give me. I'm unable to slow my breathing as I feel his grip tighten over my panties. He begins to slowly slide them down my legs until I'm fully exposed. He slowly leans his face closer until he's less than a foot from the part of me he wants to taste.

His hands gracefully glide along my inner thighs. Each time his hands get closer, until I feel my hips scooting to the very edge, like a magnet to his mouth.

He continues to tease. Then I feel the warmth of his hands gliding under my ass, gripping it tightly. The man leans his face closer and closer, but still doesn't touch me with his mouth. Instead, I feel his warm breath and lips breathing onto it, tantalizing me even more. I arch my hips closer to his mouth until I feel his lips finally meet mine.

His tongue begins to lightly touch and massage over my clit. It's so subtle the way it delicately glides. I feel my clit and labia engorging over his drooling mouth.

Then his finger goes inside me as a guttural moan escapes me. My pussy tightly wraps around the girth of his finger, while his tongue continues to strum along my clit with deft precision. The pressure on my insides goes from painfully good to feeling like I'm going to faint into an orgasm.

"Please, don't stop. Right there!" I moan, gasping for air.

When it feels too good, I arch my back up for a closer look. Then I grab him by the back of his head pulling him desperately into my wetness. He gasps for air as I pull him tighter into me. Then he hits the perfects spots with his finger and tongue. I can't hold it back anymore, screaming his name.

"Benny! Benny!" I scream until I collapse on my back.

I push him off because it feels too good, the way the flood of pleasure escapes all at once. He's watching me fall further into my orgasm, still shaking uncontrollably.

I try catching my breath, but then I feel his hands grasps onto my hips, flipping me onto my stomach with ease. I get on all fours because I want him deep inside me. I want all the pleasure he never got to finish.

I look to the side realizing that I'm no longer in a dark room. The slats of wood are neatly nailed into a tree. The same one where I lost my virginity.

The only sounds are from the thrusting of his cock as he goes deeper into me. The pace is careful and methodical, hitting spots inside me I didn't know could feel this good.

"Oh, Penny, I'm close!" he shouts, pounding into me faster.

Then his chest falls onto my back. Benny's arms come around my chest. I lean my ass into him to allow for more closeness and deeper pressure. Then I feel the manic thrusting slow to a spasmic pace.

His moan is loud and unrelenting. I feel his cum explode into my pussy. My insides begin to pulsate. I accept every bit of his cum as my own.

"Mommy! Mommy!" The squeaky voice keeps shouting. There's a banging on the door, and I open my eyes to a popcorn ceiling. It's symbolic to the nothingness that awaits my dire need for pleasure.

"Fuck," I mumble. "Give me a minute, Marcus!"

I try pleasuring myself, but Marcus won't stop calling to me. I begrudgingly get up because a four-year-old has no concept of time.

While making breakfast I can't snap out of my groggy, grumpy mood. I'm grumpy because it's the third sex dream I've had with Benny in the last three nights. I like them a lot. But I always feel weird after waking up. It's normal to be horny. But I'm so aroused right now, and it won't go away. Even looking at the greasy sausage links makes me want to fall back into a dream.

I'm groggy due to the lack of sleep. Benny and I were up until one in the morning. The medication Dad is on has him emptying his bladder every hour. It's a process helping him out of bed and then walking him to the bathroom to get him situated. I'm so thankful for Benny's help because I don't have the strength needed to do the heavy lifting.

Luckily the morning and afternoon time gives all of us a break as Dad's live-in nurse comes to help out. Her name is Dana and she's an absolute doll. She's so good to Dad that some days I think Ms. Green gets a bit jealous. His insurance only covers eight hours of medical assistance, and the rest of the time it's us kids and Ms. Green doing what we can to help Dad on his road to recovery.

It's only been a couple weeks since the stroke, but his progress has been dramatic. He's basically the same man he was before, he just can't get around. He also can't talk for prolonged periods of time. But the speech therapy that Dana and Ms. Green do each day has helped a lot.

Benny comes in from his run. He's not wearing a shirt, making things even more distracting.

"How are you?" he asks, sweat dripping down his chin.

"Fine," I mutter, unable to avoid a quick glance at his pecs. It's hard to not drool over his post-workout body. My dream felt so real, so possible.

"What's that smell?" Benny asks.

"Oh, fuck!"

I run to the stove, shutting it off while flipping the sausage links over. They're all charred to a crisp.

*Can I blame it on my sexual fantasies?*

"Goddamit!" I shout.

"Hey, don't worry about it. Look, some of them are okay," Benny says, prodding at the burnt links. "I'll eat these three burned ones and the rest will be fine. No one will notice."

It's kind of him to cheer me up, but we both know that half of what I cooked isn't edible. He also doesn't know my son very well.

"What's that smell, Mommy?" Marcus asks, cruising into the kitchen. "Did you burn something again?"

"Maybe," I mutter, taking a deep breath.

I lean down to kiss him on the head. I wipe off whatever smudge is on his forehead, admiring the beauty in his brown eyes. "Mommy didn't sleep well," I tell him. "And I got distracted. But don't worry, Benny volunteered to eat the ones that taste like rubber."

"Why were you distracted, Mommy?" Marcus asks with a confused look on his face.

"Oh, it was nothing," I sigh. "Just some bad dreams. I'll be okay."

"Why did you have bad dreams about Benny?" Marcus asks.

My hand goes over my mouth. Then I see Benny squint out of the corner of my eye.

"What makes you think I dreamt about Benny?" I ask, wanting to crawl into a cave and hide.

"I heard you, Mommy. You screamed: 'Oh Benny! Oh Benny!'"

I just look at Marcus, stunned at how well he recreated my own orgasmic tone. Benny looks away, pretending to wipe down a counter, while I remain tight lipped.

"Good morning, everyone!" Ms. Green proudly announces her arrival in the kitchen. "How did everyone sleep?"

"I slept good. Mommy didn't because she kept screaming Benny's name. But I don't know—"

I clamp my hand over Marcus's lips, shaking my head in utter disbelief.

"Honey, my dreams are private. But I'm sorry I woke you up," I say, dashing out of the kitchen past Ms. Green's smile.

I go outside for some fresh air. I take a couple deep breaths, feeling even more confused. And still very horny.

"Hey, you okay?" Benny asks, stepping onto the front porch.

"I'm not talking about my dreams, Benny."

"I didn't come out to talk about that. But whatever you dream about is fine. You don't have to feel embarrassed by it. I had my share of those dreams, too, when I was away. They're just dreams."

I chuckle because he has no idea how good the dreams are. And they're definitely not ordinary, especially with our history.

I hear the door open as Benny heads back in.

"Wait. What did you come to chat about?" I ask.

"Oh, I just wanted to let you know that breakfast is ready," Benny says, pausing to bite his lip. "And I uh, I wanted you to know that I had so much fun playing cards and talking with you last night. Maybe we can do it again tonight. That's all."

"Me too, Benny. And yeah, that would be great," I admit as we both head back in.

It was more than fun for me. It was like turning back the clock to years ago when we'd stay up late talking in the treehouse. Those were the best days because I felt safe and more loved than I ever thought I deserved.

We talked about a lot of things last night. But I was careful not to disclose too much about my relationship with Patrick. Nor did I go into the more serious topic of when he was away in prison. But for the most part it was light-hearted. We laughed a lot and just enjoyed each other's company.

----

Later that afternoon I head onto the front porch to read while Dad takes a nap. I watch as Benny gives Marcus instructions on throwing a proper spiral. His hands are still too small for a football, but it's cute seeing him try to emulate Benny.

"What time you picking up Jimmy tomorrow?" Ms. Green asks, taking a seat next to me.

"About 9 a.m."

"How do you think he's doing on his own?" she asks with a concerned look.

"I called him yesterday. We tried talking about Patrick. But he gave me nothing. I just don't know how to help him. I want him to know that grief is a long process. I want him to open up. But…nothing."

"He'll open up soon. Just like you. You kids are all blossoms. We just can't always be blooming at the same time. And that's okay. Have faith in Jimmy. He'll be okay. But how are you, Sweetheart?"

"I'm not sleeping great," I yawn.

"So I heard," Ms. Green says with a chuckle.

"Stop it, Ms. Green. It's not like that. It was just a dream."

She keeps chuckling until it turns into a cough. "Oh my. You'll have to excuse me. You two are just a site to behold. That's all."

"What do you mean by that?" I ask.

"Oh, I'm just a senile old lady. I don't know what I mean by most things. But dreams are a gateway to our subconscious. I have no doubt about that. Besides, it sure is cute seeing you two be friendly with one another again. You always made such a cute couple. And to think, a couple weeks ago you were kneeing him in the balls. Oh my lord. The things love does to us. It sure makes us crazy."

"You know we're not a couple. And we never will be, Ms. Green. He only sees me as his sister."

"Whatever you say, Penny. But don't say 'never'. Because love does funny things to boys and girls. Look at me and your dad. I'd told you it's impossible to fall in love after losing my Jonathan. But look at me now. I want every second I can get with Richard. And that's when you know. I'd do anything to keep that man alive as long as I can. Speaking of which, I'm going to go check on him to make sure his old ticker is still ticking."

Ms. Green slowly stands. "Oh, and one other thing. Don't lie to yourself either. It's not healthy. Because I know when that cute boy is out there chopping wood, you're walking by that window one too many times."

I bite my tongue as Ms. Green heads inside chuckling to herself yet again.

----

"Is he down?" Benny asks.

I nod and start laughing for no good reason.

"What's so funny?" he asks.

"Oh, it's just weird you asking me that question about Dad. I can't tell you how many times Patrick and Jimmy would ask me that question. They hated tucking Marcus into bed because they were always too worried to leave too early and get Marcus all riled up."

Benny deals out the playing cards, then pauses.

"Do you mind telling me more about Patrick? What kind of dad was he?"

"Um, I don't know how to answer that question. He was just always present with Marcus. When he gave Marcus attention, nothing else in the world mattered to him. It even made me jealous sometimes."

My laugh feels awkward and forced.

"But as your husband he treated you good. Right?" Benny asks.

His question lingers. I sense his eyes searching for mine while I aimlessly stare at my cards. Then I swallow the acidic taste in my throat.

"Yeah. He was good to me."

"I'm glad you found someone, Penny. I mean, while I was gone and all."

"What do you mean by that?" I ask.

"Well, I mean, think about the last time we were together. You know. In the treehouse."

Like I've forgotten about our final night in the treehouse, just because Patrick came into my life. I definitely didn't forget that night. I never will. It was too special, and it meant too much to me.

It was more than just losing my virginity. It's also what he told me before we had sex. The way he looked at me with desire and love, which made us something other than siblings. That's what I'll never forget. But when he left my life for so long I started to wish I could forget it, because of the heartbreak. And now that he's back, I don't know what to think, or how to feel about him.

"Penny?"

"Yeah," I finally look up from my cards, swallowing the lump in my throat.

"You okay?"

"Yeah."

"Then why are you crying?"

*Fuck, again!*

I quickly wipe at my eyes.

"I'm really sorry about Patrick. Is there something I can do to cheer you up?"

"Give me a minute," I tell him, hastily making my way to the bathroom.

The cold water on my face is invigorating, but it does nothing to revive me. I look in the mirror as my hands glide down the dark skin of my cheeks. The imperfections in my face and body are my only focus. There's the bags under my eyes, the pimples on my cheeks, the extra flab in my belly from childbirth. Even my butt and breasts don't have the same perkiness they used to have. I just want to feel desirable like I did in my dreams.

*Fuck! What am I doing?*

My mind is a jumble of thoughts. I need to get back out there and just tell him I'm not feeling well. I mean, it's technically not a lie.

It takes a couple more minutes of catching my breath before I finally head back to the living room. But he's not in there.

The clinking noises from the kitchen draw me there, where Benny is stirring something in a pot. He sprinkles in a pinch of salt while my sense of smell comes back to me.

"Are you—?" I throw my hand over my mouth, already drooling. "Oh my god! You're making homemade mac and cheese!"

Benny turns to flash an angelic smile. "I thought it would cheer you up. I don't know how to help you with what you're going through. But I figure this made you happy when you became hormonal once a month as a teen."

"Really?" I laugh at his phrasing. "Hormonal?"

"What? How should I say it?"

"Not like that," I tersely reply. "Just say what it is. It's a period. Girls do it once a month. We can't help it. It's actually a healthy thing to go through."

"Sorry."

"Don't be. This is so sweet of you to do all of this. Thank you, Benny."

It's a small act, making my favorite meal. But it's amazing how it changes my mood. We spend the next thirty minutes eating an entire pot of mac and cheese. We talk about life before Benny went to prison.

We also talk about my brother. It's something I've rarely done with Benny because it used to be too hard for both of us. But tonight, everything about Benny feels different.

The biggest difference is the way I feel when he smiles at me. It calms all my anxieties in an instant. He's even sitting closer to me. Sometimes our shoulders touch, and I can't ignore the electricity he gives off.

Eventually we both check on Dad. He's still sound asleep. I'm not sure if we'll need to check on him again, or if we can head off to bed.

"I think he'll be okay for the rest of the night," Benny whispers as we walk back into the hallway.

I nod my head as we stop in the narrow hallway. Behind both of us are paths to the end of another evening. But I don't want it to end. Judging from the shine in those gleaming green eyes, he doesn't want it to end either.

The walls feel like they're suddenly squeezing us closer to one another. I know I can't act on how I feel, but at least I can maybe dream about it again tonight.

"Good night, Benny," I say walking past him.

"Good night, Penny. I hope you have sweet dreams," he says, smiling back.

I put my hand on the doorknob, hesitating for a split second to turn it. Then I open the door.

"Hey, Penny."

"Yeah."

Benny hesitates. He bites down on his lower lip. "Um, I've had trouble sleeping the last couple nights. If you have trouble sleeping, just know I'm probably not sleeping well either."

"Okay, Benny." I'm so confused on what he's really saying.

"I'm sorry. I guess I don't know why I told you that. But, if you're having trouble sleeping feel free to come out in the living room and hang out with me, if you want. No pressure."

The lustful feeling between my thighs has my insides simmering. His words felt like an open invitation. But what do I say?

*Just say something!*

"Okay, Benny," I finally mutter. "Goodnight. I'll see you tonight. I mean, tomorrow morning. I'll see you in the morning."

When I'm flat on my back in bed, I'm wide awake.

Sleep suddenly feels impossible. I'm pretty sure Benny's invitation to hang out was for more than just talking in the middle of the night. And I may have given him no real answer. But I know what I want.

*Him!*

# CHAPTER TWENTY-FIVE

## Benny

I lay on the fold-out couch, wondering why I said what I did to Penny. But my mind can't make sense of it. It's like over the past week Penny has cast a spell over me.

My whole reason for staying back was to take care of Grandpa. That part's been easy. She was never supposed to even be here. But she is, and I couldn't be more thankful.

The best part is all the alone time I get with her after our tasks are done with Grandpa. During this time alone I feel like much more than just her brother. I'm her friend.

The reality is I feel like a completely different person over the past week. My guard is down when it's just the two of us. Then I get these feelings. They're the kind I haven't felt in a long time. But there's something even bigger brewing within me. In her presence I no longer feel like Benny McClain, the convict. I just feel like my old self—*my best self.*

The physical attraction has always been there. Denying that feeling is a lost cause for me. Every part of her mind and body drives me insane. But there's a deeper connection between us because of our history. That part worries me, because I've already broken her heart. If either one of our hearts breaks this time around, it becomes even more complicated because of Marcus.

I feel the need to tread lightly with whatever comes next. I need to remember how fragile her life is right now. Her husband has only been dead a few months. And it's clear that not having him here has brought immeasurable hurt to everyone.

My options are both complicated and simple. Either I stay here and get another sleepless night, fantasizing about being with Penny, or just say "fuck it" and see where things go.

*Fuck it!*

I walk up to her door and put my hand on the doorknob. I'm trying to decide if I should knock or just open the door when the doorknob turns on its own.

"Hey," I say, feeling out of breath.

"I can't sleep. You?"

"Me neither," I quickly reply. "Um, can I come in?"

My question hangs in the pitch dark of night, at the precipice of so much unknown. I can't see the uncertainty in her face, but I sense it.

"I can go back to bed if you're not comfortable—"

"No. Don't do that," she interrupts me. "I just don't want to complicate things even more."

"Even more? Um, yeah, I think I understand. Um…Okay. I'm going to head back," I say, turning away until her hand grabs my wrist.

"Stay. Come in and just hold me. Please, Benny," she whispers, guiding me in.

I follow her to the bed. I climb in first, lying flat on my back. As she slides under the sheets, I'm already harder than a diamond, confused about what holding her really means. She snuggles into my side, her head resting over my heart. The lavender fragrance from her hair is still alluring as she wraps her arms tighter around my torso, pressing her breasts into my side.

I want to kiss her, but we both know once that starts, we'll probably take it too far. But if she makes the first move, I'm not holding back.

Our embrace continues. I want to cradle her ass, and just the thought of this has my erection getting harder.

She pushes her leg up across my hip, brushing over my hardness. It's like she's wanting to straddle me but holding back the slightest bit. Then I feel her breathing ramp up. Her face nuzzles deeper into my neck, now smelling my scent. My hand begins to squeeze and slide up and down along her hip. My other hand goes under the back of her shirt, caressing her milk chocolate skin.

"Benny," she moans.

"Yes, I know. I want to, so bad," I whisper in her ear.

I let my lips lightly brush over hers with soft, delicate kisses. The kind that makes our insides shudder in overwhelming ecstasy. Then her lips taste down my neckline and I begin caressing her ass. My lips brush across her ear and down her neckline, tasting with a mix of lips and light tongue. We both moan, gasping for air.

I've never wanted something so much in my life. I need every part of her body on mine. I want to be inside her, to finish what we never could.

When my hand goes under her panties, her hand is quickly onto the warmth of my engorged erection. The second my fingers feel the wetness between the lips of her pussy, I'm even more manic with desire. Her moaning gets louder as I rub over her clit while she strokes me. I still remember the rhythm and change in pressure she likes. And she still knows how to work her hand over my cock, squeezing hard over the tip. If only I can get her juicy lips to taste me.

Then she hears my thoughts, kissing from my chest down my abdomen. When her lips brush over the tip, she stays there, lightly tasting and teasing me with her tongue. Then she swallows it whole. I feel the warmth and lubrication from her mouth. She's hungry to suck me off, but not as hungry as I am for her pussy.

I lay back, feeling my whole erection go further into the back of her throat. Then she pulls off and begins stroking me while sucking on the tip. I can't see how wet she's making my dick, but I feel the saliva dripping down. When I feel like I'm getting too close I pull it out of her mouth. Then I lean up to taste those lips. They're still soaking wet, making her even more satisfying to taste.

Then I pull off her lips, leaning over her ear. "My turn," I whisper.

Penny leans back, touching herself while she spreads her legs. The second my tongue touches her pussy the taste and smell has my appetite ravaging. I tease her clit with light circular brushes of my tongue. It's already engorged as I glide a little harder over it, starting at the base of her clit. Then I slowly slide my index finger inside her. The moan gets louder the deeper I go. Then I pull my finger out to taste her insides. I suck off every last bit of her juices. Then I put my finger back in her while applying a little more pressure with my tongue over her clit.

Everything about this moment is too much euphoria. I can hardly breathe with anticipation for what I'll be doing in a moment to her tight insides. But I'm in no rush. Pleasing her right now is all that matters. Making her cum tonight is everything.

Her moan gets louder as I find different angles and pressure along her clit. The lubrication coming out of her has my mouth drooling even more. Then her moan gets louder.

"Oh, fuck!" she shouts, muffling her hand over her mouth a second too late. "Please stay right there. Right there," she demands, pulling a pillow over her face.

Then her legs shake uncontrollably. She pushes my head out from between her legs. Her muffling scream into her pillow becomes the perfect climax to witness as her whole-body spasms with pleasure. It goes on and on as she tries to catch her breath.

Eventually, her vibrating body slows. Her head tilts up, staring daggers at me through the pitch-dark room. "Get over here," she demands, spreading her legs to invite me in.

The sound of a ringing bell startles us both.

*Fuck!*

"I'll handle it, Penny. Just hold that thought and I'll be back in ten minutes. He probably just has to pee again."

"Okay, please hurry," she begs.

Getting Grandpa situated on the toilet is a bit of a process. Luckily he's super groggy and not in the mood to chat. Once he's done, I help him get settled into bed. It's probably only been five minutes by the time I'm back in the room. But there's one big problem.

Penny's sitting at the edge of the bed, fully dressed in her pajamas. Her face is buried in her hands. I sit next to her, putting my arm around her. But her body is so tense.

"You okay?" I whisper.

She nods her head no, still not looking up.

"Is it because of what we were about to do?"

My question hangs in the air for far too long. That's a "yes."

"I'm so sorry, Penny."

"It's not that!" she raises her voice in frustration. "You need to read the letters I wrote you. I'm just not able to tell you. And I can't do this with you until you know. It's either that or Jimmy tells you. But I doubt that will happen anytime soon. And even when you know, I still don't know if I can do this with you. You don't understand how much you hurt me, how much I hated you. You told me to stop being a McClain when it's the one thing I was most proud to be. It's like you dis-owned me. You don't know what it's like to not feel love as a child. It stays with you forever. So no, we can't do this. This is just too fast. The wounds are still open, Benny. And some scars never go away. So just go to bed. We'll figure this out tomorrow, because I still need your help with Marcus and Dad. I'm sorry."

I sigh, wanting to find some way to rectify what I've done. But I can't. I walk out of the room, replaying the pain in her desolate voice as I go.

The pain she's endured when I was away sounds insurmountable, and somehow bleaker than what I experienced in prison. And whatever it is she can't say, is in those letters.

But one thing also stands out. She said Jimmy could tell me. But what is it he'll tell me that Penny can't say for herself? Nothing makes sense anymore.

Nevertheless, I can't change what I've done to her. Grandpa's told me that loving someone takes willingness and sacrifice. Now, that suddenly makes more sense in my world. Because for Penny, I'll sacrifice anything.

# CHAPTER TWENTY-SIX

## Benny

"What do you say we try it for a bit without the walker?" I ask Grandpa.

He's much steadier on his walker today, but I can tell he's still hesitant.

On the weekends we have no nurse helping us, so I'm giving Ms. Green a bit of a break until Penny and Jimmy get back from the bus station. I'm excited to see Jimmy, but also worried after Penny's comments last night.

"Um, okay," Grandpa finally says. "Why not."

I hold out my arms for balance. Grandpa's arms begin to vibrate as he latches on. "We'll just walk to the end of the porch and back. Come on, you got this."

Each step is done methodically, for optimal balance. The further we get the harder he squeezes and the more he groans as he runs out of breath. Then he makes it to the end.

"Not bad. Right, Benny?" he groans, still trying to catch his breath.

I'm proud of Grandpa, I really am. But I'm also still lost in thoughts of last night with Penny.

"Hmm. Not bad for an old hag," I joke.

Grandpa huffs out a laugh. "Should we do it again?"

"No. The therapists wanted you to wait until next week to do this. But it shows how you're getting better a lot faster than even they expected. How do you feel overall?"

Grandpa takes a few more deep breaths. Then I help him take a seat on the porch rocking chair. "Well, to be honest, I'm still a bit uncomfortable. I'm not used to having people bend over backwards to help with so many things. I'm also not ready to be approaching the end."

"What do you mean? You still got a lot of good years," I try to encourage.

"Oh, I think you're right about that. But when you have something like this happen, you begin to question a lot of things in your life. And I don't like having regrets."

"What do you regret?"

"A lot of things. But it's more than just regret. It's the things we still miss. I miss your grandmother. I miss your parents. I miss all the friends I lost in the war. I also have some things I still owe to Ms. Green, and myself. There's just a lot you think about when you almost die, especially with the people you love. And I don't like living in the past..."

Grandpa pauses, closing his eyes and exhaling slowly and deeply. He smiles and opens his eyes.

"You know, my mom had a great saying: 'If all we do is worry about yesterday and tomorrow, we'll keep forgetting about today.'"

Grandpa turns to look at me. He softly pats my shoulder. "I don't want to forget about today. I want to be in the moment and just soak it up with a smile. But my Lord, is it hard some days.".

"You want to talk about regrets. I got you there, old man. My life is one big fucking regret," I admit.

"I don't agree with that," Grandpa counters. "But what is it you regret most, Benny? Let's get it out of your system so we can live in today."

I let out a nervous laugh. This is definitely a conversation I'm not prepared for. "How about you go first?" I challenge.

"Well, okay. I regret not saving Madeline's life. A week before her accident she skipped a routine doctor visit because she had a headache. Maybe I should've talked her into going, but I didn't."

"What else?" I ask.

"I regret not being in town that night everything went down with the Monroes. I would've slashed your tires and tied you down until you came to your senses. Then I probably would've gone ballistic and gone down there myself to pick a fight."

"No you wouldn't have, Grandpa."

He scoffs at my remark. "You see me as a pacifist, Benny. And that's fine, because I am, now. But I'm not perfect. I drove to that house over a hundred times with my pistol. No one knows, and the Monroes never saw me because I always kept my distance. Thank God for that. But I learned something eventually. That house had a lot of pain and suffering in it. More than you and I would ever believe."

"Why do you say that? You don't know everything."

"I do know some of it, Benny. A few years after they burned our house down I was in town getting me a coffee at the diner. And you'll never guess who walked in and sat down with me."

I hold my breath, waiting for Grandpa. "Vern Manningham?" I ask, my insides cringing.

"No. It was Clarence's youngest son, Ricky Monroe. He saw me right away and sat at the other end of the diner, facing away from me. But I knew he saw me. Then, right as I finish up my coffee he comes over and asks to sit with me. I say nothing, but he sits down with me anyway. Then he does all the talking. He ends up telling me most of his life story. He said that when he was younger his mom and dad were in a serious car accident, which I knew about. But what I didn't know is the driver that hit them was a young black man that had too much to drink. And so his mama died when he was only seven. He says his daddy suffered a lot after the wreck. There was the constant neck and back pain to go along with the heartache. Apparently, it's what drove Clarence to drinking to dull the pain. It also drove him to hate people of color and join the Klan. I don't know how Clarence saw people before the accident. I probably should've asked. Maybe he was bred to be a racist from birth, or maybe he had it out for everyone of color after his wife was killed. But it doesn't matter. You see, he made the choice. He chose to not forgive. Remember that, Benny. It was Clarence Monroe's choice. Then he spewed that hatred, indoctrinating his boys to hate. And it's hard to not blame him. Because for most, it's easier to be angry than it is to forgive. Maybe Clarence saw his bigotry as some sort of justification for what that black man stole from him. But that's no life to live. And Ricky told me that his dad never knew how to show love or give love once his mama died. And that's not okay. That was the day I decided to not hate the Monroes anymore."

Grandpa pauses to catch his breath. "And the next day I drove to Clarence's house, walked up his front steps, and I apologized."

"What? For what?" I raise my voice in disbelief.

"Well, I said I'm sorry for the loss of his wife. And I told him I'm sorry for the loss of his son. Then I told him that I forgive him for doing what he did to all of us. And that was it. I left and he said nothing in return. The only other time I saw him is when Penny saw him."

"Penny saw him, too?" I can't hide the shock and hatred in my voice.

"Well, her situation was quite different. It was her own way of forgiving through helping. But I'll let her tell you that story when she's ready. Or, when you're ready to really talk to her and learn for yourself."

I run my hands over my face and cover my mouth. I want to scream, but I hold it in.

I can't believe what Grandpa is telling me. It's so out of the blue. And why would he forgive the most despicable human being we've ever met? Why couldn't he just let him be, and hate him for all eternity?

I already knew that Clarence and Ricky got off easy for committing perjury. I also knew that Clarence's health was vastly declining.

"Wait, is Clarence still alive?" I ask.

Grandpa nods his head. "As far as I know, he is. The perjury charges got waived a while ago after I told the prosecution we didn't want to file any suits. I figured he's suffered enough, just like the rest of us. All I can hope is he dies peacefully, without hate in his heart. It's what God would want for all of us."

"No! Fuck him, Grandpa!" I shout, suddenly standing over him with my fists balled up.

"Come on, Benny."

"No, Grandpa. I mean it. Fuck that guy and fuck the Monroe family! I hope he slowly dies in a pit of fire." I groan, shaking my head to rid myself of any thoughts of a happy ending for those assholes.

I just want Grandpa to hate those people as much as I do. I don't want revenge anymore. I hate these people on principle. Clarence Monroe has no regrets about what he did to our family. I just know it.

"I won't forgive Clarence, or any of his sons," I finally admit, unable to look Grandpa in the eyes.

"I didn't ask you to, Benny. You're a full-grown man now. The decisions you make are your own. But I will ask you to talk to Penny about what life was like once you went to prison."

"We have, kind of."

"No. You haven't," Grandpa replies, his tone suddenly cold.

I watch as he rubs the thick stubble on his cheek, staring daggers into my soul. His face slowly morphs into a scowl.

"What?" I finally ask, feeling confused.

"Benny, have you done the math?"

"The math? What do you mean?"

Grandpa raises his hand, then slaps at the air in frustration, gazing away from me. "You aren't stupid, Son. Talk to her. Do the goddamn math. That's all I'm going to say about that. Now please walk my old ass to the bathroom."

After getting Grandpa situated, I hear two loud honks from Penny's horn. Ms. Green signals that she can take it from here.

Outside I notice that Jimmy and Penny look apprehensive. Penny keeps glancing in my direction, and as I approach them she looks away, trudging away from me.

"Hey, good to see you," I say, my arms held out for a hug. Jimmy turns from me, walking away.

"Come on," Jimmy says, waving for me to come with him.

He's walking into the middle of the woods. Once I catch up, I look back at Penny wiping at her eyes. She quickly looks away as Ms. Green comes up to greet her with a hug.

"Hey, what's going on? Why are you walking so fast?" I ask him. Jimmy stares straight ahead, ignoring me.

"Okay. We can do it your way. I'll wait until you're ready. Penny told me you may have something important to tell me. I still don't get what's going on, but I'm ready when you are."

Jimmy doesn't even blink at my comment. He only picks up his pace, walking faster.

I'm trying to be patient. Everyone's been hinting at things that happened while I was gone. The only one who hasn't yet is Jimmy. But now he's acting weird as well.

I begin thinking about the short time I've spent with him since getting out of prison. He's been cold most of the time, and I deserved that treatment. But patience only lasts so long. Eventually people just need to shit or get off the pot.

"Stop!" I shout, grabbing his shoulder. He pulls away from me, slipping from my grip. I take another step toward him, and he swings at my face. I dodge his blow, which barely misses my chin.

"Hey! What the fuck, Jimmy! What was that for?"

His breathing becomes rapid. He scowls and grits his teeth. He's turning so red I can see veins popping out of his forehead.

"No, Benny! Fuck you! You know nothing about us!" he screams, spit flying out of his mouth.

I've never heard such rage in my brother's voice.

"We raised him! We did it for you! What have you done for us?" Jimmy hollers, pounding his chest.

Nothing he's saying makes sense, maybe because I'm too terrified to hear what he's really saying.

The words of others come back all at once, like an inescapable echo living in my head. Grandpa said I should do the math. Penny said I should read the letters. And Jimmy is telling me that "we" raised him, for me.

"Marcus?" I ask.

Jimmy nods his head, staring at me with hatred in his eyes.

"Marcus…is my son?" I ask, already knowing the answer.

Everything begins spinning: the trees, the ground, Jimmy, and even the sky. I fall to one knee, unable to catch my breath. I look up at Jimmy, who's still not saying a word. His silence answers my question.

Out of nowhere, it begins raining. The raindrops fall on my skin, but I barely feel them.

"I don't understand, Jimmy. Penny said Patrick is Marcus's father. She told me that the first day I got back. I believed her. Those were her words. Why would she lie about this?"

"I don't know, Benny."

"Then who's Patrick? Is he even real?" I beg. That's when Jimmy charges at me.

Instinctively, I put my hands up. But I'm too late for his right cross, which sends me face-first into the soil.

I let my body lay there in the mud. My hope is he'll keep on hitting me until I'm unconscious. It's what I deserve. But he doesn't.

Eventually I roll onto my side, wiping the blood from my nose. Jimmy just sits across from me, grimacing in pain. He slowly hunches over, hugging his stomach with utter despair. It's as if he's trying to cry, but can't.

I crawl over to him and put my hand on his shoulder. The second I touch him, he lets out a loud groan that turns into a whimper.

The tears come next, and they don't stop.

"Who's Patrick? Please tell me," I beg, trying to look into his eyes while he stares away. "Come on, Jimmy. You can tell me."

Jimmy takes a deep breath. Then he slowly lifts his head, narrowing his teary eyes on mine. "He was my boyfriend. I loved him so much. But now he's gone. And I miss him…*so much.*"

His voice crumbles into tears. This time the hurt is even deeper. I feel it suffocating my chest.

I hug my brother, not knowing what to do or say. I try to soothe him by rubbing his head. He's lost someone he loves dearly, something we both know too much about.

I never knew Jimmy was gay. I've known so few people in my life that are gay. But it doesn't matter who he chooses to love. Only one thing is certain, my brother was in love with this man. He still is. And if he loves him, then so do I. If he cries, I can cry too. His pain is my pain. He's my one and only. *My brother*!

Our warm embrace feels so soothing as the rain picks up. But the moment is so much bigger than just holding him in my arms. I've finally re-connected with the brother I knew before I went to prison. We've always needed each other growing up. And for the first time since getting out of prison, I can be there for him.

Eventually Jimmy leans back as the rain slows to a drizzle. He takes a swipe at his nose, and I reach into my pocket pulling out a Kleenex that's damp but still useful.

"Here, take it," I tell him.

After blowing his nose a few times he finally looks into my eyes. I suddenly realize what I've always known: Emotions have always been hard to understand for Jimmy. It's what makes him unique. But now, I think, he understands my confusion, my worry, and hopefully the reality that I do care. I always have and always will. But it means nothing, because since I've returned to his life, I've made one egregious mistake.

"Jimmy. I'm so sorry you lost your boyfriend. I am. I mean it. But I'm also sorry for being away from you guys for all these years. Shame is not an excuse for doing what I've done. And I should have been back here the second I got out of prison. I should have been here for you, Penny, Marcus, Patrick, everyone. But I wasn't. And I'm so sorry."

Jimmy squeezes my shoulder. His lips begin to tremble.

"Benny, I forgive you. But I also need to thank you. Because being there for Marcus meant the world to me and Patrick. I was never his father, but on some days, it felt like it. Me and Patrick did everything we could to help Penny raise that boy. Grandpa and Ms. Green helped, too. We loved him like a dad would. We loved him like you would've. But I know it's your turn now. So please, just do one thing for me."

"What is it? I'll do it, Jimmy. Just say the word."

"Please make things right with Penny. She still needs you. I just know it. And little Marcus needs both of you, together. It's been long overdue for Marcus to have his real dad."

Jimmy's words stick to my insides like a bee in honey. I don't think I can give Jimmy exactly what he wants. But I know I can give him some things. And I know I can give my all to Marcus.

Penny and I, on the other hand, are a different story despite our recent sexual encounter. There's no doubting I want to be with her. But can she ever truly forgive me for all I've done? And can I ever forgive myself?

I stare into Jimmy's green eyes as the rain drops drip off his eyelids. His eyes are full of so many thoughts and newfound emotions. He wants me to make a promise that changes things for all of us. But I can't do that. I can only do one thing for him.

"I'll try."

# CHAPTER TWENTY-SEVEN

## Penny

I wait by the window as Marcus tugs at my shirt, whining for attention.

"Not now, Marcus!" I shout.

I instantly regret my harshness, feeling like the worst mom.

Ms. Green takes him into her arms, leading him out of the room before he has a meltdown.

I'm a good mom, usually. But right now, I'm a nervous wreck. Jimmy said he was going to tell Benny everything. At first, I didn't believe him. But they've been gone in the woods for so long.

I should have never lied to Benny. It was stupid. But how do you explain something so complicated when you haven't seen someone for years? I love him and hate him with so much entangled passion.

It felt like the right thing to do at the time, telling him Patrick was the father. It was an out for him I'd thought he'd want anyway. I truly thought he didn't want any of us back in his life. But now I know that's no longer true. I have to rationalize hiding something so important from him.

The answer is rhetorical and simple. I still don't know what the fuck I'm doing. Maybe this is what love does to a girl—it makes them irrational and fucking crazy.

There they are, walking back through the trees, side-by-side. They're soaked to the skin and probably freezing, even though the rain has stopped. They still look like the same two kids I remember roaming the neighborhoods and backwoods of our old home. Except they're no longer boys.

As Benny takes a sharp turn toward the shed, Jimmy comes up the steps and walks into the house.

"Hey."

"Hey," he calmly replies. "Benny wanted me to tell you that he needs to collect his thoughts."

"Oh, okay," I mutter.

"I'm going to go play with Marcus," Jimmy says, walking right past me. I'm still frozen with shock.

*Ask him!*

"Wait, Jimmy!" I shout. He stops in the hallway, turning to look at me with an emotionless face. "Did you tell him?"

Jimmy nods his head.

"Everything?" I ask.

"He knows, Penny."

Before I can ask anything else, he's already disappeared into the hall. I hear Marcus screeching with excitement as he enters his bedroom.

I glance back at the shed and see Benny leaving it holding a saw and some other building supplies.

I run to the back window, watching him march out to the forest. He must be going to finish the treehouse.

Now I'm angry. I'm dying on the inside with anticipation. He just found out I lied to him. He just found out he's a father. There's also the fact that he just found out his brother is gay. So, where's he going?

I can't believe his selfishness. Why can't he at least say something to me? I need to know how he feels. But more importantly, I need to know what he wants. What are we going to make of this fractured life?

"Hey," Ms. Green says, startling me from behind.

"He knows. And now that asshole is just walking out to the woods to work on that stupid fucking treehouse. He hasn't changed one bit."

"You're wrong there," Ms. Green corrects me. "That boy is trying to turn his life around. And I'd say the news he just got is a lot to take in. Not to mention what your dad just told me. I guess he told Benny about the last time he went to make amends with the Monroes. So…." She pauses, letting out a loud exhale. "I'd say that boy has learned quite a bit in the last couple hours. Give him a little time."

My head bows down, shaking in sheer disbelief. Then I look at Ms. Green and just start laughing. I don't know why, but it's the only emotion I can express. Then I bite my tongue and march to the back door.

"Wait, Penny!" Ms. Green shouts, reaching for me. I pull away.

"Don't touch me!" I scream. "You don't know what you're talking about. You want me to give him time! Are you fucking crazy?"

"Calm down, Sweetie. I just—"

"Calm down! All I've given to that boy is time and space. And now he finds out he's a dad and thinks he can go lumberjack in the forest to burn off some steam. No! That's not happening!"

I rush out of the house as Ms. Green calls after me. But I don't care anymore. I'm a volcano ready to burst. And to think I almost slept with him the other night. What a mistake that would have been.

I have no clue what I'll say to Benny once I find him. All I want is for him to be out of my life, and Marcus's too. I know I can't take all of that away, but he deserves it. It's the only form of revenge I have left.

Revenge is a funny thing. Dad always said it's a never-ending cycle. He preached it well before he adopted me as one of his kin, and he loved reminding me on a regular basis while I was growing up. But fuck his sage advice. Fuck everything in my life!

I walk briskly up from behind Benny. His shirt is shirt off and he's busy sawing. He turns around with a look of indifference that only heightens my anger.

My hands fly to his chest with every bit of strength and anger I can muster. He falls backwards a couple steps but stays upright.

"What the fuck!" he shouts.

"What the fuck! What the fuck are you doing? You find out Marcus is your son and you come out here to blow off steam. Don't be a coward, Benny. Talk to me!" I scream, pouncing my chest. "I'm not waiting for you a second longer. It happens now!"

I watch his large adam's apple go inward as he contemplates his words. But nothing will change how I feel.

"I don't know, Penny," Benny says, bowing his head. "I don't know what to say."

I was right. He's a coward. He'll probably just tell me he needs to leave again for a while. But one thing is for sure. If he leaves us again, it'll be the last time I ever have anything to do with Benny McClain.

"I'm fucking in love with you, Penny! There! I said it!" He lets out a long exhale. "I think I always have been. But not the kind I feel toward a sister. And I can't shake this feeling any longer. But it means nothing. I just don't feel like I'm deserving of you. That's the problem. You deserve better than me—a lot better. And now that I'm a father, I just don't know what to do."

His green eyes become radiant with candor and sincerity. His stare sharpens into my soul, plucking at the threads that are barely holding my heart in place.

Every snarky reply I had is rendered useless by that four-letter word. It's something I've wanted to hear my whole life. And now I don't know what to do or say.

Every second of silence passing between us feels like an hour. Benny looks so sad. I can see the hopelessness killing him from the inside.

Wide-eyed, he takes two steps toward me, grabbing me by the arm. "Are you okay?"

That's when I notice I'm bleeding. The sleeve of my white shirt is blood-red, and I can see a small gash through the fabric just below my elbow.

"I'm so sorry. I think the saw got you by accident when you pushed me."

Benny quickly pulls off his belt, then grabs his shirt off the ground.

"How far is the closest hospital?" he asks.

"I don't know, like 25 minutes," I reply, feeling suddenly nauseous from all the blood.

Benny rips off the sleeve of my shirt and places his shirt over the wound. He begins tying the belt around it to help contain the bleeding. My arm throbs in agony the tighter he pulls.

"I have to pull it super tight, Penny. This is going to—"

"No! Stop it!" I scream. "It hurts!"

Ignoring me, Benny loops the belt over my shoulder and under my armpit and ties it off into a sling.

He puts his arm around my waist and begins leading me back toward the house.

"Relax, Benny. It's probably just going to be a few stitches."

He ignores me, hunching down to pick me up and sling me over his shoulders like a sack of potatoes.

"What the fuck!" I scream, pounding my fist on his back. But it's too late. There's no way I can squirm off with one functioning arm.

"You're too slow, Penny. We need to get you there quick. What if it gets infected? I don't want you to lose an arm."

I let out a long sigh, rolling my eyes as he quickens his pace. He's moving so fast it feels like he's gliding over the ground.

This doesn't feel real. Getting hurt like this is either a stupid accident or a humorous act by God, designed to make me spend more time with Benny.

I look through the trees and notice a half-built treehouse. It grows smaller as I hear Benny scream out commands. Then the treehouse, the one safe-haven I lost a long time ago, becomes lost once again in the distance.

# CHAPTER TWENTY-EIGHT

## Penny

"And that's it. Stitch number five should do it," Dr. Johnson explains. He stands up over the operating table and takes off his gloves. "Just sit tight for a few minutes. My nurse will be here in just a second to do one final cleaning of the wound and bandage you up so you can go home."

"Thank you."

The doctor smiles back, heading out of the room. As the door closes, Benny barges in.

I huff out a loud exhale, shaking my head.

"How are you feeling?" he asks.

"Well, they'll probably need to amputate my arm given the five stitches it took to sew up the wound."

Benny smiles and takes a seat without my invitation.

"I'm not allowed visitors."

"I don't care. You said we need to talk. Well, let's do it. I've got no weapons in my hand, unless you think I'll need one for self-defense."

I sigh again, shaking my head. "Where is everyone?"

"They're all down in the cafeteria," Benny replies, sliding his chair to my bedside.

He's right: We do need to talk. But I don't know what to say to him. I want to still be angry at him, but I've had so much time in this room to calm down and collect my thoughts. My mood swings feel ridiculous. Ever since Benny came back, I've gone from wanting to kill him to not wanting him to ever leave my side again. But there's one big problem with having him know he's Marcus's father: Wondering how our lives will ever make any sense.

I mean, we both live in different cities, 50 miles apart. I'm close to graduating. He's just beginning to live out his dream of playing football. And now Marcus is caught in the middle of it all. Maybe it's a good thing he's too young to understand all these complications. But he still needs a father in his life.

*But what do I need? Don't my needs matter, too?*

I can't take the silence a second longer. "Just tell me what you want from me, Benny."

"I don't know. What do you need from me?"

His question hangs awkwardly in the air. I don't have any magic answers, and neither does he.

"Can I ask you a question, even if it upsets you?" Benny finally asks.

"Sure."

"Why did you lie to me about Patrick being Marcus's father?"

I feel suddenly nauseous. I can't blame him for wanting to know. And now I can tell him because Jimmy's finally spoken his truths.

"It's complicated, Benny. But for a while there we thought you'd never come back into our life. And we kind of moved on. But not really. At least I never did. And Patrick was a father to little Marcus. He really was. But first Patrick fell in love with Jimmy. They worked at the same grocery store and started hanging out all the time. It was obvious pretty quickly that it was going to be romantic. And it was sweet, seeing the two of them together, and happy. Patrick was unique in his abilities, just like Jimmy. They helped each other in areas where the other one was lacking. And together the two of them helped me raise Marcus. It just happened with Marcus calling Patrick 'Dad' one day. Maybe I should have corrected him, but Patrick was just so proud. So, he eventually moved in with us and life just carried on. And then you came back into our lives again. I didn't think you'd stick around and I got scared, so I lied. I'm really sorry."

I watch Benny's face as he breathes in my words. This may not be the story he wanted, but it's our story. It's the truth that Patrick and Jimmy and I have lived.

"Was all of this in the letters to me?" he asks. "You know, about me being the actual father and Jimmy meeting Patrick."

I nod my head.

"Yes. That's what made me so angry. I thought you were actually reading them for so long and that you were just scared to write back. The day you told me you ignored every single one of my letters was the day you broke me. Then you told me to change my last name…" I stop, taking a deep breath. "But none of that matters anymore. Because now it's your choice, Benny. I'm just glad you finally know."

"What do you mean it's my choice?"

"Well, if you want to be a part of Marcus's life as, you know," I shrug.

"Penny, I'm not leaving you guys. Why would you even think I would? I want to be with Marcus. And I'm not asking. That's just the way it's going to be. I want to be his father."

I'm happy to hear that Benny wants to be a part of Marcus's life. Yet, something is still missing.

"What else do you want?" I ask.

Benny's lips tremble. His gaze at me becomes pensive. I can feel my lips trembling as well.

"I can't, Penny," he barely whispers. The ache in his words is palpable. "I mean, I want to. But you deserve better than me. My prison time scarred me. And even if we tried, I don't know how we could make it work. We're in different cities and different stages in our life. If we tried to be together...I just can't give what you deserve. We'll just have to find a way to share Marcus from a distance. For now."

My mouth is rendered useless. His words while honest, hurt the deepest parts of me. He may be thinking logically about all of our futures, but sometimes a girl doesn't want logic. She wants passion. I need his willingness, because I want Benny in my life.

"I'm sorry, Penny," he says, sniffling.

"No, you're right. I just had to ask. I mean, I can't stop thinking about what you said by the treehouse."

Benny grabs my hand. "I meant what I said, Penny. I love you. I think I love you a little too much, if that's possible. But that can't change our situation, and it can't change what I've done to you in the past."

"Then what do we do from here?" I beg.

"Well, I think we need to clear the air on some other things," he pauses, looking disturbed.

"What is it?"

"Well, Grandpa says you went and saw Clarence Monroe. Can I ask why?"

The flashback to that wretched man's face makes me nauseous. I take two deep breaths.

"I didn't go see him. It was all an accident," I say, suddenly feeling stuck. "I ran into him in town awhile back. He had a heart attack in the street. It all happened so fast."

I start to cry, picturing that vile man up close, his cracked lips on mine. I can still taste the nicotine on his breath.

"Penny, I don't understand. What happened?"

I feel lost, staring at Benny. *So lost.* It's not that I regret what I did. I just don't know how he'll react.

*Just say it!*

"I saved his life!" I blurt out. Benny's face goes pale.

"How?"

"I gave him CPR. There were people all around just standing there, doing nothing. I only did it because it felt like the only thing I could do. And I revived him. He may not have deserved my help, but I couldn't live with the guilt of watching any person die before my eyes."

Benny lets go of my hand, looking at me with disgust and disappointment.

"I hate what I did, Benny. But I don't regret it."

Benny says nothing. Then he quickly walks out of my hospital room, leaving me alone, yet again.

# CHAPTER TWENTY-NINE

## Penny

### *3 days later*

The last of the paperwork is signed. Leaving this hell hole is a huge relief. It's been three days since I told Benny about saving Clarence Monroe.

After he left, the nurse noticed some swelling around my wound. It got worse, so they loaded me up with more powerful antibiotics and ran tests to make sure it wasn't a tetanus infection. Luckily it wasn't, and the swelling slowly went away after two days. They kept me overnight for one more day to make sure I was safe to go home today.

It's a relief knowing I'll be okay. Yet, ever since Benny left, every breath I take hurts. I'm lost about how to go back to living my life now that he knows everything.

I've already spoken with Sarah. She's coming down later today to help me with Dad for the next week. My hope is that after the next couple weeks, he'll be strong enough to be on his own. Then I can officially move on with my life, without Benny in it.

The drive home from the hospital is long. We're all sad that Jimmy had to go home and get back to work, especially Marcus. On the drive home, Dad tries talking to me about a conversation he had with Benny that morning, but I shut him down quickly. I figure if Benny doesn't care about us, why should I care about him anymore?

----

Once I'm back at Dad's house, I try to stay as busy as possible. Ms. Green must feel the same way. We mop, wipe and scrub almost every square foot of the house. We have the time because Dad's taking a long nap.

Afterward, we head out to the porch to relax and read. Sarah is out exploring with Marcus. Having my best friend here is a godsend. It's more than just her companionship. I also need a break.

Marcus has been so mopey since we got back. When he's not moping, he's constantly badgering me for attention and explanations on things I cannot answer. But I can't blame him. He misses the men in his life.

I already snapped at him earlier when he wouldn't stop asking about Benny. It was stupid to take my frustrations out on him, but I just can't get rid of these anxious feelings.

My life feels like a broken compass, every path and direction leading to more emptiness. Furthermore, everyone around me is walking on eggshells. None of it is fair. I just want to breathe and not feel the hurt anymore. But I feel hopeless.

"Mommy! Mommy! Mommy!" Marcus keeps shouting as he sprints up the porch steps. I put my book down because he won't stop hopping up and down like a pogo stick.

"Slow down, Sweetheart. What's going on?"

"The treehouse! The treehouse! It's so big! I want to live there! Come on, Mommy! Please, please, please," he repeats, tugging on my shirt.

"Wow! Did Benny really build that?" Sarah asks, walking up the porch steps.

I look at Ms. Green. Her eyes stay glued to her book, but she flashes a quick grin.

"Wait," I say. "He finished building it? Is he here?"

"He was," Ms. Green replies, still staring at her book.

"Come on, Mom. Let's go look at it," Marcus begs.

I follow him toward the treehouse. Once I'm halfway down the steps he's already sprinting the quarter mile to get there.

"I'll hang back for a bit," Sarah hollers.

The walk to the treehouse feels odd for some reason. I'm feeling apprehension and something else. Maybe it was that brief grin from Ms. Green. Or maybe it's how everyone has been so quiet around me since we got back.

Then I see it at the top of the hill, peeking out at me through the pine trees.

Memories instantly flood my psyche. There's so many of them at once. I can't believe what I'm seeing.

The closer I get, the more the color stands out. It's so red it begins to overwhelm my memories. My mind flashes back to the one place I escaped to so many times as a kid. It's the place where Benny learned everything about me, and I learned so much about him. But more than anything, the treehouse is the birthplace of my love for Benny McClain.

Once I get to the base of the tree, I slowly climb my way up the ladder and crawl through the opening. Marcus is in his own world, digging through what looks like a treasure chest filled with endless, brand-new toys. I gaze around the treehouse. Finding words to describe what I'm seeing feels impossible. The outside was gorgeous, but the inside is otherworldly. Almost every detail is identical to the treehouse we once had.

I smell the fresh coat of varnish on the walls and ceiling. There's a sign in one of the corners that reads "Penny's Nook." Nearby, there's a bookshelf full of books. Next to it is a brand-new wicker rocking chair, almost identical to the one I once had. Even the reading lamp, coffee table, and daybed all look about the same. There are even glow-in-the-dark stickers scattered around everywhere, just like I remember.

Everything feels brand-new and immaculate. It's like I've traveled back in time. Yet, something doesn't make sense. This treehouse was half-built at best before I got hurt. There's no way Dad helped. And there's no way Benny could have done all of this in 72 hours. Nor is it possible he would want to do such a thing.

I keep circling around the room, noticing so many small details both in the layout of the treehouse and the overall floor plan. It feels so homey. Then I notice a basket with a bow in the nook area. I remove the ribbon and tissue paper, wrapped around a stack of hundreds of envelopes.

"Oh my god!" I screech.

Every single letter is open. All of them are addressed in my handwriting to Benny McClain at Montgomery Penitentiary.

Then I notice a single envelope, taped to the handle of the basket with a note on it.

**To Penny. Please read.**

The envelope looks brand new, unlike the hundreds of other envelopes in the basket. I slowly open it, taking a seat in my rocking chair.

**Dear Penny,**

**I'm sorry for my reaction at the hospital. Processing so many life-changing things in a 24-hour period didn't bring out the best in me. But on my way home I ran into someone I never expected to see. It felt like a curse at first. But perhaps some curses aren't always what they seem to be.**

**This chance encounter has given me a new perspective on what's important in life. And what's important is loving and living in the moment. You see, I've already missed too many moments in my life. I'm done with that. I'm finally ready for today, and more todays to come.**

**Living in the moment means being vulnerable, knowing it's okay to fail. Because to know how to truly love is to also**

know how to forgive. You taught me that. And forgiveness within myself will allow my love to flourish with no bounds.

All of your beautiful letters have now been read. I'm finally able to understand what you've been through and why you worked tirelessly to keep in touch with me. My only hope is that it never felt like an obligation. Because even if Marcus never came into this world, it wouldn't change how I feel about you. Nothing could ever alter my feelings for you.

The blessings have been in front of me all along. I have Marcus, OUR beautiful son. I have the blessings of Ms. Green and Grandpa, loving me like their own son. Then I have my amazing brother. I can finally see how Jimmy and Patrick did more than help raise Marcus. They also supported you through so much.

All that's left is winning you back. I want you in my life. I'll fight for you, protect you, and do everything within my power to support your dreams. But most importantly, I'll never stop loving you, if you'll let me in one more time.

My path to closure is currently in progress, but I hope to see you very soon. And when I'm back, I promise to give you all of my heart, and at the same time, hope you'll give me the blessing of yours.

Love Always,

Benny McClain

I read the letter again and again, tears flowing out of me the whole time. My heart is trying to decipher so many things at once. But perhaps some things don't need to make sense yet.

What's most important now is that Benny sees me as Penny McClain. He didn't write this letter to his adopted sister. He wrote it to the mother of his child, and a woman he's madly in love with.

The words written here are to the same girl that could never stop loving him, no matter what. And he loves me in the truest sense possible. I finally *feel it*. He wants to love me like I want to love him. For eternity.

# CHAPTER THIRTY

## Benny

My clammy hands are sticking to the steering wheel, and my heart is pounding. The final turn to my destination leaves so much out of my control.

I park my truck and close my eyes. The memories flood my mind: The sound of a fist pummeling a skull. The sound of a single gunshot whizzing past my head. The sounds of clanking chains and the helpless feeling of living life constrained by shackles. Wishing these memories away forever is not possible.

The anger still lives inside me. I can't deny that. But today the anger feels different. The metaphorical shackles on my soul feel less permanent, and a little less constraining.

I'm at Monroe Farms for one reason, and one reason only: to break free.

I walk up to the front door, noticing little things on my way. The wooden porch creaks loudly as I walk on it. The wood exterior looks dry and dilapidated. Even the paint is fading and chipping off. The other difference is I don't recognize any of the cars parked out front.

I knock loudly on the screen door and take three steps back. The door slowly unlatches as goosebumps electrify my body.

"Hi," the most innocent sounding voice says.

The little girl has a head full of long blond hair. She leans her face up to the screen door. "Who are you?" she says with a sour look.

"Um, is your mommy or daddy here?" I ask, trying to soften my voice.

Then a woman appears. "Hi. Can I help you?"

"Yes. I'm Benny McClain. You guys were expecting me today."

The woman just tilts her head at an angle, causing her long dark hair to fall over her shoulder. It's then I notice the stethoscope around her neck.

"Let me go talk to them. Give me a moment, please."

"Of course."

The woman dashes away while the little girl remains, frozen like a statue, still looking up at me.

"What's your name, Sweetie?" I ask, kneeling down to her eye level.

"Brooklyn," she whispers, looking suddenly shy.

"That's a beautiful name. Are you from New York?"

"What's a New York?" she asks, frowning at me.

I giggle under my breath as the dark-haired lady reappears.

"You can come in, Benny," she says, her arm welcoming me into the house.

I step inside as the little girl dashes away, giggling.

"Just have a seat in the living room. They'll be down in just a moment."

I take a seat on the couch and look around the room. All the walls are vacant of decorations, except for the one behind me. I stand up to take a closer look at the framed photograph there. It's a picture of Ricky Monroe and a woman with bright blond hair. He has one arm around her waist and the other over her pregnant belly.

"Hey, Benny," the voice startles me from behind.

I turn around. Standing six feet away with his hands in his pockets is Ricky Monroe.

"Thanks for coming. Can I get you something to drink?"

"No, thanks," I reply, clearing my throat.

"Please, have a seat," Ricky gestures toward the couch. I sit.

"Um, thanks for coming."

I nod my head, again looking around the room. He's already thanked me for coming. This feels awkward sitting in this house while he's being so hospitable. I still don't even know why he wanted me to come over when I ran into him at the hospital a couple days ago. And I still don't know why I was so quick in agreeing to this.

"John will be down in just a second. Can I ask you something?"

"Sure," I reply.

"Did you know we've been looking for you, for quite some time?"

I quickly shake my head no.

"I didn't think so," he says, rubbing his hand along his chin, deep in thought. "It's so odd how I finally ran into you at the hospital."

"I don't understand. Why were you looking for me?" I ask.

His mouth opens. Then our attention is drawn to the creaking of the stairs. Down walks a large man I think I remember. Then I see his blond hair, except it's much shorter than I recall. But it can only be one person.

*John Monroe!*

I quickly stand up. Maybe it's my protective nature taking over like a reflex. He regards me calmly and keeps walking towards me, extending his arm in my direction.

"Benny," John nods his head.

I look down at his hand. It seems premature to shake this man's hand without knowing why he wants to see me. But he refuses to back down, so I shake his hand anyway. My squeeze over his hand is harder than I've ever given a handshake in my life. But he needs to know I'm not scared, even if that's a lie.

John takes a seat, giving a quick glance at Ricky.

"Why did you guys want me to come here?" I finally blurt out.

Ricky nods his head at John, who opens his mouth to speak. He's interrupted by a scream from behind.

Another blond haired three-foot-tall beauty runs into the room and tackles John's knees. She looks quite a bit younger than Brooklyn. Her pacifier flies into John's lap. Another woman runs into the living room, swooping the little girl into her arms.

"I'm so sorry," she whispers apologetically.

I quickly stand up. "It's okay. Who are you? My name's Benny McClain."

"Oh, excuse me. I wanted to give you guys privacy. But I'm Tiffany Monroe. I'm John's wife," she says, quickly shaking my hand.

"Nice to meet you, ma'am. And no worries on the little one interrupting us. I got one of my own, so I understand."

She smiles back, pulling the little girl up to her hip.

I notice John nodding his head for her to leave. She smiles at me one more time before scampering out of the room.

"You have kids?" John asks, looking surprised.

"I do. A little boy."

"How? You know what, never mind. Benny, there's a reason we asked you to come here today. Well, actually there's a couple reasons."

John clears his throat again, looking even more nervous.

I look at Ricky as he gets up from his chair to go sit next to John. He puts his hand on his shoulder while John rubs his temples. Then John locks eyes with me.

"Benny, have you heard of the term 'shell-shocked'?" John asks.

"Um, not really."

"Well, I fought in Nam. I did two years in that jungle. And I've seen things that I wish I could un-see, if you get my drift."

I nod my head, seeing the pain in John's face. But I still don't understand why Ricky was so adamant about having me come here today. What does his brother's suffering from the war have to do with me?

John clears his throat. "I've been seeing someone to help me process the things I want to forget. I would have never done counseling if not for my wife, but I've been doing it. And it's been helping with the shell shock. And the thing is, it's brought some other memories out of me. The one's I've been trying to bury away for quite some time now. But I just don't, um…I—"

"I don't understand," I interrupt.

"Tell him, John," Ricky encourages his brother, rubbing his shoulder.

John bows his head and takes a long breath in and out, then locks eyes with me.

"It's about the night you came here. You know, after we did what we did at your house. You see, I wasn't unconscious when my dad hit you with the butt of his gun. I was definitely dazed. But I know what I saw. And it's the exact same thing Ricky saw. That gun went off the second the butt of that gun flew into your head, and that shot killed my brother. I know you know this already. But you need to know that I'm culpable for the prison time you served. I may have convinced myself otherwise by living in my own denial that I was knocked out cold. But I saw what happened. And I just laid there, pretending to be unconscious while my daddy was screaming for Terry to wake up."

He pauses again. "I'll never forget that scream, for as long as I live. I'll take that with me to the grave because I'm just as much to blame as any one of us. I just needed you to know that. And I need you to know that I'm a changed man. And I'm incredibly sorry for all I've done to you and your family. You don't need to forgive me because I know I don't deserve it. But I just need you to know that I'm sorry. I'm truly sorry, Benny."

I look into his eyes with astonishment as another tear drips down John Monroe's face. He quickly wipes it away, sniffling to try and catch his breath.

The last thing I remember of John Monroe is me smashing that rock across his head. I really did think I knocked him out cold, or maybe even killed him. It's all my memory knows of him, not this demoralized, sorrowful person staring back at me.

"Keep going, John," Ricky says, patting his shoulder.

*There's more?*

John sits up taller, clearing his throat again and taking another deep breath.

"When I was in Nam, I fought next to the people I was groomed to hate. I didn't know any better. Not that it's an excuse, but I just believed what my daddy said growing up. But something changed in me over there. I had one black fella in my platoon named Damon. He was my Sargent. And he was an older fella that I kept my distance from at first. Man, I hated taking orders from him. But I had no choice. And a couple months into my tour, something happened in the jungle. We were getting massacred from both sides and our platoon got separated. Me and another private were basically in a fishbowl waiting to die. It felt like we were surrounded at all angles. I eventually just threw myself flat on the ground playing like I was dead after I took a couple bullets in my arm and back. I figured it was my only chance. But the next thing I know I hear our gunfire coming to life and my Sargent yelling for us. Then Damon, by himself, dragged my ass out of there while my surviving platoon mates laid down heavy fire. He dragged my ragged ass about a hundred yards, saving my life. The other private didn't make it. The next day I went to thank him, and you know what he told me? He said, 'Don't thank me, Johnny Boy.' That was his nickname for me. He said he was my brother. But he didn't just say it, Benny. *He meant it.* A black man that had known me for maybe a couple months risked his life for mine and called me his brother. He didn't know all the terrible things I've done to people like him. And I didn't deserve to live that day. But I did. And now I get to wake up every single morning with my wife in the same bed as me. I get to see the beautiful smile of my baby girl. And it's all because of a black man. But I no longer see him as a black man. I only see Damon as one thing: *my brother*."

John stops suddenly and shoves his hand over his mouth. I just sit there as more tears streams down his face.

The old me would enjoy watching this man suffer through his demons. But I only feel one thing towards John: complete and utter sympathy. It's all too much to process at once.

"I need to step outside for a moment," I finally mutter, standing up quickly.

The two of them stare as I hurry past them. Once outside, I collapse on the porch railing, trying to catch my breath. My heart feels like it's going to explode out of my chest. The screen door opens behind me.

John hands me a glass of water.

"Thanks," I mutter, still trying to catch my breath.

I take a long drink and look into his eyes. I forgot how tall he is.

"There's another reason we brought you here, Benny. I don't know how to explain this. But we want to give you something. It doesn't right what we've wronged. But we feel it's something we need to do. And we sure hope you'll accept it on behalf of our family. It's to all of you, including Ms. Penny."

He holds out an envelope to me, and I take it with reluctance.

It's the way he said her name. A woman this very man once called a nigger. Now he refers to Penny with so much respect in his voice.

*Ms. Penny?*

"You know what she did, don't you?" I ask.

John quickly nods his head. "I do. She saved my dad's life. I know he may not have deserved more time on this earth after what he did. But believe it or not, he's a different man now. The memory loss has changed him into a different person. He's also gotten more time with his grandchildren. He's even apologized to me and Ricky for the type of father he was."

John bows his head and shakes it side to side.

"That sister of yours did something incredibly selfless. I still can't believe it. But we're thankful to be getting more time with our dad. You see, even with his memory going in and out, we've made peace on a lot of unspoken strife in our family. If I ever see her again you better believe I'll thank her."

John's voice breaks and he quickly disappears into the house. I look at the blank envelope with the words "McClain Family" written on it. I tear it open and pull out a check.

The screen door squeals open again, but I can't tear my eyes from the long line of zeros staring back at me.

"We don't want it, and we don't need it," Ricky says. "We took your home from you, and a lot more. It's the least we can do, for now."

"I can't take this," I tell him. "It's not happening."

"Yes, you can," Ricky says. "And you will. Whether you need it or not, we know a family with a heart like yours will make good use of it. Besides, you got a son now. Pay for his college, invest it, or talk it over with your family and decide together what you'll do with it."

"Ricky, this is seventy-five thousand dollars! Our house was maybe worth half that when it burned down. Plus, Grandpa got the insurance money. We don't need it."

"Like I said!" Ricky raises his voice. "You all will find a good use for it. We trust you. And we're so sorry for what we've done. Especially to you, Benny. Now go on now. Just take it before I change my mind."

Ricky quickly turns around to head inside.

I look down at the check one more time to see if I'm reading it correctly. It's then I notice the signature on the check.

"Wait!" I shout.

"What?"

"The signature on this check. It's signed by your—"

"Dad agreed to it," Ricky says. "It may have not been his idea, but he agreed to it when we reminded him of all we've wronged. Then we reminded him what your sister did in saving his life. Then he didn't hesitate. He signed that check a few seconds later."

"But Ricky. Is he of sound mind?"

"He was a couple weeks ago when he signed the check. But now he's not awake much."

"So the lady with the stethoscope. That's his nurse."

Ricky nods his head.

"Yep. That's his hospice nurse. He's upstairs sleeping. He's not doing so well. They said he'd pass away a couple nights ago. But that heart of his just keeps ticking away. He always was a stubborn old asshole."

I don't know what to say as Ricky stares at the ground.

"Can I talk to him?" I blurt out.

"Are you sure? I mean, you can if you want. But he's likely asleep still."

I nod while trying to swallow back the throbbing tension in my throat. It's a weird feeling to regret what I've asked, but at the same time knowing I can't back down.

"Come on." Ricky waves me in.

I follow him up the creaky stairs as Brooklyn races by me. Ricky shouts at her to slow down, but she's in her own world. When we make it to the top floor, Ricky walks into the first room. I pause at the doorway, not ready to go in just yet. I can see John and Ricky sitting at their father's bedside.

I try to calm my nerves with deep breaths, but it's useless. It's time to just face this demon.

I walk into the room and face the bed, looking down at Clarence Monroe's emaciated face. He has an oxygen mask over his mouth and nose. His head slumps to the side the slightest bit. His chest moves faintly up and down.

The wrinkles and splotches on his pale skin make it plain to see: This man is dying through his last breaths.

"What does he remember?" I ask, unable to hide the fear in my voice.

"Not much now," Ricky says. "But when we tell him about things, I feel like he remembers some of it. It's either that or he's just trying to oblige us. We're not sure."

"I need you two to leave the room. Can you do that for me?"

When they say nothing, I walk to the closest window and look out at their farm. I can hear the brothers murmuring behind me, but I can't make out what they're saying.

"The room is all yours. We'll give you a few minutes," Ricky finally says.

"Thanks," I whisper as they leave.

I take the seat closest to Clarence. I watch the mask fog a little with each straining breath. His eyes twitch every now and again, like he's lost in a dream. But his chest is the part of him I can't stop staring at. I can't help but wonder when his last breath will be.

My wonderment has me thinking about the last few months for the Monroe family. I've only been given pieces of their story, but the brothers speak of their dad in a way of finding peace and closure. It's the opposite of what I've always wanted—until maybe today.

The strength to utter a single word feels like moving mountains. I clear my throat over and over again, and close my eyes, picturing the beauty of one woman. I picture her chocolate skin, her smiling face, and the aura of her kind spirit. Then it happens. I feel what I need most in this fleeting moment: Penny's courage.

"I know you're about to die, Mr. Monroe. And I can't tell you how badly I've always wanted you to suffer. Perhaps it's because you always wanted me and my family to suffer. I guess that's the definition of revenge, right? I don't know why you hated certain people like you did. My grandpa thinks you suffered a lot. But he also thinks you should be forgiven. So does everyone in my family, I think. And I don't know if I can do that and truly mean it. But I know I can try."

I'm suddenly startled. His head moves slightly, side to side, and his eyes crack open. I lower my face, hoping he can see me. The closer my face leans in, the more his pupils dilate. He takes a loud, wheezing breath, then another. I lean my ear closer and closer to his dying mouth.

"I...I...am...ssss...sorry."

I slide my chair away from him, looking at his still half-opened eyes while he's gasping for life.

He was unconscious the whole time I was talking to him. I was sure there's no way he could hear me. But now he's awake. He's looking at me like he heard every last word I said. And he just uttered the three words that will change who I am, and who I want to be, *forever*.

Not knowing what to do or say, I stand up tall. It feels good to look down on him as a lightness settles over me. My lungs open up fully for the first time. The shackles within me unlock, falling to the ground with more weight than I've ever imagined. I look at this man and can tell, by the look in his eyes, that he meant what he said. He is *truly sorry*.

"I forgive you. Please go in peace," I say, my whole-body tingling.

I walk out of the room knowing I never need to be back here. I never need to see any of these people again. I am free.

When I get to the front door I notice the collection of people in the living room. There's kids and family members, most of whom I don't know. But as I put my hand on the doorknob, I feel the eyes of John and Ricky Monroe on me. I turn to look at them, sitting side-by-side with their children in their arms. I feel the need to say one more thing.

"Ricky, John." I stop to catch my breath. "I'm sorry about your brother. And I want you to know I've just forgiven your father for what he's done. And I want you two to know that I forgive you. Please live your lives with your beautiful families. And please know I no longer have hate in my heart for you people. I want you and your family to just promise me one thing.

You live the rest of your lives with kindness in your heart and not one worry about the McClain family. We all forgive you.”

I drive away from Monroe Farms for the last time. I take one final glance into my rear-view mirror. Their house slowly disappears behind a pluming cloud of dirt and dust, and I can feel my world shifting from darkness to light.

As I drive to Grandpa’s, I think about fatherhood. It’s a piece of my life that’s been nothing more than a jumble of puzzle pieces, connecting and disconnecting.

I barely knew my father. Then my grandfather took over that role and did his best. It’s a role I’ve accepted and denied from him over and over again. And now I have the opportunity to hopefully embrace that role with Marcus.

The Monroe kids on the other hand didn’t get a fair shake with their father. But at least they’ve said their goodbyes and made their peace with him—something they’d never have if not for Penny’s bravery. She gave them final moments like today. Yet, she lives her own life, not knowing how courageous it was to give that man a few extra breaths. And it’s given me the chance to be free of the poison that’s controlled my heart and mind for far too long.

Her kindness leaves me wondering about the pieces to the puzzle that make up her life.  She’s had an equally difficult upbringing but survives each day with such grace and beauty.

I pull up to Interstate 59 knowing I’m only about 30 miles from Grandpa’s place. There’s so much I have to share with Penny. But instead of going south, I turn north, heading away from Grandpa’s house—not to be a hero, but to be like Penny McClain. To be selfless.

# CHAPTER THIRTY-ONE

## Penny

The four of them drive off. The dirt kicks up. The fishing rods jingle around the bed of the truck as I wave at Marcus. He frantically waves back with a beaming smile. He's so excited to go fishing with his grandpa, Ms. Green, and Sarah.

I wanted to go with them, but they were adamant about me staying behind. The truth is I don't want to be alone for the next few hours. But I guess they wanted to give me a break.

I walk into the house and aimlessly look around. Dinner is already made for tonight. My homework is already done. Even the house is clean as a whistle. I'm bored for the first time in forever.

I'm excited to head home next week and get back to normal. Dad's progress has been quite dramatic over the last few days. The help he once needed with simple tasks around the house are now things he does on his own, albeit a slow pace.

We're still going to have a nurse come help for a few more weeks, but I'm excited to get back to my studies. My teachers were able to mail me all of the work I needed for the first week of school. Now, getting through this final semester and being a teacher feels closer than ever. I could be student teaching as early as next fall.

Things seem good for most of the McClains. However, one thing is still clearly missing: Benny. His note was a relief at first, but with each passing day I get more anxious. I need him back.

It's been a week since he left me in the hospital. All I know is he's had some communication with Dad. Dad told me the other day that he's taking care of some important family business. He wouldn't elaborate any further.

The letter he left me in the treehouse said many beautiful things. But the part that stands out is him searching for closure. The specifics of that could be many things. But I figure he'll tell me when the time is right. What our life will look like from there is anybody's guess.

I decide to go on a long walk because I need some fresh air. It's the one thing that helps settle my racing brain. I do my usual three-mile route. The only difference is I finish my walk at the treehouse.

I've been up here with Marcus for a couple hours every day for the last few days. It feels weird being up here on my own. I sit on the day bed and crack open a book. The silence is odd but also refreshing. The only sound is the whistling, melodic breeze blowing through the trees.

It's astonishing what this confining space above the ground gives me. It's more than just safety. It allows me to recharge my battery. It helps me remember what it felt like to be in Benny's arms up here. Those are the kind of memories I want to relive every single day.

I lay down and let my mind drift away. The first place my mind wanders is the night I lost my virginity. We never got to finish what we started, but I guess we did it long enough to create Marcus.

The thought of him powering over my naked, fully exposed body ignites all the best feelings within me. But the act of sex is not what I remember most. It was the desire in his eyes. The look of lust and hunger over my naked body. It was bigger than need and want, it was love.

----

The faint squeaking of a chair has my eyes cracking open. I turn away, trying to keep my eyes sewn shut. But my senses did more than just hear. They saw a faint silhouette.

I quickly sit up, sliding myself backwards to flinch away. I blink a few times because this doesn't feel real. The man in the rocking chair is the same man I was just dreaming of.

"So, what do you think? Paul and I finished it," Benny says, gesturing around the room as he comes to sit next to me.

I quickly dive into his arms without a second thought. Hugging him feels like the most natural reflex. I squeeze his hardened body, hearing the air leave his lungs. I don't care if I'm hurting him. His closeness is the final antidote to everything I need in my life.

"I missed you," I softly whisper. My lips brush across his ear for a split second. The smell and taste of him is overwhelming.

He breathes in the scent of my neck, while I do the same to his. He leans back to look in my eyes.

"I missed you more," he admits, his tone full of sincerity.

"And I'm sorry, Penny. I'm sorry I left so suddenly. But it turned out to be a blessing. You'll never believe who I ran into at the hospital the day I left you."

"Who?"

"Ricky Monroe."

"What do you mean? What happened?"

"He said he's been looking for me. And he said I need to come to Monroe Farms to talk to him and John. He looked so desperate. And I don't know why, but I said yes. I went there a couple days later, and we talked. They reminded me that you saved Clarence Monroe's life. They said it allowed them to make peace with their father. And it also gave them the opportunity to give their kids more time with their grandpa. You gave them that, Penny. You did that."

"So you're not mad at me?" I whisper.

Benny shakes his head.

"I was at first, but now I'm not. If anything, you should be mad at me. I'm so sorry for how I reacted. But now I truly see what you've done, and what you've given to others, including me. And I realized, it doesn't matter what people deserve. It matters that we do the right thing when the opportunity arises. Your selfless actions are what drove me to go see them. But there's more, Penny."

Benny leans in closer and his hand tightly grabs hold of mine.

"They apologized to me. All three of them."

"What do you mean, all three of them?"

"Ricky, John, and even Clarence. The crazy thing is Clarence is in rough shape. He was basically on his deathbed. And for all I know his very last words were an apology to me, and all of the McClains."

I feel my body tingling from head to toe. My heart feels like a live drum beating beneath my chest. I have so many more questions, but I'm too awe-struck to speak.

"Say something, Penny," he begs.

"I don't know what to say," I mutter, feeling out of breath. "What did you say when they apologized?"

Benny smiles. But this is no ordinary smile. There's a residual pain in it.

Then he bows his head down to collect his breath. His head slowly tilts up until his crying eyes find mine. I feel the heat and moisture build up in my face. Then Benny straightens his posture, breathing out a loud breath.

"I told them I was sorry for the loss of their brother. Then I told them I forgive them, that we all forgive them. And that I want them to live their life with kindness and no guilt. Then I left, knowing I never have to return. I did it, Penny."

Our bodies collide into the perfect embrace. The hug is so desperate, our hearts so close to one another that letting go is impossible.

"I'm so proud of you. But Benny, you need to be proud of yourself!" I shout into his ear, feeling his arms go tighter around my body.

We soak in each other's tears. I feel the weight coming off his shoulders, and mine to. But it's more than just relief. Between Benny's broad shoulders is the showcasing of his true heart. It's all I've ever wanted, and now it's all mine.

Our hands begin moving over each other's backs. Then I let my hands dig through his fluffy brown hair. I lift my face above his ear to breathe in the scent of his scalp.

Benny's hands begin touching more and more of me. I do the same to him, not caring what part of him I touch. I want every last bit of him, and he wants all of me.

Everything happens fast, but it feels right. His hands massaging my breasts. My hands on his hardened stomach and chest. I want so badly to kiss him, but I can't. Not yet.

I suddenly pull away from his touch. Benny gives me an apologetic look.

"I'm so sorry, Penny. I should have asked for permission."

"I want this, Benny. I want you. But not without assurances. We have no plan for tomorrow. Marcus has a father he desperately needs that lives an hour away from him. If we do this, it only complicates things. I just need something more from you. I don't know what the solution is...."

My voice trails off, not knowing how to continue.

I close my eyes, trying to will the proper words to come. But then I feel his warm hands over mine once again. They squeeze into me as I envision his hands delicately wrapping around my heart. I open my eyes, and his loving gaze takes my breath away, yet again.

"Penny, I'm not leaving your side, ever again. You hear me. You're coming with me. We're going to live together, not as brother and sister. We're going to make a life for our family. And I'm not taking 'no' for an answer. You hear me."

"But Benny—"

"We'll work it out, my love. You'll transfer your credits over. We'll have more money than you'll ever need. Please, Penny. Let me be with you. Let me fall deeper in love with you. Because I choose you, and Marcus. I want to love you so deeply. And I want your heart, all of it, until it takes its very last beat."

His words break through my core, leaving me stunned. Instead of responding with words I let my lips fall onto his.

Our clothes are off in a matter of seconds. All of his bare weight goes on my chest and hips. Our tongues taste each other's lips and mouth with life-or-death desire. The moans we share are years of pent-up need for lust.

Benny rolls me on my side, spreading my legs. His girthy fingers lather over my clit. He slips one finger in to tease me, then slides his fingers out and goes back to my clit with more pressure. I can feel it engorge to his touch. The wetness inside me is now all over his fingers. It feels too good!

Benny's lips go back to caressing mine as his fingers continue to brush over my clit. The combination of touches has me craving to suck his dick. But I can't leave when it feels this good.

Then his mouth comes off my lips. He flips his body around until his face rests over my pussy. In the blink of an eye his cock is inches from my mouth, begging to be sucked. The only option is satisfying my hunger.

I slurp over the tip of his cock while my other hand strokes it. The saliva spills naturally out of my mouth as he moans louder. Meanwhile his tongue continues to do it's magic over my clit, making me moan. The better it feels the deeper I try choking down his dick.

Then it shocks the back of my throat. His cum explodes into my mouth with no end in sight. But I don't care. I keep sucking the tip of his cock until I've swallowed him dry.

"I'm sorry," he whispers, still gasping to catch his breath

"It's okay. We got time. They won't be back—"

"Until 6," Benny interrupts, his smile suddenly mischievous. "I know. I helped plan their little fishing trip so we can get some time alone. Here, Penny. Lean back, spread your legs, and get comfortable."

My insides simmer again to the confidence and controlling nature in his voice. He desperately wants to pleasure me.

Benny's fingers spread me open as his mouth breathes heavily over my clit, letting his lips and tongue barely brush over. I watch his eyes staring intently at mine, seeking a reaction for where I like his mouth to touch. Each time he teases my clit it sends an electric wave of euphoria through every part of me.

Then I lean up, grabbing him by the back of his head, pulling him into me. I stare at his tongue while it lightly massages my clit. Then it brushes along and around the inside of my labia as he slips his finger back inside me.

Seeing him taste me up close is unlike anything. At times I have to pull away and catch my breath. But eventually he can't stop. I feel him hit the perfect angles on my clit with a more intense pressure than before. It has me moaning and shaking as I reach the peak.

Then I feel it. The orgasm hits as my legs strangle around his face. He keeps his finger inside and his mouth over my clit as I cum into his mouth.

The orgasm carries on. My whole body keeps spasming uncontrollably. I can't see anything; I only feel the warm wave growing stronger over my body. My vision is blind to the highest form of pleasure I've ever felt in my life.

It takes a while for my breath to come back. Then I feel his body come up to my face. I open my eyes, looking at his glowing lips smile. His grin has my heart overflowing with emotion. Then I feel the poke on my thigh. I glance down at his full erection.

"Oh my, Benny," I seductively whisper, still trying to catch my breath. "We're not done, are we?"

"Before I make love to you. I want you to know something," he whispers, leaning closer until his lips are inches from mine.

I feel his hand slide over my bare chest, until if finds the perfect resting place over my heart.

"You didn't have to wait for me, but you did. You never gave up on me. I promise to never give up on you again. You are everything I need to be complete, Penny McClain. You are the greatest blessing in my life. And I love you. I've always loved you to the moon and back. Now, let me love you to the moon and back again."

"Yes! I love you, Benny!"

His lips and body fall on top of me. My legs spread, inviting his power into me. I'm still so wet as his cock slowly slides inside me. It hurts, but feels too good at the same time. After sliding in a couple inches deeper, he slows down, letting me catch my breath and position my hips at a better angle.

"Sorry," I whisper. "It just hurts a little."

"It's okay. Take your time, my love."

His tone is so patient and endearing. I look deeper into his green eyes while they meld into mine, overflowing with affection. Then I pull him by his ass into my hips. When he gets further inside me, I feel his strength over power my body. He rides into my wetness with a moan of dire need.

I arch my hips further up into him to let his cock touch different parts of my insides. He begins riding deeper into me as my pussy wraps tighter around his cock.

"Don't stop, Benny!" I shriek with pleasure. "Please! Please! Don't stop!"

I kiss his lips and watch his eyes marinating in desire. Then he goes faster and deeper into me. I wrap my arms around him, pulling him closer than ever.

The pressure of his bare body on mine means everything. It's more than just want and need for touch. It's how our souls are becoming one. And the lust, while perfection, is only the beginning blossoms to our ever-growing love.

"I'm close," he whispers, gasping for air.

"Please cum inside me. Please! I want your cum!" I scream, until I feel his body lose control inside mine.

My entire body can't stop shaking, and neither can his. He screams into my ear as his cum fills up my insides. I dig my fingers into his rock-hard ass, making sure every last drop of cum is mine to own.

Then he fully collapses his weight over me. His pulsating cock is still deep inside as I soak up every last drop of his seed. Together, we hold each other in an embrace so special, and forever unforgettable.

----

We're still giddy during our walk back to the house. The smiles on our faces feel permanent. But the best part is keeping him so close at my side. We can't keep our hands off each other. It makes my mind, body and soul feel whole again.

Then I feel his body go rigid. His arm flies across my chest.

"Wait!" Benny demands, staring toward the house.

"Whose car is that?" I ask, staring at the yellow Volkswagen Beetle parked in the driveway.

"I don't know."

I believe him, but I feel like he knows something I don't. We watch a tall black man in a plaid shirt walk from the car to the corner of the house where we can't see him.

"Penny, just stay back."

"No!"

"Penny, trust me. I think I know who it is. He's not a danger. But can you just hang back for a quick moment? I just need to make sure."

I let out a loud sigh. "Just tell me who you think it is."

"Well, I'm not sure, just give me two minutes," Benny says, backing away from me as he jogs ahead of me toward the house.

I follow Benny to the Volkswagen, noting the license plate.

"California? We don't know anyone from there," I mutter to myself.

Once I get around the house, I freeze in my tracks. I watch Benny and this strange man having a tense conversation. Then Benny shakes his hand. But he doesn't just shake his hand, it's the way he does it. He puts both hands around the man's hand, and practically bows down with gratitude.

I suddenly can't move. Even my face feels numb. Realities that feel impossible begin to play in my mind.

The man has curly greyish black hair sprouting from both sides of his blue baseball cap. He's wearing thick glasses and there's something about him that looks familiar.

Then he turns his body fully in my direction and his eyes lock on mine, just as I notice the bouquet of flowers he's holding. He adjusts his glasses, leaning down to grab his flowers he's just dropped. He stares at me like I'm a ghost.

Every curve and indentation in his shocked face remind me of only one person: my late brother.

It's how I'd picture the older version of Marcus in his 60s. But it's not Marcus. It's the person I always thought had left my life. But he's here, and now he's walking toward me.

He comes to a halt, inches from my face. I can't breathe because now I'm lost in his eyes. They're a carbon copy of both my brother's and my son's own eyes.

He reaches out to delicately touch my cheek with the back of his hand. His eyes glow with wonderment as our skin touches. It's like he's touching his daughter for the first time.

"Penny? I thought I lost you. Is it really you, baby girl?" he asks, tears pouring down his cheeks.

I say nothing and frantically nod my head. Then his whole body careens into mine, knocking the air out of me with a hug like I've never had. It's from a man I thought never wanted me. But this man holds me like a father desperate to hold his daughter.

"Daddy," I whimper in his ear.

"Yes, it's me, Honey," he whispers, nodding his head.

We hold onto each other, too overwhelmed to process what's happening. I notice Benny walking away.

It takes a while until we've stopped crying to carry on a conversation.

His full name is Calvin Marcus Jones. He's a retired Marine. He currently works as a butcher in the North Park suburb of San Diego. He was born and raised in Boston and being from Boston turns out to be the only truth my mama ever told me. Everything else was a bunch of lies.

The truth is he never left us. He fought in the Korean War and came back to an empty house. He spent years searching for us, only to find my brother's obituary years later. He was never able to find me because my last name had changed when Benny's grandpa adopted me.

His life, while tragic, did turn around. He remarried about 15 years ago. Now he's a proud stepdad to 18-year-old twin girls. He's so excited for me to meet my stepsisters, Sasha and Tiffany.

"But, Daddy, how did you find me?"

"Oh, Sweetie. It's a miracle. Apparently, your boyfriend here was quite persistent. He went door to door through my old Boston neighborhood. He covered a good ten blocks trying to find me, but I wasn't living there. Luckily, he left notes and pictures of you at all the houses where he didn't speak to anyone. One of those notes got to my best friend, Darren. The second I found out where you were I drove all the way out here in a day."

The two of us start laughing. I glance behind me to smile at Benny, who's peering down from the front porch with a look of endearment.

"That boy is in love with you, isn't he?" my father asks.

I wipe my eyes, trying to collect my breath. "Yeah. He's something else."

Our attention turns to the sound of a honking horn. We watch as everyone pulls up from the fishing trip.

I take my father's hand, squeezing it with every ounce of love I have in me. "Are you ready to meet my other dad, and my mom?"

"Yes. It would be my honor, Penny."

Dad slowly gets out with his cane and directs everyone else to stay put in the truck. He hobbles his way up to us, a look of confusion on his face. But his look quickly morphs into something else. I watch as his eyes fill up with moisture and his head tilts the slightest bit.

"Dad, I'd like you to meet someone. This is Calvin Jones. He's my other daddy," I say, unable to utter another word.

I watch as my dad's cane falls to the ground. Everyone's mouths hang open, looking at one another with disbelief. Then Dad's hands reach out to Calvin, grabbing his shoulders for balance.

"So, you're Penny's daddy?" he asks, lips trembling. "I hope you don't mind that I raised your baby girl. She needed help. And I did my best. I mean…*we*! *We* did our best."

"I know. She told me how wonderful you people are. I don't know what to say. But thank you Mr.—"

"My name is Richard McClain. And I should be thanking you, sir. Raising your daughter has been the greatest blessing I never saw coming. She's so beautiful. So smart. So kind. And a wonderful mother. She's the best of all of us."

The truck door slams shut. Calvin lets out a loud gasp, stumbling backwards for balance. His hand slaps over his heart. The smile on his face is so wide, and so much like my brother's. It's then I realize what I've yet to tell him.

"I'm a…" Calvin whispers, unable to utter the most perfect word.

"You're a grandparent, just like us," Ms. Green chimes in, walking up with Marcus holding her hand.

I suddenly realize that my dad's both have their arms around each other. But it's not just for balance. It's because they're already family.

One is an old white man who saw beauty in a damaged young black girl. The other is my real father. He looks at all of us like he's won the lottery.

I grab Marcus's hand, slowly walking him up to meet his newest grandpa, and lean down on one knee to look into his eyes. There's confusion, but also a look that is every bit my brother, and every bit his grandfather.

"Marcus, Honey. Do you remember how I told you I have two daddies? Well, this is my other daddy. His name is Calvin Jones. He's your grandfather, Marcus."

Marcus says nothing, peering up at his newest grandfather with curiosity. Calvin slowly goes down on one knee, taking the hand of my son as I hear sniffles all around me.

"I'm so happy to meet you, young man," Calvin says, shaking Marcus's limp hand. "I'm sorry I'm crying, but they're happy tears. You see, I'm so happy I found your mama. I thought I lost her, but I didn't. She's my baby girl."

Calvin smiles through the tears while taking my hand over his chest.

"I don't understand. How did you lose her?" Marcus asks, squinting with confusion.

"It's a long story. One day I'll tell you. For now, I just want to be with you all. But only if that's okay with you."

"Do you want to come see my treehouse? Benny built it for me," Marcus tells him.

Calvin can only nod, smiling wider as he wipes away more tears. Then he takes Marcus's hand. I watch as the two of them quietly walk to the treehouse. Ms. Green looks on with teary eyes, her arms draped around Dad.

Then I feel Benny's arms wrap around me. His lips kiss the top of my head. He holds his lips in that perfect spot while I melt into the most profound happiness.

Benny's given me so much good in one day. All I have left to give is the one thing that's been his all along: my heart.

# CHAPTER THIRTY-TWO

## Benny

### *15 months later*

I watch from the back porch. First, it's Calvin and Penny sharing a long hug with one another. Then I watch as Ms. Green and Penny share a moment. Their faces stay close to one another in intimate conversation, their smiles serene and content. Their dress and gown are so formal and breath-taking.

I want to hear what they're saying, but some things are meant to be private. Penny may not be with her biological mother, but she's found a strong black woman who's already taken that role with pride.

She also has Calvin in her life. He may live on the other end of the country, but he phones her often and has committed to visiting her at least twice a year.

A loud slap on my back nearly knocks me over.

"Thanks, asshole," I say, giving Paul a playful smirk.

"Oh, you're fine, Benny. You still got one good leg. Besides, I just heard the news from your grandpa. Can I still call you Benny? Or do you only go by Coach now?"

That label does have one hell of a ring to it. I shake Paul's hand, still in shock that I've been hired by the Eastern Alabama University coaching staff. I'll be the Assistant Offensive Coordinator. It's a big deal, given how rare it is for students to be hired onto the staff with no official coaching experience.

"I'm always Benny to you. We're teammates for life," I tell him, holding up the ring on my finger.

Paul grabs my hand, pulling me in for hug. "You'll always be my QB one," he whispers.

I'm sad that Paul's moving to St. Louis in a couple of weeks, but I'm elated for his future. After we won the national championship, he was drafted by the St. Louis Cardinals in the first round of the NFL draft. He'll likely be a year-one starter playing professional football in a few months.

His future could easily have been mine. I led Eastern Alabama to a national title in my one year as an eligible Division One starting quarterback. My last play was a perfect fade pass in the endzone with no time on the clock to give us the win. It was the most memorable few seconds of my life, until a 300-pound defensive end landed on my knee, tearing away the ligaments. I knew my playing career was over, but at least I went out a champion.

I'm three months removed from surgery after the national title game. I'm still getting used to hobbling around on one leg. Luckily, the doctors say I'll be able to walk normally in few months. But playing competitive sports is no longer an option.

Most nights I think about what could've been with my football life. It's hard not to. However, I can usually escape that dark hole by holding onto Penny. She and Marcus are my world now.

"He's here! He's here!"

I can hear Sarah's scream from the front yard. I hobble my way through the house and step onto the front porch right as

Jimmy and his boyfriend get out of the taxi in their tuxes. The first one to greet Jimmy is none other than Penny.

We all miss Jimmy ever since he moved out on his own about a year ago. But the void is different for Penny. She worries about him a lot. But the reality is Jimmy is a fully capable adult who's now living his best life.

He works at a manufacturing plant in Montgomery that builds car parts. However, he no longer works on the assembly line. Instead, he uses his math and engineering skills to design ways to make the assembly line more efficient.

He's also recently started seeing someone he works with, a guy named Charlie. He's very coy about their relationship because most people in the southern belt frown on homosexuality. Jimmy is used to it, though. And what's most important is that he's so happy having Charlie in his life.

When I make it to the porch steps, Jimmy races his way up to give me a hug. I grab the railing just in time to avoid falling flat on my back.

"I miss you, Benny," Jimmy whispers, wrapping his arms tighter around my back.

"It's so good to see you," I say, leaning back to look him over, head to toe. "You look—"

"Like a hot piece of ass!" Penny shouts.

Jimmy blushes while I laugh.

"Yeah, I've never worn one of these before," Jimmy explains, adjusting his bow. "Charlie helped me pick it out. Where's Grandpa?"

"I don't know. Probably still doing his make-up," I joke.

"Where's Marcus?"

Then we hear it, Marcus chanting Jimmy's name as he quickly rounds the corner of the house. I watch as the two of them run into each other's arms. Jimmy lifts Marcus into the air, swinging him around like a helicopter.

"You ready?" Penny asks, greeting me with a kiss.

"Yes. How about you?"

She lifts on her tippy toes, wrapping her arms round my neck. I lean down to kiss her, feeling like the luckiest person on earth. Then I lean my forehead onto hers, absorbing those chocolate brown eyes.

"Let's do it."

----

The music starts up. I stare out at the small audience of maybe 20 guests, all close family and friends. I try standing tall the best I can with my hands crossed over my cane for balance. Then I glance to my right. Grandpa slowly walks up behind me, taking his rightful place in the center of the aisle.

Grandpa looks over his shoulder at me and Jimmy. "Boys," he nods his head, smiling his way through the nerves.

The music suddenly shifts to "Canon in D." The audience slowly rises. Ms. Green gracefully makes her way down the aisle in her long white wedding gown. Penny is glued to her hip, their arms hooked around each other. They're both already crying, blotting their eyes with tissue.

When they get to the end of the aisle, I watch as Penny kisses Ms. Green's forehead. The kiss is long and heartfelt. Then she leans down to whisper something in her ear. No one can hear what they're saying, but it's a long message. Ms. Green just keeps nodding her head as the tears pour out. Then she kisses Penny on the cheek.

The wedding ceremony for Grandpa and Ms. Green still feels like an unexpected event. It was the first news we got the last time we visited a couple months ago. We were elated to find out that Grandpa had proposed. The only trouble is the news Grandpa gave us a couple weeks later.

The cancer is already in his lymph nodes. They took a chunk of it out, but there's not much more that can be done. According to his doctors he has about six to twelve months left to live.

I look at the both of them, wanting so much more time for them. But I also realize that Grandpa is 82. He's lived a long, fulfilling life. Well over a decade of that life has included loving Ms. Green.

He's dealt with tremendous tragedy in his life. But he's stayed the course with his unwavering commitment to family. Grandpa's given so much to all who have crossed his path. He's made enemies into friends. He taught us about true forgiveness and love. But most importantly, he lives his life with a smile. You'd never know he's close to the end by the way he looks at Ms. Green.

I still wonder how Grandpa shaped himself into the person he is. After all, he grew up and raised two diverse families in one of the most racist places in America. But he chose to never acknowledge color, difference, or hate. Instead, he chose to grace people with love; to see the best in *all people*.

The two of them pull out their vows. Ms. Green goes first.

"Richard McClain!" she bellows his name with pride, her smile brighter than a thousand suns. "I moved in across the street from you over ten years ago. I was an angry and bitter widow, still suffering in my grief. And I wanted to hate you because, well, I used to hate a lot of things. But you were my neighbor, first and foremost. You treated me with hospitality and respect. You saw past the color of my skin and the sadness in my soul. And you helped me find the best parts of me, even the parts I thought I had lost forever. You were always so unselfish and kind. But most importantly, you taught me that it's okay to love again."

She pauses, letting out a long exhale. Her eyes go from her paper up to his face.

"Thank you for coming into my life. Thank you for sharing your beautiful family with me. I love them unconditionally as if they were my own, because they are now. They're all so different and beautiful in their own way. But more than anything….They're you. They're you, Richard McClain. You see, you make everyone feel better. You make everyone feel truly loved. And I know what's left of our time together may be short. But together, we'll make it special. Together, we'll keep living every second of every day. Because today, I'm no longer

Clara Green. I'm Clara McClain. And I'm so proud to finally call you my husband."

I can't see my dad's face, but I'm sure he's a teary-eyed mess like everyone, including me.

"Can I kiss this woman right now? Please!" Grandpa begs the pastor, who scowls. He starts to speak as Grandpa lunges for Ms. Green's lips. Everyone goes from crying to laughing in the blink of an eye.

I almost lose my balance because I'm laughing so hard. This old crazy man couldn't wait for the kiss-the-bride part. And I don't blame him in the least. He's found his second love in life.

After three long smooches, Grandpa pulls back, still grinning as he reaches for his vows. Then he takes a couple long breaths to compose himself.

"Clara McClain, we share this beautiful day with more than our family and friends here today. We share this day with loved ones smiling down from heaven. And I assure you, their smiles are further igniting the love we have for one another. Your words were so kind, my love. But the truth is, you all make me a better person. You all make my capacity for sharing love feel infinite. Because I want to give you all the eternal happiness I've found in this life. Because when your days are numbered, you learn to live in these perfect moments and soak them up for all they're worth. That's why I vow to do what I've always done since you came into my life. I'll make you smile. I'll make you laugh. I'll make you cry. I'll love you with everything I have left to give. And I'll always be by your side, until I've taken my final breaths. It's more than just my duty as your husband, it's my duty and my honor, as your best friend."

Grandpa puts his paper in his pocket. Then he takes a moment to dry his eyes with his handkerchief. The Pastor gives the final parts of his sermon. But my eyes are focused on one thing, and one thing only: my best friend. I mouth my favorite three words to Penny as the Pastor makes the announcement to kiss the bride.

----

"Are you nervous?" Penny asks, leaning her head up from my shoulder.

I caress her cheek. "A little," I whisper, still lost in her beauty.

Penny's hair is tied up. She's wearing a beautiful amethyst necklace she got from Ms. Green. It hangs down just above her breasts. It's distracting in the best way possible.

Jimmy taps me on the shoulder.

"Can I say something before you speak?" he whispers in my ear.

I'm surprised. Speaking to a crowd doesn't sound like something he'd ever do. But the look he gives me is serious and self-confident.

"Yes, of course. I mean, I was going to speak here in a second, but you're more than welcome to go in my place. Here, just give this a jingle," I say, handing him an empty wine glass and fork.

Jimmy wastes no time jingling the glass for everyone's attention.

"Hello! Hello!" his voice booms, surprising everybody.

I look around as conversations give way to silence and murmuring.

"Hello! I just needed to tell you all something important. Grandpa and Ms. Green are my heroes. I actually have many heroes here today. And a hero to me is much more than being a savior. My heroes believed in me when others would only see weaknesses and differences. But I'm not weak. I'm only different. And I'm proud to be different. I'm proud of who I've become because of people like Grandpa and Ms. Green. And I'm proud to share this day with you all. So please raise your glasses for the bride and groom."

I can't stop staring at my brother. The confidence in his posture, his words, and his intense gaze at the audience is shocking to me. I'm so awe-struck Penny has to elbow me to get my glass in the air.

"To my heroes!" Jimmy shouts.

The audience shouts the words back in unison. Then I watch as my brother's face crumbles away with emotion. He begins crying uncontrollably. Perhaps he's overcome with happiness. Or maybe he's realizing that his grandpa, who's much more than just a father figure, won't be around much longer.

I get up to go hug him, but Penny's already beat me to it. She holds him tightly, rubbing his back and whispering comfort in his ear. It makes him only cry harder.

Then it hits me. In my 25 years of life, this is only the second time I've seen my baby brother cry. Emotions and understanding them may still be hard for him to process. But today, I feel like they make perfect sense to Jimmy. Whether he's wallowing in happiness or sadness is irrelevant. Emotions like these are meant to be expressed. They're meant to be shared with the world. Like Grandpa once said, "Emotions are blossoms from the roots of love."

----

It takes quite a while for the dust to settle from the wedding. The dancing, eating, drinking, and partying were all perfect— an evening we'll never forget.

But now my stomach is tied into knots. I watch Penny walk over in her turquoise-colored Mod Shift Dress. The happiness radiating from her face has my heart finding an even deeper love for this stunning black woman. I take two deep breaths as she gets closer. I know it's time.

"Hey, Sweetheart. Come on a short walk with me," I tell her.

Penny hooks her arm around me. We slowly make our way into the pitch darkness of the forest.

"Are we going to the treehouse?" she asks.

"Maybe."

I can't hide my smirk as she hooks her arm tighter around my waist. Our walk to the treehouse is mostly silent. She's probably exhausted. I, on the other hand, have never felt more nervous in my life.

When we finally get to the ladder, Penny gives me a playful look of exasperation.

"How the hell you getting up that thing on one leg?"

"Watch me," I challenge, chucking my cane aside.

The strength in my arms allows me to pull my weight up. I use my one good leg to swing up each rung of the ladder. It's exhausting, but I finally get to the top ahead of Penny. Then I slide my butt to the edge of the day bed.

"Take a seat," I tell her, patting my hand on the bed.

"What's going on?" Penny asks.

"I just thought a perfect night like this could only get better if I brought you up here. You see, there's something I was going to ask you when we got back home. But I don't want to wait a second longer."

I slide my hand under the mattress until I feel the box. My other hand grabs her left hand.

"Penny McClain. It's no secret I want to spend my life with you. I want to have your babies and make you feel like the happiest woman on earth. And we're here in the treehouse because it's the place where I first fell in love with you. And it's the place where I'll ask you to be my wife. Because I promise to do everything within my power to love you more than any other man could ever love a woman. I know I can give that to you. Because when I'm with you, I'm the happiest man on earth. You see through my faults, loving me for who I am. So I'm begging you to give me your hand in marriage. Please marry me. Please be my forever."

Penny's hands go over her heart as she gasps. I grab her left hand, sliding the ring onto her finger. Her smile becomes angelic as the tears trickle down. I lean my face up to hers, cupping my hands around her cheeks.

"Marry me, Penny."

Her lips go into mine. I pull her into me, then we both pull away, gasping for breath.

"Is that a yes?"

Penny nods her head laughing. "Yes! Yes! Of course, Benny! I love you!"

We kiss again. Then we make love under the light of a full moon. It shines through the treehouse with a brightness like I've never seen on any other night. It gives light in our world that once had so much darkness.

Now, our future begins. Once upon a time she was my sister, and now she's my best friend, and forever my wife.

# Epilogue

# Penny

## *5 years later*

The long flight from San Diego has us all exhausted. However, as we drive up, I get a burst of invigoration seeing Mom and Dad.

"I'll handle everything," Benny confidently says. "Go hug them."

I fly out of the car the second Benny pulls over. I run into Mom's arms first.

"Oh, Penny," she calls out. "Oh, I missed you, Honey."

I wrap my arms around the woman we used to call Ms. Green. After marrying Dad, she requested that we all call her mom. It felt weird at first. We'd been calling her Ms. Green for over a decade. But this is her rightful name to all of us.

I pull away from Mom to hug my other father.

"Penny, Sweetheart. I'm so sorry for your loss," Dad says, sniffling to fight the tears.

"Thanks, Dad."

I start looking around the cemetery because I recognize their car, but don't see Jimmy or Charlie.

"They're already up by the gravestone," Mom says, adjusting the veil on her black hat. "I think they wanted a moment alone with your dad."

After getting everything situated with the kids, we make our trek to Plot 87. The number 87 is by no means a random coincidence. It's the age of his passing. My dad, Richard McClain, lived five years past his cancer diagnosis. He defied the odds of every doctor and fought to live out every last breath of his life.

It's been three months since he's passed on. The eulogy had to be delayed because of everyone's busy schedules. I think it's given us all time to accept his passing and move on like he would want us to.

There are still moments in the day I feel numb, knowing he's no longer here in the flesh. Yet, I still feel his presence every single day. Whether it's the little idiosyncrasies that remind me of him in Benny, or the similarities I see in my children, I know he's here with us.

Benny and I are now a proud family of five. We had twin boys two years ago. Baby number four is set to arrive in a couple months. He or she has been kicking around in my belly all morning long. I'm hoping for a girl.

I took two years off from teaching to have the twins. Their names are Richard and Patrick. They're such a blessing to raise alongside their big brother. Marcus looks after them as if he's the third parent in the family. He's a great big brother, just like his daddy was.

Meanwhile, Benny is the one who brought us to San Diego. He was hired on at the University of San Diego, where he's now the youngest head football coach in Division One history. It's been a bit of an adjustment coming from the south. But the west coast lifestyle is growing on all of us. Furthermore, we enjoy living in a more progressive part of the world that's more accepting of interracial families.

Together, we recently started the McClain Family Trust after more money was passed on to us from the Monroe family. Its major financial beneficiaries are the NAACP and Special Olympics. It's two organizations we're proud to support because they fight for equality and inclusion of all people.

When we all get closer to Plot 87, we start to slow down. Jimmy and Charlie are both hunched down by Dad's gravestone. Their moment with Dad feels too intimate to break up. After a couple minutes they both start waving for us to join them.

It's the first full family reunion since he died. It feels good sharing hugs and kisses, but it also means uncovering our wounds. I watch as Benny and Jimmy share a moment together. They break away from a long hug with reddened eyes and faces still wilted with sadness. It breaks my heart seeing them cry, but I know how important it is for them to share these moments together.

"Hey, y'all!" Mom shouts, getting everyone's attention. "Before we get started with the eulogy, I have a note here. Richard wanted one of the kids to read it. He thought Benny might want to, but really any of you can read it aloud."

After Benny puts our boys in the stroller, he walks up to Mom and grabs the note. She whispers something in his ear.

"Really?" he asks, clearly surprised.

Mom nods her head with a smile.

I watch as my gorgeous husband and the father of my beautiful children stands before us all. He's clearly in pain, but Benny is courageous. I know he can do this.

"Mom just told me I'm the first person to read this—" Benny pauses, biting his bottom lip. He's trying so hard to keep it together, but he just can't. Then I watch as Mom goes up to stand next to him. She grabs his hand for reassurance.

"It's okay, Benny. Take your time. You got this, Son."

Benny smiles at her while slowly getting control of his breath. Then he turns to face the rest of us, showcasing those tender green eyes.

"Thanks, Mom. Before I read his note, I wanted to tell a quick story about Grandpa. I think it encapsulates the person he was, and still is to all of us. You see, our twin boys were maybe three months old. And this was still my first rodeo with babies not sleeping. Penny was asleep on the other end of the house because I wanted to give her a break, and a full night's sleep. But my beautiful boys wouldn't stop crying. I tried everything until I broke down and called Grandpa at two in the morning. I was just beside myself, venting about how hard parenting newborns and working full-time truly is. I told him I feel like I'm failing as a father and husband because I can't always be around, and when I am, I don't always feel like I'm doing the best job. Because the truth is, as a parent you always want to do better for your kids. I get that now. You would do anything for their happiness. *Anything*!"

Benny stops. He begins chuckling and sniffling at the same time. His eyes remain glossy as he glances towards the sky in remembrance. Then his smile grows even wider.

"And then Grandpa gave me the best response ever. It made no sense at the time, just like a lot of his life lessons when I was younger. But he said, 'Benny, there's no magic wand or formula for being the perfect parent. Allow yourself to screw up and make mistakes. Be vulnerable like you're being with me here tonight. Because all it takes is effort and vulnerability. They're just more blossoms blooming from the roots of love.'"

Benny bows his head.

"I get it now," he says, his voice beginning to break. "We're all perfectly imperfect. And love makes us strive for perfection. And it's okay, as long as we're vulnerable to one another. Grandpa taught us so much that we'll never, ever forget!"

Benny raises his voice as tears pour out of him. "I love all of you so much! And I don't know how to live without my grandpa. Because he was more than just a grandpa. He was my father. He was my shining light. My crutch when I only had one leg. And I know he'd be proud of who we've all become. So today, in honor of the man who became my father, let's be vulnerable together. Let's shower each other with love to get through this grief. And let's never stop talking about him. For he may not be here in person, but he's engrained in all of us. Thank you."

I run up to Benny, hugging him while we sob. Then I feel arms come around us from every direction. We all embrace together, in the name of vulnerability.

"Penny," Benny whispers in my ear. "I need a break. Can you read his letter?"

"Of course, my love. I'll do anything for you."

It takes a couple minutes for everyone to collect themselves. Benny's speech could have moved mountains. The power in his words will live on in our hearts, forever.

I hold the envelope with Dad's note tightly in my hands. I turn around to face my family. I can't help but marvel at all the blessings before me. Then I close my eyes, taking the deepest breath I can take, willing my father's courage into me. On the exhale, I feel an electricity take over my body. Then a large gust of wind kicks up.

My body feels like it's going through an awakening. The best images of my late father begin replaying in my mind. Then my hand begins to tingle from the pressure. I look down at my hand, seeing nothing. But I feel the spirit of his hand wrapping around mine. His presence gives me the courage to pull out his letter.

**Dear McClain family,**

**Thank you for eulogizing my life. Eighty-seven years is a long time to be around. I've seen lots of good, and lots of bad in my time. But please remember that good outweighs everything. Because the good is in all of you.**

**To my children and grandchildren, all I have to say is thank you. Thank you for being the wings of an angel. You all are the reason I fly high each day. You give me a happiness and contentment that knows no bounds, even in death. My love for you all is forever engrained in your hearts.**

To my Clara McClain: You are the wife and mother I never saw coming into my life. The love you showered upon me, and my family means everything. Thank you for loving me up until the end. I can't wait to see you when the gates of Heaven open. But please take your time. Keep living your life and spreading the beauty in your soul to others.

Today, you all are allowed to grieve my passing. But you must also celebrate my life, today and for all your future days to come. Because my whole life was a daily celebration of loving you all. And I never once took it for granted.

So make sure you keep living in the moments of each day. Soak up the blessings all around you. Live your journeys, applying the lessons I've taught. Because there's limitless potential in all of you to do good. You'll see beauty in differentness. You'll see blossoming love, overcome the weeds of hate. But most importantly, you'll see yourself, taking pride in your reflection, loving who you are, just like I'll love you, forever.

Love always,
Richard McClain.

THE END

Thank you for reading my story. I would greatly appreciate your time by leaving a review on Goodreads and Amazon. After a quick message from the author, I'll also encourage you to keep reading for a sneak peek at my other book, *The Girl in the Red Wig*. This book is available on Kindle and in paperback.

# A Message from the Author

Thank you again for giving my book a chance. I sincerely hope the message in this story lives on through the kindness and good deeds *you* put forth into the world.

Writing is my passion and I'm truly honored to share it with the world. If you'd like to learn more about my author journey and upcoming book releases, please subscribe to my mailing list by visiting www.timothykylebooks.com.

Lastly, I'd greatly appreciate your support by leaving a review on Amazon and Goodreads. For new authors like me, it helps us grow our readership and improve as writers.

# Sneak Peek

# The Girl in the Red Wig

# Prologue

# David

I look out into the backyard as the water runs down our sliding glass door. The multiplying water droplets make everything outside so blurry and distorted—the full moon, the light post by our shed, even the stars look different when the water trickles down the glass in the middle of the night.

The crash of thunder has my whole body flinching. The wrenching pain in my stomach spreads upward, slowly creating a suffocating pressure over my chest and throat. It's like an incurable flesh-eating disease, devouring what's left of my insides. Luckily, there's not much left.

Everyone else is asleep. I only know because I've checked multiple times. Sleep has felt impossible lately. I can close my eyes for prolonged periods of time, but falling into a bliss of unconsciousness only feels like a fantasy.

How does a twelve-year-old boy sleep into a dream or alternate reality? That's what I want—to blink and wake up in a new life. The kind of life where people aren't unfairly taken away from you in the blink of an eye.

*"The roads were slick. Six inches this way, and we're looking at a totally different outcome," the police officer said to my father.*

The words keep playing back in my head. Each time, it's like barbed wire slowly scraping through the inside of my chest. Then I hear the screams of a grown man as he collapses to his knees, begging. I wasn't meant to hear those words preceding his screams, but I did. I'm glad I did. It showed me the true evils of the world.

*"Twelve, twenty-one, eighteen, thirty-six. For emergencies only," my dad told me when I was younger.*

The numbers to the safe click as I rotate the knob. I grab hold of the metal handle, surprised by how cold and heavy it is in my hand. I'm sure this qualifies somewhere under the umbrella of emergencies—no longer wanting to live. But if I left this world to escape the pain, would I even find her? Perhaps that's a risk worth taking, albeit selfish to Dad and Angela.

I walk back downstairs, feeling the weight of my world in my right hand. I close my eyes and lean my forehead into the sliding glass door. This sharp, cold sensation sends a shiver down my spine and may be the last feeling I experience.

The Glock 19 goes up to the side of my head. My index finger becomes clammy as it traces along the trigger. I close my eyes. Then, my countdown begins.

*Five, four, three…*

Our aluminum trash can clanging to the ground has my attention. I put the gun on the counter to take a closer look outside. All I can see is a shadowy figure. The figure then walks under the light post by our shed.

*It's a girl!*

I know this girl. I rarely ever see her, but I know her. But there's something off. She's huddled under the thin eve of our shed roof.

A white light flashes, giving me a split-second vision of the girl. Another thunderous roar from the sky follows the lightning. I watch the young girl shiver in her pajamas, soaking to the bone.

Millions of questions run through my head. The first is why a girl my age is in my backyard in the middle of the night. Or why her lips move to a conversation she could only be having with herself. But those questions are suddenly unimportant. The intriguing part is the way the light post shines down upon her fiery red hair. It's odd how it doesn't look damp despite the rain coming down harder. In fact, it has a translucent red glow that has my eyes transfixed. It's *so red*.

It takes another minute or two before I gather the courage to head outside with my umbrella. The closer I get to her, the more I feel the need to slow my approach. She's huddled against the shed siding with her back to me. All I hear is the indistinct mumbling of words and water pelting the shed.

"Hey! Hey! Are you okay?"

The wind kicks up. The rain goes sideways, pelting the shed harder. There's still no response. She won't turn around, and her shivering worsens. I take another tentative step closer while positioning the umbrella at an angle to keep her dry.

"I know who you are," I tell her as I peer around to see her face. "Can I help you?"

The girl slowly turns around, looking at me like she's lost. But she's not lost in the physical sense. She couldn't be. She's my neighbor. It's her mind. She's here in front of me, dripping wet and wide-eyed with fear. But she doesn't seem to recognize me or even see me. Her line of vision goes over my head to an alternate reality. It's like she's lost in a dream.

"I'd like to help you," I tell her again—still nothing.

I'm running out of options. Talking to her is going nowhere, and the temperature is dropping by the second. The only option is to lead her into the shed to dry her off and see what's happening.

My trembling hand slowly extends out to her shoulder. I know a boy is not allowed to touch people like her. But I just don't care. All I feel is the innate need to help her. It's what Mom would do without a second thought.

The second my hand touches the sleeve of her shirt, she flinches and lets out a loud gasp. Then, her other hand slams down on my wrist, squeezing it with an ungodly amount of strength. Her entire body begins to shake violently.

"She lives! Go find her! She lives! Go find her!" Her whisper is loud and raspy. *It's terrifying.* But more than anything, the pleading tone in her voice has my whole body chilled.

The same words keep pouring out of her. Each time, it's a more desperate plea than before. Her hand continues to dig into my wrist as I feel her panic in my chest.

The need to no longer live becomes a distant memory in this moment. And to think, I was two seconds away. Mom was only six inches away from living. It's ironic how something so small and minute can be the threshold between living and dying.

Eventually, she lets me guide her into the shed. Once we're in there, I take stock in my situation. It's the middle of the night. I have no way of helping her or understanding the meaning of her words. All I have is a gut feeling. A feeling that's overflowing with clarity. It's a resounding truth I feel in the marrow of my bones.

I will live a little bit longer. Maybe to help. Maybe to just listen. But most importantly, I'll do as Mom would have done.

# Acknowledgments

This book may be a work of fiction, but it's also a sad reminder. Hate exists in both our past and current world. But so does love and compassion. My hope is the reader leaves this book feeling inspired by the power of love, forgiveness, and hope. If you believe in the message of *The Tree House* than prove it by doing one thing and one thing only: Be kind to all.

*The Tree House* would have never blossomed in my imagination without the privilege I had in working with people who have special abilities and unique talents like Jimmy. This book is meant to uplift those that are not seen, not heard, or treated as less. Everyone deserves a spotlight, and everyone deserves love.

Lastly, I'd like to send my sincere appreciation to my entire Arc and Street Team. I'd like to specifically recognize my PA, Nicole. Your support and positive attitude means the world to me. To my editor, Robrt Pela, thank you for your tireless efforts in making this story into my first real book. To my cover designer, Abby Simmons, thank you for creating a cover that's the perfect representation of my story. And lastly to my wife, for always believing in me. Support from the person I love and respect the most means everything. I love you Emmy! "Don't ever change!"

# About the Author

Timothy Kyle is a longtime native of Phoenix, Arizona. He's a proud husband and father to three rambunctious pre-teen girls. When he's not writing or making ridiculous social media content, he's pursuing his other passion in life as a tennis coach.

Timothy received his master's degree in exercise science in 2009. He worked for the next decade in the non-profit and education sectors that support individuals with *special* abilities. He's a proud advocate of the special needs community and of women's rights.

*The Tree House* is his first book. His other book is *The Girl in the Red Wig*. If you enjoy his writing, he'd love for you to visit www.timothykylebooks.com and subscribe to his mailing list, so he can keep you in-the-know on his next projects.